Disco for the Departed

Disco for the Departed

COLIN COTTERILL

Published by
Soho Press, Inc.
853 Broadway
New York, NY 10003

Library of Congress Cataloging-in-Publication Data

Cotterill, Colin.
Disco for the departed / Colin Cotterill.
p. cm.
ISBN 1-56947-428-1
1. Paiboun, Siri, Doctor (Fictitious character)—Fiction.
2. Older people—Fiction. 3. Physicians—Fiction.
4. Coroners—Fiction. 5. Laos—Fiction. I. Title.

PR6053.O778D57 2006
823'.92—dc22   2005055462

10   9   8   7   6   5   4   3   2   1

To Siri and Soun, who, despite all the tragedies, have survived and grown and now have two beautiful daughters. To Poki and Panoy from Loong C.

Contents

Guesthouse Number One

D r. Siri lay beneath the grimy mesh of the mosquito net, watching the lizard's third attempt. Twice, the small gray creature had scurried up the wall and ventured out across the ceiling. On both occasions, the unthinkable had happened. The animal had lost its grip and come plummeting down with a splat onto the bare concrete of the guesthouse floor. For a house lizard this was the equivalent of a man coming unstuck from the ground and falling up with a crash onto the ceiling. Siri could see the stunned confusion on its little puckered face. It looked around to get its bearings, then headed once more for the wall.

For over a month, Dr. Siri Paiboun, the national coroner, had been wondering whether his new incarnation might be disruptive to the natural laws of animal behavior. The peculiarities could have started before, but it wasn't until the mongrel from the ice works began to build a nest in his front yard that he took any notice. She somehow managed to drag old car seats and cement sacks through his front gate and mold them into a very uncomfortable-looking roost. And there she sat patiently, day after day, as if waiting for an unlikely egg. A week later, the paddy mice at the back of the compound formed what could only be described as a gang and started terrorizing his neighbor's cat. This morning, as he was leaving his house in Vientiane for the trip up-country, he'd looked back to see a hen on his roof. As there was no sign of a ladder, he had to assume the thing had flown up there. And now the lizard. Even if these were all coincidences, it was still very odd. Ever since Siri had discovered his shaman ancestry, a lot of strange things had happened in his life.

He worked the nail of his pinky finger around the inside of his mouth, counting his teeth once again. It was a habit he'd fallen into a few months earlier when he'd found out he was different. All there—all thirty-three of them. The same number of teeth as old Prince Phetsarat, the magician; the same number as some of the most respected shamans in the region; the same number as the Lord Buddha himself. Siri was in hallowed company. But even though he had the right number of teeth, he hadn't yet taken control of his abilities.

Only recently, Siri had learned that he hosted the spirit of an ancient Hmong shaman—Yeh Ming. Until then, he'd always thought the contact he'd had with departed souls in his dreams was some kind of mental illness. He hadn't bothered to try to interpret their messages, hadn't even realized that the spirits in his dreams were leaving clues to the causes of their deaths. All that had changed the previous year. Yeh Ming had become more active—woken up, you might say— and had drawn the attention of the malevolent spirits of the forest. These evil spirits, these *Phibob*, were gunning for Siri's ancestor, and as Siri was his host, Siri was suddenly in the line of fire. Supernatural fireworks were spilling over into his life.

Very little could really shock the old surgeon anymore, but he never ceased to be amused by the mysterious events happening around him. His own life seemed to grow more fascinating every day. While others his age had begun to wind down like clocks as they tottered into a frail twilight, Siri had been reborn into a period in which fantasy and reality were interchangeable. Every day was a kick. He felt more alive than ever. If this were truly some kind of senile insanity, it was one he was secretly enjoying: one he was in no hurry to recover from.

That May, Siri had arrived at his seventy-third birthday, still as sturdy as a jungle boar. His lungs let him down from time to time but his muscles and his mind were as taut as they'd been in his thirties. His head boasted a shock of thick white hair and his likeable face with its haunting green eyes still drew flirtatious smiles from women half his age. None of his friends could imagine Dr. Siri Paiboun running out of steam for a long while yet.

The mosquito-net-covered bunk bed in which Siri lay watching the lizard, stood on the floor of Party Guesthouse Number One in the cool northeast of the People's Democratic Republic of Laos; the year was 1977. "Guesthouse" was hardly an appropriate name for the two-story building designed by Vietnamese rectangulists a few years earlier. It looked nothing like a house, and its inmates were certainly not guests. It was mostly inhabited by those who had sinned, ideologically, against Party dictates. Here, the village heads, government officials, and army officers of the old Royalist regime were lulled into believing they had been invited for a holiday in the mountains of Huaphan province, an educational visit to revolutionary headquarters.

Earlier that evening, Siri and Nurse Dtui had sat drinking coffee with a group of men from the south who once held senior ranks in the Royalist police force. They still assumed they were merely attending a seminar and would soon return to Vientiane with a new, enlightened understanding of the Marxist-Leninist system. The mood had been jolly as they sat on the ground-floor veranda on uncomfortable red vinyl chairs. The men had spent their first afternoon doing "getting to know you" activities and still wore their paper name tags stapled to the tops of their shirt pockets. Each man's name was followed by the word "officer," then a number. As if unwilling to break rank, they'd sat in numerical order around their small circle of chairs.

Siri had listened to them boast of their good fortune in seeing a part of the country that was as alien to these urbanites as any foreign land. They spoke of the locals as a tourist would of Africans or peculiar Europeans. Little did they know their brief excursion to the provinces would likely extend to months; in some cases, years. Little did they know they were to be trucked from the comparative luxury of the guesthouse to a site some eighty kilometers away near Sop Hao on the Vietnamese border. There they would be assigned to work gangs to rebuild roads, repair bombed bridges, and help the local peasants till a booby-trapped land littered with unexploded ordnance. In the evenings they would sit around blackboards in study groups beneath the yellow light of beeswax lamps. They would learn the dates of the most famous battles, the numbers of casualties, and the names of the great leaders of the revolution. This, and often much, much worse, was Lao reeducation.

Eventually, either by sincere personal choice or through desperation, they would swear undying devotion to the Cause. If they were convincing enough, they might one day be returned to their families. If not, the families would be invited to travel north to join them. Only women who truly loved their husbands and were prepared to forgo the luxuries of city life accepted such an offer. The majority fled across the Mekong to take their chances on the Thai side.

But these jolly men on the guesthouse patio as yet knew nothing of this. They still saw the purpose of their trip as a simple conversion, like switching a motor's consumption from regular gas to diesel. They imagined they'd learn a little about communism, have a guided tour of the caves, and go home with snapshots to put in an album. They'd said as much during their chat with Siri and Dtui.

"So, what's a pretty thing like you doing so far from home?" Officer Three had asked of the solidly built young nurse whose nickname, "Dtui," meant "Fatty." He was a portly red-faced man who'd learned how to talk to women in dark nightclubs. He'd been staring at her chest since they arrived.

"I'm with my boss," she said, nodding in Siri's direction.

"Dirty weekend by the looks of it," said Officer Four, nudging his neighbor in the ribs. Dtui and Siri blushed in unison, bringing great howls from the men.

"That would be nice," Dtui countered with a typical Lao Band-Aid smile that covered no end of emotional cuts and bruises. "But it's work, I'm afraid."

"Work, eh? That's what I always told my missus when I was going off for a little weekend R and R," Officer One confessed proudly. "What *work* is it you do exactly?" Dtui frowned but didn't snap. Siri was impressed by her composure.

"I'm a nurse. My boss is a surgeon." She decided nothing would be gained by telling them she was Siri's trainee at the morgue, and that he was the national coroner of Laos.

"So they're here playing doctors and nurses," said Officer Two, producing even more exaggerated laughter from his mates.

It occurred to Siri that these men were trying too hard, being too blokey, and the reason was obvious to him. They were afraid. Despite their bravado and their unreasonable expectations, they were in enemy territory, and all they had as a weapon was this false camaraderie.

Siri was concerned about their families. He wondered how their wives and children would survive with their breadwinners breaking rocks on a road gang. "Is the Justice

Department taking care of your kin while you're up here?" he asked.

Officer Two thought that was a very funny question. "They haven't paid us a brass *kip* since they took over." There were no coins in Laos, so a brass *kip* would have been worth even less than a paper one. That, in turn, presently stood at six to the U.S. cent. On the occasions there was money available, a policeman under the new system would have received seven thousand *kip* a month plus a small rice ration.

"Then how do you live?"

"Oh, we have resources. Some of us managed to put small nest eggs together under the old regime. We sent money out of the country. We anticipated the damned Reds coming in and messing things up."

"Look, I don't want to throw you gentlemen into some hysterical panic here but I'm one of those nasty Reds who spoiled your party," Siri said.

Officer Two blushed. "Really? Sorry. You didn't look like . . . Then, what are you doing here? I mean . . ."

To undo the damage, Officer One hurriedly asked Dtui where she and the doctor were based.

"Mahosot Hospital."

"Then you're a long way from home, too."

"You aren't kidding," Dtui said. "I haven't been outside Vientiane for twenty years. It's so exotic up here." She cast a sideways glance at Siri. "I'm looking forward to seeing my first pog."

"Your first what?"

"Pog. My ma used to tell me about them when I was little."

Siri looked away so the policemen wouldn't notice his smile.

"Can't say I've ever heard of them," the officer confessed. "What are they?"

"You can't be serious. You haven't heard of a pog? I admit they're rare, but up here in the northeast the animals are never penned up. They all roam around together—the chickens, the dogs, the goats, the pigs. With animals being the way they are, there's a fair amount of experimentation that goes on, if you know what I mean."

Siri could control his face no longer. He got to his feet and walked over to the front steps to look at the full moon reflected hazily on the surface of the pond. He chuckled under his breath but made it sound like a cough.

Dtui continued at her most convincing best. "And here in Huaphan, probably due to the altitude, or, some say, the sulfur in the water, on occasions, the union of a randy male dog and a sow produces . . ."

"You cannot be serious."

"I swear on my brother's life. I've seen the photos. They have the face of a pig and the paws and tail of a dog. I can't believe you don't know about them."

"Yeah, I've heard of 'em," said Officer Four.

"You haven't," said Officer Two.

"Now you mention it, I might have seen one on a farm just outside Tha Reua. Didn't know what it was, though. Odd-looking thing," recalled Officer One.

"That's right," said Dtui, "and up here they're everywhere. If you see one around perhaps you could grab it for me. I'd love to take one back for my ma."

"No problem," said Officer Four, "I imagine they're really easy to catch."

"Well, I'm afraid we have to get up early," said Officer Two, who obviously knew his curly tail was being tweaked. He stood and stretched painfully like a first-time jogger. The others stood also. "We have an hour of tilling to do starting at six in the morning."

He still sounded like a tourist on an adventure holiday.

Siri walked back to the group. "You be careful where you dig. There are unexploded bombs all over this area."

The officer chuckled. "I very much doubt they'd send us into a minefield, Doctor."

"You just be careful. I don't want to spend tomorrow sewing legs back onto foolhardy policemen." Although he said nothing more, Siri could think of few more effective mine-clearance techniques than sending a chorus line of corrupt Royalist policemen across a field with shovels.

"Have a good night's sleep, you two," said Officer One with a wink. The others laughed and walked off to their dorm room, leaving Siri and Dtui alone on the patio. Dtui poked out her tongue when they were out of sight.

"Creeps," she said.

"Just victims of the money culture," Siri said. "They'll change. Taking away a man's comfort strips him down to basics, lets him see what he really is. Suddenly finding one-self with nothing can add a dimension. If they survive the cold and the hunger and diseases up here, they'll be more real than they are now, more humble."

"Ah, you'd find primroses in a pile of poop, Dr. Siri. I'm sure you would. But they won't change."

"Have a little faith, Dtui."

"Once a pig, always a pig."

Siri raised his bushy eyebrows. "Unless it's a pog."

Once their laughter had died down, they sat looking up at the crags that blended into the night sky.

"Do you think we'll get a chance to do some sightseeing?" Dtui asked.

"Who knows? We don't even know why we're here. They might have us bumbling around all over the northeast. Why, where do you want to go?"

"Ma says there's a temple up near Xieng Khaw with a relic of the Lord Buddha." Siri gave a wry smile. "What?"

"Which particular relic is it this time, Nurse Dtui? A tooth? A severed toe? An eyeball?"

"You're an old cynic," she huffed. "I'm not telling you."

"Cynicism has nothing to do with it, dear. It all comes down to mathematics and physiology. Just count the temples around Asia that claim to have an actual bit of the Lord Buddha or his footprint. If all their boasts were true, his holiness would indeed have been a sight to behold. There he'd be, plodding around the countryside with feet the size of water-urn covers, a couple of thousand teeth crammed into his mouth, and toe- and fingernails shedding like the hair off a rabid dog. It doesn't bear thinking about. No wonder people followed him."

Dtui shifted to the far side of the table. "Where are you off to?" he asked.

"Nowhere. Just don't want to be sitting beside you when the lightning hits you."

Siri laughed. "You obviously haven't been paying attention at your political briefings, Comrade. Unless you count the politburo, there are no gods. Even if a real one were able to sneak under the Party barbed wire, he'd be a grounded god. They've decommissioned fire and brimstone."

"No God? I bet your old Karl Marx didn't make this scenery."

"Heretic."

"It is lovely up here though, Doc."

"It certainly is, when you have time to enjoy it."

"When you aren't dodging bombs, you mean?"

"That's all I did for ten years. That and put together people who hadn't been so lucky."

"When do you think they'll tell us why we're here?"

They'd been given short notice to get to Wattay Airport with their equipment. Judge Haeng had told them nothing of the mission, just the name of the person who'd contact them the next day.

"Comrade Lit should be here by nine tomorrow."

"And who's he again?"

"Regional commander, Security Division."

"Right. Did you know him when you were based here?"

"I don't recall the name. But when all the senior comrades and the ranking army officers moved down to Vientiane, a lot of young bucks were promoted in a hurry up here. Cadres were flying up through the ranks at such young ages I heard the regional quartermaster was still in diapers when he arrived at his office. They had to confiscate his rattle before they could get any work out of him." Dtui chuckled. "I don't know. I might have seen this Lit fellow around," Siri went on.

"Does he know you've brought your cuddly and gorgeous assistant?"

"I'm sure he'll be delighted."

Again, the calm around them lulled the two into a peaceful silence. An amateur fisherman cast his mushroom-shaped net out into the inky black pond. The squirrels chirped like sparrows with sore throats. Dtui looked toward the staircase behind Siri.

"Doc."

"Yes?"

"At the top of the stairs . . ."

"I don't know."

"How do you know what I'm going to ask?"

"You're going to ask why there's a partition up there with an armed guard sitting in front of it."

"Ooh, you're good. Did your spirits tell you what I was thinking?"

"No need. I read your mind myself. You're insatiably curious, so it was only a matter of time before you asked. I also heard you flirting with the guard."

"He wasn't very sociable."

"You mean he wouldn't tell you what's behind the partition?"

"Not a word. I hate mysteries."

"No doubt we'll work it out before we go."

But now, on his lumpy kapok mattress, drowsily watching the moths fly clockwise around the bulb he, too, was contemplating the mystery behind the plywood partition. Access to a small upper wing of the building was blocked. From the grounds he was able to estimate there were three or four rooms up there. He wondered what was so special about them. He clawed his fingers through his thick white hair and sighed. It was some time after 11:00 PM and he feared he'd be unable to find any sleep at all. There was too much on his mind. And if he didn't think himself awake all night, *they* would certainly keep him up. He reached for the ancient white amulet that hung around his neck on a tightly woven white plait of woman's hair. As his fingers made contact, a surge of energy ran in a current the length of his body. He could suddenly hear *them* even more clearly, chattering in the distance. His feelings and instincts had begun to take on tangible form. Spirits he once encountered only in his sleep had become bold. Some even appeared in daylight, often at the most inopportune moments. Even before the old Russian Mi-14 helicopter had landed that afternoon, he could feel the souls of the thousands killed during the war. They passed through him like sightseers at a historical palace, deciding whether he was a shaman they could trust.

All around Guesthouse Number One, their voices could be heard: mothers calling their children in from the open fields, old women crying for the old men they'd left behind, toddlers giggling—too innocent to realize they'd been dead for many years. How could Siri sleep with such an accompaniment? Then, as if things weren't already bad enough, at about midnight the awful disco music started up. It destroyed any hope of sleep. He wondered what type of people would start dancing in the middle of the night and how anyone could enjoy such an ugly Western din. Or perhaps this was one of the Party's torture techniques to punish the officials from Vientiane. He could think of few things more cruel.

The Red-Tag Bag Room

Geung Watajak had been born in October 1952 in a village on the outskirts of Vientiane called Thangon consisting of a temple and a tiny collection of wooden huts that blew down in the wet-season monsoons. Its only reason for appearing on maps at all was its ferry, which labored back and forth across the Nam Ngum River, sending people to and from the great reservoir. Few travelers stopped in Thangon for any other reason, but a village had grown up there nevertheless. Despite its proximity to the capital and the constant stream of passing gentry, it was very much a hick town.

Beliefs were simple there. According to the locals, there were only two categories of mental infirmity: slow as a tree growing and fruity as a bad batch of plum cider. Thangon had itself one of each. Auntie Soun had briefly been the shaman for the region before she completely forgot how to release the evil spirits back to the forest. They became bottled up inside her like soda gas until one day she flipped her lid. She became renowned for wild solo rantings and spontaneous acts of flashing.

Geung, on the other hand, had been a very quiet baby, one of seven children. He displayed the physical characteristics of Down syndrome so just one look at his face and everyone knew there was no point in sending the boy to school. It's true he was a slow learner but that might have been because nobody ever tried to teach him anything. Only his mother called him by his name. His father, brothers, and sisters all called him Moron. It wasn't said in a nasty way, and Geung reached eighteen years of age still thinking it was his mother who'd got it wrong.

As the Watajaks were a farming family, their routines were repetitive and uncomplicated and that suited the happy boy. Hard work built up his slowly developing muscles, and being around his family all day gave him a feeling of loyalty and belonging. But that security came to a sudden end on the day his father took him and two of his siblings to Vientiane to find them work. They were big enough and cost too much to feed. It was time for them to give a little something back to the lazy man who had gone to all the trouble of siring them. Their mother had no say in the matter.

The sister got work in a bamboo-and-corrugated-tin nightclub out on Hanoi Road by the market. The sad fact was she'd earn most of her salary with her feet in the air, but a fourteen-year-old farm girl with no schooling had to think herself lucky to have any kind of paying work. Geung's younger brother got a job at the bus terminal touting for passengers, collecting tickets, and hanging out of the door of the speeding bus announcing where it was headed at the top of his voice.

But his father knew that finding work for Geung was going to be the biggest challenge of all. Who in their right mind would want to take on a moron? But not only was the old man a layabout, he also possessed the nerve of the devil. He took his eighteen-year-old son to Mahosot Hospital, where he offered the boy's services free of charge in exchange for food scraps and a floor to sleep on. Hospitals, after all, were supposed to look after sick people. He reminded the hospital employment section of this fact, and the clerk on duty made the fatal mistake of displaying a moment's hesitation before saying no. So when she left the office at the end of the day, she saw young Geung sitting alone on the wooden bench out front. He had a newspaper-wrapped parcel on his lap.

"Where's your dad?"

"Home," he answered in a matter-of-fact way.

"Well, you can't stay here. You know that, don't you?"

He smiled, showing a line of teeth that looked as if they'd all been borrowed from different people's mouths. When she arrived for work the next morning, Mr. Geung was sitting in the same position, and the next day, and the next. Each day he smiled, displaying his unmatching teeth, and wished her good health, and his newspaper parcel got smaller and smaller till all his dried fish was eaten. So it was that Geung Watajak became an unpaid member of the staff at Vientiane's newest hospital.

As it turned out, there was a job that *normal* people were unable to do for any period of time. It was in the clearing room behind the hospital laundry. It had driven off four applicants in two months. It was the place where red-tagged bags arrived from the wards and operating theatres. The tag denoted soiled items. This generally meant blood and excrement but there were often other little surprises wrapped hurriedly in the sheets and blankets. Over the five years he worked there, Geung could likely have put together several complete human beings from all the spare parts.

His task was to rinse through the red-tag linens and surgeons' rubber aprons, and take out the bits and pieces before sending the laundry off to be boiled in industrial washers. He was given a small room to sleep in and coupons to use in the staff canteen. He never complained about his gruesome work or his lack of income. This was his destiny. Every now and then, his father would make a very brief appearance on a "salary collection run." Although Geung had no money to give him to take back to the farm, the old man would bring a little fruit and a baton of sticky rice in bamboo along with interesting news of people who only barely registered in Geung's memory. The young man never asked to return home.

Geung's uncomplicated honesty endeared him to the nurses and other medical staff. He became so popular that one of the doctors, Pongruk, decided it was time to rescue him from the red-tag bag room. Since Geung had first come to Mahosot, the Americans had rented Laos and most of the people in it. The colonizers' money paid government salaries, bankrolled the military, and set up selected pockets of infrastructure in an attempt to hold off the advancing Reds. USAID funding had sent Dr. Pongruk to Bangkok and Washington to learn the trade of forensic medicine. Upon his return, he was to set up a new morgue on the hospital grounds.

Apart from Dr. Pongruk's wage, there was one more half salary available that the Lao authorities envisaged would pay for the services of a part-time nurse. When the doctor told them he'd found someone very competent to work full-time for the small salary, they were delighted— until they found out whom the doctor had in mind. Like most other people, Dr. Pongruk had been appalled when he found out Geung had worked for all those years without pay. He understood that, due to his condition and lack of written qualifications, the hospital couldn't hire Geung officially in any capacity. But slavery had died out in Laos by the end of the Lan Xang kingdom and he wanted to pay Geung back somehow.

The interim American administration agreed that this would certainly be the right thing to do, so the doctor set about training Mr. Geung as his morgue assistant. He showed infinite patience and put in many extra night hours to get Geung to a point where he was proficient at morgue duties. And the young man took to the job with great enthusiasm. He could take off the cap of a skull without grazing the brain and snip through ribs as if they were chalk with his long-handled cutters. He carried bodies and their errant parts around the lab like a caring member of the deceased's family.

The doctor told his wife one night, "It's a bit like using *kee see* sap to seal the planks of a boat. You have to be patient till the resin takes hold, but once it sets you couldn't prize it apart with a mallet and chisel." So when Dr. Pongruk and his wife floated across the Mekhong River one night to escape whatever the communists might have had in mind for academics, they left behind a morgue assistant with a knowledge of the procedures of autopsies second to no one in Laos. But there was no longer a coroner for him to work with. The morgue was shut. For six months, Geung was returned to the red-tag bag room. He didn't complain or see it as a demotion. It was his destiny.

Then one day, Dr. Siri had arrived, Nurse Dtui was pulled from the wards, and the morgue came alive again. They needed Geung's expertise, and very soon the three became a team. It couldn't, however, be called a team of forensic professionals. Siri had been a surgeon all his life but had never conducted an autopsy and didn't particularly want to. He sought the retirement he thought he deserved and was very reluctant to commence this new career. They'd spent that first year learning and guessing. Even now, with no lab, no modern equipment, and no textbooks outlining up-to-date techniques, the Mahosot morgue was often a scene of rampant experimentation. If it hadn't been for Siri's gift—his ability to communicate with the spirits of the dead—there would likely have been some very serious mistakes made.

Their shared experience had brought the three colleagues very close together. To Geung, Dtui was a sister, and Siri a grandfather. Although he couldn't explain his feeling, Geung loved them like no one else in his life. Even when he wasn't sure what was going on, he suffered along with them. He enjoyed their victories and cried at their sorrows. He was as sensitive to their emotions as a barometer in an airship. They trusted him, and his honesty prevented him from making promises he wouldn't be able to keep. That, in turn, increased the value of the ones he did make. Honoring promises took precedence over everything else in his simple mind. Before they'd left on this latest trip, Comrade Dr. Siri had made him promise to look after the morgue until they came back.

His duties were simple when the doctor was away. The hospital could accept no more than two bodies at a time. Geung would be responsible for storing them, bunk-bed style, in the single freezer. There was unlikely to be a sudden intake of corpses requiring an autopsy. The dengue outbreak in the Vientiane basin was spreading fast but there were no mysteries as to how it did its deadly deed: fever, lethargy, bleeding, and death. The morgue only handled unexplained fatalities at the state hospitals and the odd murder referred by the police.

When they took on cases, Geung was indispensable. But he was not a mortician and could only perform his tasks in the presence of a doctor. All he was allowed to do while Siri and Dtui were away was dust, sweep, chase away cockroaches, and stand guard over the office. He took his role seriously; he'd even brought a blanket and pillow from his room and was ready to spend the night in the cutting room, an unlikely sentry.

He was the angel of peace. Anger and aggression had never been a part of his makeup, and he could feign neither. He was no scarier than a Chinese dumpling. So, when the two surly-looking men in uniform marched through the morgue entrance and called out his name, he greeted them with a smile that vanished when he saw their weapons.

"Wha . . . wha . . . what can I do for you, C . . . Comrades?" he asked.

They pointed their pistols at him and pulled their triggers. After a split second of astonishment, Mr. Geung fell to the floor like a ripe jackfruit from a tree.

A Restaurant with No Food

Siri's early-morning thoughts were disturbed by the rousing refrain of Patriotic Work Song Number Seventeen, "We Shall Hoe for the Republic," written by the president himself.

"Oh my lord. Now what?"

Bones cracked as the doctor eased himself to a sitting position, half in and half out of the mosquito netting. If he'd slept, he certainly had no recollection of it. Now that he was seventy-three years of age, time had acquired a value, and he'd just given away six hours of the stuff without getting anything in return. He got to his feet and staggered, dull as a stack of pillows, over to the window.

Through the gap in the green nylon curtains he could see the singing policemen, with their farming implements over their shoulders, climbing onto the back of an army truck. Although their warders stood well back and held their weapons down at their sides, they appeared no less threatening. Each movement was directed by the shriek of a whistle. The inmates stood with their eyes front, and the truck headed off along the dirt track. The song vanished into the mist along with its choir. All around, the crags melted into the fog like some gray Chinese watercolor. The sun wouldn't break through for another two hours.

Siri showered under a cold spout in the communal

bathroom. Stale water that smelt of carbolic and dirt squirted up from the loose tiles under his feet. He dressed and walked to breakfast, passing the solitary guard who nodded, half asleep, on a fold-up chair in front of the plywood partition.

"Good health," Siri said, but got no response.

The dining room contained twelve wonky tables without cloths, several framed black-and-white photos of the heroes of the revolution, and Dtui.

"Morning, Doc."

"Good morning. How long have you been down here?"

"About an hour. Couldn't sleep."

"Me neither." He sat opposite her in the silent room. "I feel we may be expected to sing for our breakfasts."

"This is a creepy place, isn't it?"

"You feel it as well?"

"Probably not the way you do. I don't get ghosties creeping into my bed in the middle of the night. But this building makes me feel strange. Plus, I've never . . ." She scrunched up her nose.

"Never what?"

"Never, you know, slept by myself before."

"Dtui, I feel this is another pog."

"No. I'm dead serious. I've always been with Ma—or in the nurses' dorm. Can't say I feel very safe up here by myself."

"You're going to have to get used to it. I dread to imagine you in Moscow announcing that you're unable to sleep alone, although you'd certainly be a popular import. You won't have your ma or the nurses with you in the Eastern Bloc, you know."

"If I get there."

"I have no doubt."

Siri looked over his shoulder to see whether there was any chance of service. He was a little embarrassed at raising Dtui's hopes again. Of course there was doubt. She'd recently taken the exams for applicants to advanced schools in the communist countries in Europe. For several years she'd studied secretly, not wanting to give the hospital administrators the idea she was smarter than they thought she was. Initiative could be interpreted entirely the wrong way in times such as these. She'd taken politics, medicine, and Russian, and stood an excellent chance of beating out medical students who had suffered since their teachers floated away across the river. The only fear Siri had was that she'd be elbowed off the list by relatives of the faithful cadres.

She had to play the game. Siri taught her what to say to fool the interviewers. He was an expert. He'd been playing communist charades for most of his life. His faith in the system had long since evaporated as he'd watched a perfectly good doctrine destroyed by personalities. What should have been a tool was being used as a weapon and he felt little pride now in his forty-eight-year membership in the Party. Dtui needed these three free years in Moscow more than most. With all the student grant money and the possibility of part-time nursing work, it would be a rich harvest for an impoverished Lao. But most of the scholarships went to those with connections, and the only person Dtui knew with influence was Siri. Unfortunately for her, he had refused to be sucked down into the same corrupt bog that had claimed most of his comrades in recent years. He hadn't called in favors from members of the politburo or used his position with the Department of Health. He had, however, insisted his way onto the board that vetted the scholarship applications. He was certain, if things were decided on merit, Dtui would be on her way to the Soviet Union in the new year. His presence on the committee increased the odds of fair play. But nothing could be taken for granted in the People's Democratic Republic of Laos.

Siri looked around the stark shadowy dining room but saw no signs of life. The seminar attendees were off blowing themselves up, and it appeared the staff wasn't expecting other guests. The evening before, there had been nothing available in the kitchen. Now the empty stomachs of Dtui and her boss were grumbling back and forth across the breakfast table. It was probably these sounds that caught the ear of a large lady wearing an apron over camouflage fatigues who had appeared in the doorway.

"What are you doing here?" she asked.

"Waiting for food," Dtui told her.

The woman's sandals flapped against the loosely tiled floor as she approached the unexpected guests. "Why aren't you out with the others?"

"We aren't on that tour," Siri told her. "We're on the three-day, two-night, padlocked-historical-temple package."

She stared at him, her expression as empty as the National Bank.

"Sorry," he conceded. "We're here at the invitation of the Security Division. We'll be staying for a few days."

"Hm. Nobody told me." She folded her arms as if challenging them to suggest otherwise.

"Sorry! That's my fault."

The voice came from behind the woman, and they had to lean back in their chairs to see its owner. He was a tall, lean young man in glasses. He wore the green uniform of a Lao People's Revolutionary Party policeman, but there were no badges or epaulets attached to it. He smiled as he rounded the obstruction. "Dr. Siri?"

Siri held out his hand. "Comrade Lit?"

"Sorry to have kept you waiting." The two men shook hands. Siri and Dtui noticed Lit's withered right index finger. It seemed to curl up like an unwatered plant.

"Not at all. We weren't expecting you till nine."

The large woman interrupted their greetings. "This isn't good enough, Comrade. You know I need a P8.8 at least three days before I can accept new guests. The night staff should never have taken them in without it."

"You're quite right, Comrade Sompet. I have the requisite form right here. This was something of an emergency. I apologize." He handed her the form, and she marched out of the room, still grumbling under her breath.

Comrade Lit remained standing. "Well," he said, looking across the table at Dtui.

"This," Siri said, "is my assistant, Nurse Chundee Vongheuan."

She smiled. "You can call me Dtui, Comrade."

"We were just about to start eating the flower arrangements," Siri said. "Would you care to join us?"

Lit laughed. "Not very nutritious, I'm afraid. They're all plastic. Let me take you both somewhere else for breakfast."

As they drove through Vieng Xai in his Chinese jeep, Lit pointed out the towering cliffs, locally known as karsts, that housed famous caves. "That's where General Khamtay lived and where the military strategies were all put together," he said. "Over yonder is the home of the prime minister."

The tour was for Dtui's benefit. Siri had visited all the caves during his long years in the northeast and knew exactly what elaborate chambers and tunnels these turrets of limestone contained. But to Dtui there was nothing to distinguish one tower from the next. American planes flying low back and forth through this valley for years had been confronted with the same problem. Even the crags that were bombed late in the war had held up to the random seeding of five-hundred-kilogram shells. It seemed incredible to Dtui that two million tons of bombs could be dropped in the communist-held territories without inflicting so much as a bruise on any of the leaders.

Vieng Xai was an odd place for the capital of the new regime. The streets were laid out in a wide grid, enclosed by the crags beneath which the old soldiers had spent ten years of their lives. This was the view they had seen every day from their caves and to them it represented freedom. Four years earlier it had been a vast, empty expanse of rice fields. For fear of daylight raids, the locals hid until the sun went down and came out to tend the fields at night. But with the cease-fire, the comrades emerged from their mountains and began to build their dream. They'd imagined constructing a grand city as a fitting monument to their years of struggle.

But Laos was more than Huaphan province. It was a country of some three and a half million people. There were no available current figures, and as many as five hundred thousand might have fled to Thailand, but the bulk of the population remained in and around the capital. Once the Pathet Lao had marched triumphantly into Vientiane to claim the country for communism, Vieng Xai suddenly seemed remote and inaccessible. To run a country, you had to be where the people were. They weren't in Huaphan, and they didn't appear to be in Vieng Xai. Two more guesthouses and a market were under construction here but the bamboo scaffold was green with moss. There was a feeling that this was a project on hold, a dream that had been half forgotten at sunrise.

Beside the market site stood a single shop that sold *feu* rice noodles in bowls deep enough to bathe a small baby. Siri and Dtui ate heartily with their left hands and fought off flies the size of coat buttons with their right. Lit had already eaten so he watched his guests conducting their breakfasts as he told them why they were there.

"We probably wouldn't have found it at all," he began. "Every now and then, rocks at the top of the karsts come loose. Some that were hit by rockets take their time before falling. We think that's what happened in this case. A big hunk of rock came crashing down onto the concrete path we'd laid from the cave to the new house. You'll notice, Doctor, most of the senior comrades have built houses in front of their old caves."

"Hm. Not wanting to leave the womb. It's common in primates," Siri said. "And whose cave are we talking about here?"

"The president's. He's due back here in a little over a week so the Party really needs to work out what happened before he arrives."

"Right," Siri said. "So the rock struck the concrete path . . . ?"

"And there it was, sticking out of the broken section."

"What was?"

"The arm."

"And is there a body attached to it?" Dtui asked. She wiped her mouth with a napkin and abandoned the last of the broth to the flies.

"We don't know."

"Why not?" asked Siri.

"Well, the arm's sticking out of the concrete so if there's a body in there, we'd have to break up the rest of the path to get to it."

"And you can't do that because . . . ?"

"Because there are very strict regulations about making alterations to government-initiated structures. We had to submit the request forms to Vientiane to ask for permission. They said we had to wait for you."

"I see. I hope you've covered the arm. The flies up here have quite an appetite."

"We tied a plastic bag over it. I'll take you up there when you're ready. We can stop off and pick up a couple of laborers and tools on the way."

"Then, let us not keep our cement person waiting. Finished, Nurse Dtui?"

"Ready when you are, Dr. Siri."

You didn't have to travel very far out of Vientiane before the road turned to pebbles and potholes. Traveling in a truck was like falling down an endless flight of uneven steps in a coffin. They'd passed the turnoff at kilometer 6 where the old U.S. compound had been recycled into a resort for communist politicians. They'd just reached the intersection that led to the National Pedagogical Institute at Dong Dok when Mr. Geung came around. He was thumped out of his stupor when the front wheel dropped into a deep rut. Although his mind was still back at the morgue, he found his body lying on a blanket on the wooden boards of an old truck. Above him were the open sky, a vicious June sun, and two rows of knees. He lay in an aisle of black boots that stank of polish. The toe caps penned him in so tightly he could do nothing but lie still stiffly and wonder where he was and whose were these legs that ended at the knees? He lifted one arm and waved, which produced an immediate response.

"Sergeant, the Mongoloid's awake."

There was a loud cheer and laughter, and a gruff voice yelled above the sound of the motor, "Get him up." Bodies leaned over him, and hands reached down to pull him into a sitting position. From there he found himself staring at two rows of smiling soldiers. He smiled back. The sergeant was at the end of one row.

"Your name's Geung, right?"

Mr. Geung had had little contact with the military but he'd been to parades and played soldiers when he was young, so he knew what he should do. He saluted. There was another loud cheer and half the men saluted back. Two of them shifted sideways to make a space on the bench for him, then pulled him up. He could see unfamiliar fields bouncing past the truck, buffalo with no mud to wallow in, many different shades of brown everywhere.

"Damn, boy, I thought you were dead," the sergeant shouted to him. "Never seen a man dropped by an empty gun before."

"You f . . . frightened me."

"Just messing with you, son. Just a little joke."

"I fainted."

"You sure did."

"Wh . . . wh . . . where are we going?"

"Nam Bak."

The name meant nothing to Geung. "Why?"

"Top-secret mission." The sergeant put his finger to his lips to show there was a need to keep quiet about it. Geung felt very important to be going on a top-secret mission, but he'd made a promise. He got clumsily to his feet and walked to the tailgate, using the chests and knees of the seated soldiers for support. The sergeant caught hold of him before he vanished off the end of the truck. "Now what do you think you're up to?" the old soldier asked.

"I . . . I . . . I . . . I have to g . . . guard the morgue."

"No you don't, son."

"Yes. Yes I d . . . do. I promised Comrade Dr. Siri a . . . a . . . and Comrade Nurse Dtui."

"You don't work at the morgue anymore."

This was a serious revelation to Geung. "No?"

"No."

"Where d . . . d . . . do I work?"

"You'll find out."

"B . . . b . . . but I . . . I pr . . . pro . . ." The words began to collide again and Geung's head spun.

"Geung, younger brother, I don't want any trouble from you. You understand?"

"I . . . I . . ."

"Just go back to your seat and enjoy the journey. You'll like—" But before the sergeant could say another word, Geung passed out again, this time across the laps of the Third Division of the Lao People's Liberation Army Infantry on its way to the north to hunt out insurgents.

Concrete Man

The jeep pulled up in front of the president's compound, and Siri looked up the slope at the pretty pink-and-green villa that nestled in among the towering cliffs. Carved out of the rock opposite was a one-and-a-half-car garage, and where the steps began to wind upward, an ornamental heart-shaped pool had been lovingly fashioned from a bomb crater. It was all so creepily quaint.

"You know, Doc?" Dtui said as they started up the concrete steps. "All this time I had visions of you lot living up here like cavemen, wrapped in bearskins. I didn't dream it would be so—civilized."

"Surely you didn't expect the president of the republic to have had to hunt for his breakfast with a bow and arrow?"

"It wouldn't surprise me, given how hard it is to find breakfast up here."

Lit led them to a walkway that wound up to the cave entrance. Up the incline a little way, a boulder the size of a bloated buffalo lay on a bed of flattened itchy fruit blossoms and poinsettias. It must have given the concrete one heck of a thump when it landed, then bounced into the garden. The force of its impact had tilted up a long, straight section of the three-foot-wide path, causing it to snap at various points. Now it lay in sections, like carriages after a train crash.

Ahead, a small canvas tent had been erected over the path between two of the sections. Lit lifted the canvas from its frame to reveal a mummified arm protruding from one side of a wide gap in the concrete. It was covered in a transparent plastic bag tied to the wrist. Its palm was up and its fingers bent into claws. From its position, Siri estimated that the body, assuming it was still attached to one, would be lying on its back inside the unbroken slab of concrete.

"Well, I suppose we should get cracking," Siri said to the two workmen who'd followed them up. Both had stonemason's chisels and metal mallets.

"How would you like it, Doctor?" one asked.

The section that lay before them was over six feet long and two and a half feet deep. Siri pondered for a moment. "I think we should attack it from the sides. Here, I'll give you some marks to guide you." He used a block of white limestone to score a line on either side of the broken section of pathway.

"Uhm, Dr. Siri," Lit asked, "wouldn't it be easier to go in from the end where the hand's sticking out, or from the top?"

"Easier, yes, Comrade Lit. But not as beneficial."

"I don't think I understand."

"Nurse Dtui will explain it to you."

Dtui was shocked out of her daydream. "Will I?"

"Certainly." This was Siri's way. He often threw her in to see if she'd float. He wouldn't come to her rescue until he was absolutely certain she couldn't bob to the surface on her own.

"OK." She looked at the peculiar scene and quickly ran through the possibilities in her mind. "Right!" she said. "If there's a body, it'll be faceup. Judging from the state of the arm, it's mummified; ergo, it would have shrunk."

Siri smiled and she knew she was on the right track. She continued with more confidence.

"As he probably didn't get inside the concrete after it was set, we have to assume he was deliberately buried in wet cement—or fell in. That means the cement hardened around him. As the body shrank, a mold would have been left of the original person. That mold could tell us as much as the body itself. So we don't want to damage the concrete too much. Dah dah," she sang. "I don't hear clapping."

Lit and one of the workmen did indeed applaud. The security chief looked at her with undisguised admiration. "Very well done," he said. "Yes, excellent."

Siri, still smiling, was looking more closely at the hand. He removed the plastic bag and took a closer look at the clawed fingers. The skin was the color of dark chocolate, not so unusual in mummified bodies. He knew a body at this stage of mummification wouldn't reveal many secrets. But the palm of this hand seemed several tones lighter than the back of the hand.

The workmen began to chisel along the dotted line he had drawn as carefully as an archaeologist at an ancient dig.

"Gentlemen," Siri urged, "it's concrete. At the rate you're going, you won't get through it until the year 2006. Smash the hell out of it, for goodness' sake."

And smash they did. They worked from either side while Lit, Dtui, and Siri sat at the foot of the karst. A feeble sun had finally burned a hole through the northeastern mist but hadn't yet warmed the land. Dtui and Lit filled the following hour with their friendly chatter while Siri dozed. The young couple seemed to have a great deal in common. Both had spent the later years of their lives caring for a sick parent. Dtui told Lit that her mother, Monoluk, had cirrhosis, and that they were presently living at Siri's house. She explained that the doctor didn't like to live alone and he'd managed to gather a peculiar collection of waifs and strays to share his large Party bungalow. Lit's father, on the other hand, had lost both his legs and a length of intestine to a bomb that exploded beneath his feet. A few months ago he'd succumbed to his injuries.

Both Lit and Dtui had taken every opportunity to study. Lit had attained his position, despite his relative youth, by working his way through the public service texts. Dtui had memorized numerous medical books in self-taught English. Then, when American aid vanished, she'd gone through the same subjects in self-taught Russian. Her dream was to join the twenty-five hundred Lao presently studying in the Eastern Bloc and to send home whatever she could save to her mother.

Their conversation was terminated by the sound of a loud crack. Siri looked up from his slumber. The workmen had succeeded in prizing the top layer of the slab loose with crowbars. The concrete lid broke in two as they lifted it off the base.

A mummy, as if in frozen horror, lay shriveled within a shell of concrete that it had once filled. One arm was by its side; the other held high above its head. Its knees were bent slightly and it seemed to be dressed only in a pair of nylon football shorts that were now several sizes too large for it. Their brilliant red contrasted sharply with the almost black-chocolate surface of the corpse.

But what shocked the onlookers most—even Siri who had seen death in many forms—was the expression of agony on its face, in which a huge gaping hole had taken the place of its mouth. They had no doubt this had been a torturous death—and no accident.

"What . . . what happened to its face?" Lit asked in horror.

Siri took hold of the concrete lid of the accidental tomb and heaved it back to study its interior. The mold was completed there, providing an almost perfect concave mask of the head. Where the mouth had attempted its muffled cry for the last time, a tube of cement curled downward. Embedded at its base were the missing teeth.

"I think this explains the hole," Siri said, not looking up. The others came over to peer within. "It would appear the final breaths of our friend here were of liquid cement. When it hardened and the body began to shrink, the teeth remained in their original position. I wouldn't be surprised if we found more cement in the lungs."

"My God," Lit said. "You mean he was alive when he went into the concrete?"

"It looks that way," Dtui confirmed.

"What a terrible way to die. Who could have done such a thing?"

"I'd have to suppose, judging from the size of the original body, that it was somebody of enormous strength," Siri replied.

"Or several people," Dtui added.

"Yes, indeed. Good point. Comrade Lit, do you think the president would object if we used the meeting room in his house as a makeshift morgue?"

"I have the key," Lit told him. "But he'll be here next week for the concert."

"If we haven't worked this out by then, we never will, son. It doesn't take me that long to concede defeat."

Judge Haeng came back from another half day of fussy domestic disputes in his courtroom. A city whose criminals and potential criminals had all been incarcerated, in which crime had been abolished, was a dull place for a magistrate. He walked past the desks of the Justice Department clerks, who sat sweating into their clunky typewriters. They nodded with little enthusiasm as their young boss went by. In the year since he'd taken up his position fresh from Moscow, he hadn't spoken to any of them civilly. Usually he addressed them through Mrs. Manivone, the senior clerk. When he approached her desk, she stood politely and smiled her meaningless smile. She wore a neatly ironed khaki blouse and a black *pasin* ankle-length straight skirt. Usually, she was equally unruffled.

"Good health, Judge Haeng."

"Has he gone?"

"Who?"

"The freak at the morgue."

She sighed. "If you mean Mr. Geung, they collected him last night. He should be there on Wednesday."

"Good. Excellent." He set off for his office.

"It's just . . ."

He turned back. "What?"

"Well, I'm not sure I understand, Judge. Everybody's very fond of Mr. Geung."

"Fond? Fond? Are we running a government department or a home for social outcasts? I'm very fond of my grandmother"—Mrs. Manivone didn't believe that—"but I wouldn't give her a responsible job in the national morgue. What image would foreign visitors take home if they came and saw a moron working for the state?"

She had a number of possible responses to that but, under her breath, all she managed was, "One of compassion?"

"What was that?"

"I don't think Dr. Siri's going to be very pleased about it when he returns."

The judge sauntered back to her. "Oh, you don't?"

"No."

He leaned on her desk and raised his voice so the others could hear. "And remind me—does Dr. Siri work for the Justice Department?"

"Yes, Judge Haeng."

"And am I the head of the Justice Department, missy?"

Manivone once again reminded herself she had three children to feed. "Yes, Judge Haeng."

"So, does he do what I tell him, or do I do what he tells me?"

"Well, neither, in fact, as I've seen, Comrade." It was a rash comment, albeit true. She knew there was a Party slogan on its way.

"Now, don't get fresh, Comrade Manivone. Every bee in the socialist hive is as important as the next. But if the worker doesn't show respect to the queen, the honey does not flow as sweetly. Remember that."

"Yes, Judge Haeng."

He looked around at the clerks, whose heads snapped back to their work. He smiled and walked smugly to his office. It would have been a spectacular exit had the door handle not stuck again. He swore at it and finally fought his way into the room before slamming the door.

"God save the queen," mumbled one clerk to the muffled laughter of his colleagues.

As the truck drove farther and farther from Vientiane, Mr. Geung's anxiety level increased. Some of the soldiers feared that something might burst inside him. To them he seemed like an animal caught in a trap, one who might bite off his own foot in order to escape. Even the sergeant felt a pang of guilt as he watched Geung shuddering on the bench. But he had his directive: delivery to a work team in the north. The order had come from the Justice Department so he was in no position to argue. Once the sun had gone down, their prisoner stopped responding to the soldiers' questions, and no attempt to cheer him up was productive. They couldn't comprehend the magnitude of Geung's feeling of guilt for letting his friends down, or how terribly lonely and sad he was.

The unit was to spend the night at the Eighth Battalion camp just outside Van Khi. The truck pulled into the fenced compound and Geung looked up to see the gate close behind him. There was no escape.

The Missing Moron

An autopsy has one purpose: to solve mysteries that surround a death. If, after three hours, the original mysteries remain and have been supplemented by even deeper mysteries, one should begin to consider the procedure a failure. Siri and Dtui looked at each other with every new unanswerable question and shook their heads. Admittedly, the condition of the corpse made their task a good deal more difficult. The cement had been laid in late January so the body had slowly mummified over the subsequent five months. Everything had contracted to the point that wounds or any traces of disease would have become hidden in the tight carapace which the skin had become or the tangle of knots beneath it.

However, three small oddities had presented themselves right away. First, clenched tightly in the right fist was a key—a long, thin type with a circular top and an uncomplicated shape at the bottom. Second, and no surprise to either of them, the corpse's teeth were pink, indicating the man had probably died a violent death. Third, sticking up from the concrete where the victim's chest had laid, they found a long broken fingernail, although the corpse's own nails were trimmed short. It was coated in some type of varnish that had kept it in good condition. They could only conclude that the nail had originally been embedded in the victim's skin.

These peculiarities had been comparatively easy to spot. The others took longer. For example, they hadn't discovered the bullet hole in the chest until much later, and only after a meticulous inch-by-inch fingertip examination of the skin. Siri was able to insert a French crochet needle deep into the minute aperture but couldn't make contact with the bullet. They decided that they would have to wait to make an internal examination.

There were a number of characteristics that suggested the man wasn't Asian. The bone structure of the face and the fullness of the lips suggested that the corpse was negroid. Siri assumed that to a degree this could have resulted from postmortem distortion but the skin itself was darker than he'd ever seen due to mummification. The corpse's teeth confirmed Siri's hypothesis. Dtui had been able to carefully chip the concrete away from them to reveal the shape of the palate. The upper incisors formed a deep U, and that strongly suggested the dead man had been of African ancestry.

The dissection of the body hadn't produced a great deal more information. Dtui and Siri were mystified by such a neat hole with no trace of a bullet. The channel didn't pass completely through the body, but no amount of searching had turned it up. This they added to their list of questions.

Lit came to hear their findings. He sat with them around a thermos of tea and three tin cups on the veranda of the guesthouse. It was four in the afternoon and surprisingly quiet. They hadn't yet got around to discussing the victim.

"Looks like the policemen got lost," Dtui said, noting that the trucks hadn't returned. Siri hadn't thought to tell her of his suspicions as to their fate.

Comrade Lit was more forthcoming. "The American lackeys won't be back tonight," he told her quite casually.

Siri was used to the labels the Party attached to the officials of the old regime, but he saw Dtui's eyebrows rise as if she was seeing a different version of the chief. She shouldn't have been surprised. A cadre didn't rise to the position of security head at such a young age without knowing how to tightrope walk along the Party line. It was an ever-swaying line and it was easy to fall off.

"Why not?" Dtui asked.

"They've been transferred to a camp," Lit told her.

"Really? I didn't see them loading their suitcases onto the truck this morning."

"No."

It was a no that Lit anticipated would mark the end of this line of inquiry, but he didn't know Dtui.

"How can they be transferred without their belongings?"

Siri could see her stepping very close to the edge. Lit had been most polite all day, but staunch Party members didn't expect to be questioned; they weren't used to it.

"I think we should talk about our cement man," the doctor said.

But Lit wished to continue. "They won't need belongings where they're going, Nurse Dtui."

"No belongings?" Dtui stood at the very edge of the crumbling precipice. "No clothes? No toiletries? No mementos of home?"

"No."

"Why on earth not?" There was suddenly a vacuum between the two.

"Because they have to learn to live without them."

"Live without clothes? It's cold up here at night. They'll catch their deaths."

"That may be the case. Those who aren't able to adapt to new conditions naturally become their victims."

Siri tried again. "I think we should—"

"Adapt? What? Do you expect them to grow thick body hair overnight?" She had plummeted down into the chasm and was beyond saving.

Lit straightened in his seat and spoke loudly. "We aren't animals, Comrade Dtui. Of course we provide them with a blanket each and basic supplies. But we expect the early days at Seminar to be hard for the corrupt American lackeys who have lived fat lives bleeding the masses. Their own excesses have softened them. We're giving them an opportunity to become valuable members of society."

"Through hard labor and cruelty?"

"Dtui!" Siri raised his voice. He was becoming annoyed, not by the questions, which he considered valid, but because she'd failed to recognize the right time to keep her mouth shut.

Lit was on the attack now. "Your type never takes the trouble to understand."

"My type? And what exactly is—"

"Shut up!" Siri smashed his tin cup down hard onto the table. Tea bounced out of it and splashed across the varnished wooden surface. "Both of you. I didn't travel four hundred kilometers to argue ideology. We're here to discuss a crime, and a horrible crime at that. Would you both mind showing a little professional discipline?"

It was the closest Dtui had ever seen her boss come to throwing a tantrum. She suspected he was bluffing but she knew she'd pushed too far. "Sorry, Doc. You're right."

Lit still glared at her but spoke to Siri. "You're right, of course, Dr. Siri. What information do you have for me from today's inspection?"

With a sigh of relief, Siri described the condition of the corpse and the peculiarities they had found. Dtui kept silent.

"In conclusion," Siri said, "it appears that the gentleman was shot, then, still alive, was held under the wet cement until he, in effect, drowned. It was certainly the cement that killed him, although I imagine the gunshot wound would have weakened him considerably. It punctured a lung."

"And you believe he was black," Lit added, now nothing more or less than a sober investigator of crime.

"I wouldn't bet my life on it but I strongly suspect so. That would have to make him Cuban."

"Why?" Dtui asked, breaking her silence.

"The only dark-skinned foreigners you're likely to find up here are Cubans," Siri said. "Mr. Castro has been very generous with aid and personnel. There used to be a joint Cuban-Vietnamese hospital project not far from here."

"They're still here," Lit told him.

"Really? Is Dr. Santiago still in charge?"

"He's managing the hospital aid money, I believe. I wouldn't say he's in charge of anything."

"Ah, good. I know him well, or at least as well as two men can who don't share a common language. It might be a good idea to pay a social call on the good doctor and see if they lost any Cubans around the time the path was laid."

"Then, er, I can leave that line of inquiry up to you, Doctor?"

Siri thought it odd the security man would relinquish his role in the investigation to a mere coroner but didn't bother to ask why. He enjoyed a bit of detective work. "Certainly."

"Good," Lit said. "Then I should get back to my office. I'll check in with you the same time tomorrow. I've arranged for the kitchen here to provide you with food three times a day. The staff won't have much else to do for another week." He stood and nodded.

"Until the next batch of lackeys arrives," Dtui told Siri. If Lit heard her, he ignored the comment and walked away. Once his jeep reached the dirt road, Siri glared at Dtui and shook his head.

"What?" she asked.

"You haven't spent very much time around communists, have you?"

"You're a communist."

"There's a vast difference between being a paid-up member of the Party and *being* a communist. Real communists take life quite seriously. If you don't agree with their doctrine, then you're the enemy."

"Their doctrine? Dr. Siri, you're one of them. It's your doctrine, too."

"And there were long periods when I truly believed. In fact, I still think a well-run socialist system could rescue the world from its lethargy and selfishness. But it's something people should come to of their own accord, through common sense . . ."

"Not torture."

"Correct. But it isn't a situation you're going to change by attempting to shout down people like Comrade Lit. Nobody shouts louder than a Red."

"So how's it going to change?"

"It'll burn itself out."

"But before then a lot of people are going to suffer."

"And I don't want one of them to be you. So keep that pretty mouth buttoned. And that's an order. You aren't going to make a dribble of a difference. You know what they say about loose tongues."

"They fall out?"

Siri laughed. He never had been able to maintain an effective show of severity for any sustained period. Dtui sulked but she understood. She knew Siri's views had been derived from years of trying to make changes from the inside and failing. His relationship with the woman he loved and was faithful to for almost forty years had brought him into the Communist Party and kept him there. But he'd been distant enough from it to see the Pathet Lao become the lapdogs of the Vietnamese, just as the Royalists had slobbered around the heels of the French and the Americans. He was resigned to the fact that his Lao brethren were destined always to be the fools of some bigger fools. He wasn't a terrific example of a man who knew when to keep his mouth shut, but Dtui knew he didn't offer advice lightly.

That night, exhausted though he was, Siri still rolled sleeplessly from side to side on the lumpy mattress. So many ghosts were calling to him from the fields. Impressionable young cadres were among them. He'd put many back together in field hospitals after their encounters with the Hmong resistance. They were telling him, "Look at us. What good did it do? All you did was fix us up so we could go and be killed in the next battle." They were right. He didn't want to listen to them. He wanted to sleep, but in sleep he'd have to face the malevolent spirits who lurked in the dark alleyways of his nightmares.

In the starless blackness of the chilly night, even with his eyes wide open, he could see none of the ill-matching furniture and not even the hand he held out before him. An invisible beetle was fluttering against the mosquito netting and he focused his attention on the buzzing of its wings. By imagining he could see it, by listening only to the buzz, he believed he could hypnotize himself asleep. And he was almost right. The voices had stopped, he was dipping in and out of consciousness, and at exactly the moment he was about to fall, the infernal discotheque started up again. Even though it seemed to come from afar, the tremor of the bass worked its way across the ground like an earthquake, reaching the second floor of the guesthouse. It vibrated through the bedposts, through Siri.

What had happened to his country's youth, he wondered, that they had developed such awful taste in music?

This wailing of tortured Americans, could it be deemed music at all? He lost count of the number of grating tunes he had to endure before he finally found the sleep he craved.

In the sleep world it was quiet, a rare quiet for his dream. A crow sat high on a wire beside a sparrow. They were a long way above the ground. This was a wire that could only have existed in a dream, because a T-28 fighter passed beneath it, strafing the fields with its guns. Bombs plunged into the paddies and sank into the mud, none exploding. It was a silent dream without even the accompaniment of music. The crow preened the sparrow as if both were unaware of their positions in the caste of birds or their proximity to a battle. They were engrossed in one another. Nothing else seemed to matter. It was a peaceful scene: the birds preening, the T-28 strafing, the nonexploding bombs tumbling.

Siri was suddenly shocked to find himself standing outside his mosquito net. He was shuddering, clad only in his undershorts: a slightly chewy smorgasbord for carnivorous insects. He had no idea why he'd left the sanctuary of the mesh or why he was standing there. Now light from a full moon oozed through the curtains, and he saw that in the vacant bed on the far side of his room, a child lay. She was about four years old and malnourished. When Siri walked over to her she looked up at him.

"When did you get here, darling?" he asked. "Why don't you have a mosquito net?"

She smiled. When she spoke, her voice seemed older than her apparent age. "I don't have much time, uncle."

"What can I do?"

"Take notice of what you see," she said.

There was a rumbling sound and the ceiling came crashing down on their heads. The floor beneath them gave way and they tumbled slowly downward like leaves falling from a tree. A cockerel joined them in their descent. It looked into Siri's eyes and crowed hoarsely.

A pale light was seeping in through the nylon curtain. Above Siri's head, the corpses of a dozen flying beetles lay bottoms up on the top of the netting. Although the spirits had been known to spring trick endings on him, this second awakening had a feel of reality about it. The falling chicken crowed again and was joined by a howling dog. From somewhere close, the sound of a *klooee*, a green bamboo flute, began. It was a simple tune, executed with technical accuracy but with little heart. As he listened, he squirmed around under the quilt to discover which of his bones and muscles would ache that day. He had no say in this. He often overexerted himself in his dreams and suffered for it the next morning. But today, even as he stood, everything seemed to work fine.

He walked over to the spare bed and looked at the unruffled quilt that covered it. For no logical reason he could think of, he pulled it back. There was nothing there. Of course. This was real life. What did he expect? He was in the process of putting it back when he squashed something beneath his bare foot. He heard the squelch and wondered whether he might have put the nonsticking lizard out of its misery, but it was just a berry. It had fallen from the dish of fruit on the table. It was a small red currant. He'd seen its kind before but couldn't put a name to it. A few years earlier he would have thrown it out. But everything that happened these days seemed to have relevance to some other thing. There were no coincidences. "Take notice of what you see." He wrapped the berry in a sheet of tissue from the roll on the table and put it into his bag.

* * *

Mr. Geung had heard of Luang Prabang and Dr. Siri's adventures there from the doctor himself. It was a place, like Paris, like Mrs. Kit's Broom and Brush Factory, like the moon. These were all only words to Geung. Visiting them was unthinkable and unnecessary. He had his own world and had no need to visit any other. So, when the convoy arrived in Luang Prabang province, he was neither impressed nor glad to be there. The journey had been a bone-jarring ordeal for all of them, but especially for Geung

Hopelessness sat heavily upon him. As he was unable to cope with all the new information he was being exposed to, he sat where he'd been put, on the wooden bench, and stared, bemused, at the passing scenery, a mountainous vista like nothing he'd ever seen in his limited life.

Whenever the truck stopped and the soldiers all climbed down to stretch their aching muscles, Geung followed them off into the forest to relieve himself. He'd become so docile and uncommunicative that the soldiers had begun to treat him more like a kit bag than a prisoner. He'd off-load himself from the truck and they'd stand him in a corner. They'd lead him to the mess tent or to the bunks. Wherever they put him, they knew that's where he'd be if they needed him. There was so little thought invested in him that by the time they reached the barracks at Xieng Ngeun, he'd been totally forgotten.

The sergeant ran up the wooden steps and knocked on the frame of the open door to the officers' rec room. He walked straight in and found his superior officer reading the *Huksat Lao* newsletter.

"Captain Ouan, sir?"

"What is it?"

"The retarded man."

"What about him?"

"He's gone."

"Gone where?"

"We . . . we don't actually know, sir. When the trucks arrived here, he wasn't on any of them."

The captain threw down his paper. "You were supposed to be keeping an eye on him."

"Yes. I'm sorry. He was in the habit of climbing up onto any truck he felt like. We got used to him just being there somewhere."

"Oh, you did, did you? When was the last time anyone saw him?"

"Just before Xieng Ngeun. We stopped to shoot rabbits."

The captain sighed. "Well, he isn't likely to go far, is he, Corporal? Take a jeep back and find him."

"Yes, sir." He saluted but paused before leaving. "Actually, it's 'sergeant,' sir."

"Not anymore it's not."

The Amateur Interpreter of English

The old Pathet Lao driver was at Siri's disposal for as long as he was needed. The jeep pulled up in front of the new regional hospital in Xam Neua at 8:00 AM. Four years earlier, this capital of Huaphan province had been a pile of rubble and splinters. Not a house had remained standing after a dozen years of blitz. The noncombatant Air America forward air controllers had guided in the bombers and choreographed the destruction, but it was mostly Lao and Hmong pilots with their fingers on the buttons. It was a symbolic gesture. The civilian inhabitants had fled long before the city was flattened.

But now a new city was taking shape with pretentious boulevards as wide as the Champs-Elysées and grand plans for another communist show town. The hospital was a temporary field of whitewashed barracks while the staff all waited for a move to a more splendid home. The front office housed the administrators, and Siri and Dtui found Dr. Santiago buried behind a rockery of files and books. He was a skinny man around Siri's age with a hairstyle modeled on that of Albert Einstein. He wore porthole spectacles with glass as thick as the bottoms of gin bottles. A cigarette burned in an ashtray beside him and he seemed to hover there in its smoke. Obviously, he was used to people walking in and out of his office because he didn't look up from his work when the visitors arrived.

"Dr. Santiago?" Siri said when he spotted him through the canyons of paper.

"*Da?*" The old Cuban still pored over his lists. Siri wasn't surprised to hear him speak Russian. After almost ten years as head of foreign medical aid in Huaphan, Santiago still refused pointedly to learn Lao or Vietnamese. He spoke Spanish, English, and Russian fluently and had reached an age when he considered himself sufficiently full of languages. He hadn't asked to come to Laos, or to work with the Vietnamese, whom he disliked. He certainly wasn't about to make an attempt to cross the cultural divide. He was the expert, and everyone had to make the effort to communicate with him. All in all, not unlike Siri, he was a stubborn but engaging old coot.

"*Dosvidanya,*" Siri said. It was his only Russian word and he wasn't actually sure what it meant.

Santiago finally looked up and squinted through his glasses. It seemed to take him a few moments either to focus or to place his old friend in his memory. "Dr. Siri? Is that you?" he asked in English. He jumped up from his chair and ran around the desk to embrace a respected colleague. They smiled and laughed a lot as they hugged, but Dtui noticed they weren't actually conversing. On the journey, Siri had told her that he'd worked with Santiago, on and off, for five years without the benefit of a common language. Siri spoke French and Vietnamese quite fluently but he, too, had reached his linguistic quota. When there was no English/Lao interpreter available, the two had merely observed one another's surgical skills and socialized with the aid of diagrams and mime. It had been such a peculiarly pleasant relationship, Siri wondered whether a common language might have spoiled it in some way.

Siri finally broke away and pointed to his assistant. "Nurse Dtui," he said.

"Hello, Dr. Santiago. Pleased to meet you," she said in English.

Both Siri and Santiago looked at her with astonishment for a few seconds before the Cuban went across to hug her also. It was a culturally inappropriate gesture that seemed to fit into the spirit of the moment. He told her she spoke English well.

"I read and write," she said. "I don't really speak it." It was true. She'd never used the language to converse. It was just a medium for study. In fact, she was a little surprised to find it coming from her mouth so happily.

He assured her that whether she read it or spoke it, it was still the same language. And, from that moment, despite the fact that she'd never heard herself using it before, English became their language of communication and Dtui its novice interpreter. She knew her pronunciation was awful, but Santiago had no problem with that because his own accent was equally horrible. He, too, had learned English from American textbooks. Siri was full of admiration for his talented assistant.

Throughout the morning, the two old doctors caught up with each other's lives since last they'd met. Santiago was spending more time on administering Cuban aid, he told them, and had less and less time available for the job he was actually trained for. Farmers continued to get blown up in their fields, and there were fewer and fewer qualified medical staff members to care for them. There were under a hundred qualified doctors in the entire country so the PL medical staff was spread thinly to fill the roles of the Royalist physicians who'd fled to Thailand. Santiago had funding but nobody to hire.

Through Dtui, whose confidence increased as time passed, Siri finally got around to the mystery of his cement man. The Cuban thought about it for a moment and asked whether he was certain the incident had taken place early that year.

"January 21, to be exact," Siri told him.

"Dr. Santiago says that if it had been a few months earlier, he'd have had two very good candidates for us," Dtui said. "At least that's what I think he means. But he reckons that by last October, they'd already gone back to Cuba."

"They completed their tours?"

"Not exactly. He says it's a little complicated. They came in 1971 to help with the setting up of some project at kilometer 8."

"Xieng Muang," Siri said. "That's the hospital. It was an amazing project. They had to drill out the centers of two mountains. They built two complete hospital wards that were invisible from the air but were able to accommodate a thousand patients. It was an impressive piece of engineering. The Vietnamese military took care of the labor; the Cubans provided nurses and orderlies."

"He thinks you may remember the two men he means. Their names were Isandro and Udon."

"Odon," Santiago corrected her.

"Sorry, Odon. He says they were here from the beginning."

Siri nodded his head. He'd only been invited to Xieng Muang from time to time to help with surgery, and on those occasions he'd always brought his Lao team with him, but he did recall the sight of black orderlies running around the wards. He'd had no opportunity to talk to them.

"While the work was going on," Dtui continued, "Dr. Santiago says they took care of the wounded in temporary caves here and there. Isandro and Odon were part of that project. They were the head nursing orderlies. When the Kilometer 8 Hospital was ready, they moved everyone into the mountains. After the two of them finished one four-year tour, they volunteered for a second. It seems that was quite unusual. Most of the Cubans were in a hurry to return home. But these two were good workers and they had made friends with the locals. They'd studied the Lao language, even acquired a taste for the local food." Dtui added, for Dr. Siri's benefit, "Of course, I might be making half of this up."

"So why were they sent back early?" Siri asked, ignoring her disclaimer.

There followed a long spell while Dtui clarified points with the old Cuban.

"Apparently," Dtui said, "there were complaints."

"Who from?"

"A senior Vietnam Army officer said one of the men, Isandro, was making advances to his daughter. He made it very clear: if he found the man anywhere near her again, he'd shoot him."

"And Dr. Santiago passed this message on to Isandro and Odon?"

"He says he did but they defied him. They said they weren't afraid of him or the colonel. He couldn't believe it. The situation just got worse and worse. The doctor couldn't have Cuban workers getting shot by a Vietnamese for messing around with his daughter, so he had no choice. He ordered them home."

"And is he absolutely sure they went?"

"Absolutely."

"And no other dark-skinned Cubans went missing from any other Cuban projects?"

"He says this was the only one in the region."

"Could you ask Dr. Santiago to describe Isandro for me?"

Again Dtui and the Cuban doctor went into a huddle.

"As far as I can make out," Dtui said, "he was built like a tree—tall and broad shouldered like an American basketball player—and strong."

Siri shrugged. This wasn't at all the description of their cement man. Dtui asked about Odon.

"This is more like it," she told Dr. Siri. "Odon was smaller. Santiago says he was ugly as a goat but had a permanent smile that endeared him to everyone. He says it's unusual for the natives—and I guess that includes you and me—to get along with dark-skinned foreigners, but Odon and Isandro really made an effort and people responded. Then he said something I couldn't really get—something like 'more fool the natives' but don't quote me on that."

Siri considered Odon a more likely candidate than his bigger friend, but as they'd both left Laos, it appeared he'd either have to look elsewhere for their mummy's identity or prove that for some reason one of the orderlies had stayed behind.

Although there was an enormous refrigerator in one corner of the office, upon inspection it was found to contain nothing but jar upon jar of culture specimens. It was a fascinating collection, they all agreed, but the contents were not likely to be particularly filling. So Santiago invited his guests to join him for lunch at the new Lao Houng Hotel. He gladly abandoned his paperwork and seemed rejuvenated by this unexpected visit. As they were leaving the building, the Cuban stopped to speak to a nurse who looked too young to have completed the nursing certificate. Siri noticed the old man take her hand in his and give her a rather unprofessional peck on the cheek. Although the girl blushed, she didn't pull away as one would expect of a Lao girl receiving an unwanted kiss. It appeared there was still a Latin fire burning in Santiago's grate.

They ate bland Vietnamese food beneath huge posters of unknown Chinese film stars and joked about the new Oz of Vieng Xai. Then, as they drank warm, lightly scented beer for dessert, Santiago turned his attention to Dtui. He asked if she was a qualified nurse. When she said she was, he asked whether she thought her "Papa Siri" would be able to spare her for a day or two. It appeared that after the cease-fire they had moved the Kilometer 8 Hospital outside the mountain and into some old French buildings that stood in front of it. It was still a hospital but nobody working there had more than six month's basic medical training. Dr. Santiago was expecting two new Cuban doctors to arrive before the weekend but, as things stood, he was desperate for somebody who could make decisions. The doctor went there whenever he was able, but he believed they really needed a big sister on the site.

She put the proposal to Siri.

"What do you think?" he asked.

"I don't know. I'm just a nurse."

"Dtui, you'll never be *just* a nurse. I could probably play detective here on my own for a bit—but the decision's yours. The living always take precedence over the dead in my book. Just don't tell any spirits I said that."

She turned back to Santiago and asked how certain he was the Cuban doctors would be there by the weekend. He told her he was positive. She told him she would help, and then translated her decision for Siri.

"Good for you," he said. "I'll come by and lend a hand whenever I can. But I'm sure you'll have the place organized in no time. And Dtui . . . ?"

"Yes?"

"You won't forget these bodies are alive, will you? Don't try to store anyone in the freezer overnight."

"Dr. Siri!"

"Sorry."

Mr. Geung wasn't designed for walking. His ankles turned outward and his legs were short. But the notion had entered his mind that he should walk back to Vientiane. He knew it was far, but not that it was over three hundred kilometers by road. He knew he didn't have any money in his pocket to pay for a bus ticket, nor did he have a concept of how else he could get to the morgue to keep his promise. So, when the soldiers stopped to take a pee, he walked to the last truck in the convoy and looked back at the road that snaked down through the mountains. He took a deep breath, as the doctor had taught him, and set off for home. Nobody noticed him go.

After only five minutes, he was alone on the deserted road. Mr. Geung wasn't one for doing things alone. He was good at joining in with others or doing what he was told, but he had hardly a trace of initiative. The trucks were barely out of sight before he realized he wouldn't be able to undertake such a journey by himself. He needed a friend. He needed a logical friend to keep him company. And, as if by magic, he looked back over his shoulder and saw Dtui just a few paces behind him. It was a relief. She was the most sensible woman he knew and he was sure she'd guide him back.

"I . . . I'm sorry, little sis-ter," he said and smiled at her.

She laughed and took his hand, and walked with him along the badly potholed road. At one point she whispered into his mind that the sun was directly overhead and they didn't have hats. They decided to walk through the groves of peculiar trees, keeping the road within sight. Having her beside him gave him confidence. As they walked, he reminded her of all the jokes she'd told for the past year. She was impressed that they'd remained stored in his memory. He didn't know where he'd be without Dtui and her common sense there to guide him.

The image of Mr. Geung appeared so clearly in Dtui's mind it was as if he were there in the room with her. She opened her eyes and looked around. In the closetless room her clothes hung from the four posts of the bed like pallbearers. The darned holes in the mosquito netting gathered the mesh into fairy stars, adding to her feeling that Guesthouse Number One was mystical in some way. The *klooee* piper played the same dirge over and over in the distance and, even in late afternoon, the mist had begun to roll against the glass of the window. She realized she must have dozed and dreamed of her friend, but she felt uneasy for him.

She knew that but for the mystery guests in the far wing and the staff sitting around in the empty dining room, the guesthouse was deserted. Siri would be down on the veranda describing their visit with Dr. Santiago to the small-minded security head. What a letdown he'd turned out to be. Before he'd suddenly turned into a raging communist Nazi, Dtui had even considered him as a prospective mate. His cool smile and lean frame fitted her ever-shrinking list of requirements. Unfortunately, she held firmly to the belief that the man for her had to have a mind of his own, an increasingly difficult order to fill. Now that she had ruled him out, she thought it best to opt out of the evening's briefing downstairs.

But her room was overwhelming her with bizarre thoughts and feelings, so she decided to get away from it. She had two tasks that would keep her occupied for an hour or so. First, she would try to get through to Vientiane on the single guesthouse telephone. About a month earlier, two men in old army uniforms with TELEPHONE COMPANY written across the backs in laundry ink had come to install a phone at Siri's bungalow. It was another Party reward for Siri's self-less contribution to the Cause. She knew if it hadn't been for her mother and the need to keep in constant contact with her, he would have told them where to stick their telephone. "Another intrusion," he would have called it.

Before the men had left, they wrote down the four-digit number, one that just happened to end in three nines, and assured them all there would be a connection the following day. In fact, it had been two weeks before they heard that distinctive Lao dial tone—a sparrow trying desperately to escape from a crinkly paper bag. Now Dtui was able to check on her mother every few days. It put her mind at ease. Of course, she had to yell her guts out to be heard. Siri was so impressed at the size of her lungs he'd wondered whether the telephone was actually necessary.

And there was something that had been worrying her about the autopsy. She took her sturdy Soviet flashlight downstairs and, after ten minutes of shouting over the phone, she walked out the back way and headed for the president's house. There had been no reason to lock the door of the meeting room. The body still lay in segments on the plastic tablecloth. The story of the Cuban orderlies had stuck in her mind. There was no way the body in front of her could have belonged to the amorous basketball player, but what about his goat-faced friend? What if he hadn't gone home? What if the smaller man had somehow been left behind and found himself in trouble?

As no logical alternatives occurred to her, she began to run the flashlight beam across the torso. She was used to Siri's ongoing discussions with his subjects during autopsies, so she began her inspection with, "Excuse me, Mr. Odon, I was wondering whether perhaps you had a little more to tell us than you have so far." She'd noticed something at the initial inspection, three marks—almost parallel lines—beneath the left armpit. At the time, she'd merely noted them as interesting. The contraction of the skin had left many such grooves, but there had been something strangely regimented about these three. Their oddity had lingered in her mind and she wanted to satisfy her curiosity.

She shone the beam onto the right side of the chest. It was more deteriorated there, harder to recognize, but after pushing at the leathery hide with her fingers, she had no doubt. Three furrows in an identical position to those on the left—symmetrical. Nothing biological could explain such marks. The body had been scarred in some type of ritual. It certainly did have more to tell.

Siri had arrived at the point where he was prepared to wake up the guesthouse supervisor and complain about the damned noise. Three nights he'd been there, and every night the foreign devil music had blasted out at midnight. Surely the youth of Vieng Xai had better ways to spend their time. Surely the senior cadres of the region ought to clamp down on such bourgeois Western decadence. He couldn't work it out. Perhaps Huaphan had too few people left who really cared.

As sleep was hard to come by, he went over the points raised at his meeting with Comrade Lit. They'd drawn up a list. One: check the date of departure of Isandro and Odon. Two: locate the Vietnamese colonel who'd made the complaint to Santiago. Three: get information about any other projects in the region in which dark-skinned foreigners were involved. Siri broadened the search to include Vietnamese mountain tribesmen even though he was quite sure the dead man was not Asian.

Somewhere between numbers seven and eight on the list, order finally gave way to sleep. The crow and the sparrow returned for a dream sequel, still on their wire above the valley, still preening one another. But slowly, one by one, other sparrows came to rest alongside them. One settled beside the first and attempted to flirt with her. She rejected its advances and returned to her crow. This caused a terrible kafuffle in the sparrow community, and they flapped and fluttered and squawked and it seemed an assault on the crow was inevitable. But, before they could attack, the crow enfolded the sparrow in his broad black wing and the two of them dropped. There was no attempt to fly away. They merely dropped like stones into the valley below and deep into the soft mud of the fields.

Siri was awakened, not by the weak morning light through his window, but by the whimpering of a child. He thought of the girl he had seen in an earlier dream but the bunk opposite was empty. This child was more real, and seemed to be closer, so close he even raised his netting and peered under his bed. He went to the door and looked out into the empty corridor. But there was no doubt the sound came from inside his room. He touched the talisman at his neck. It could sense tricks from the malevolent spirits. They'd fooled him before. Their black magic had almost killed him on two occasions. But the white stone hung still and cool. This was no black magic. It was a sincere cry for help from some other troubled soul. But, with no clues and no way of responding, Siri could only lie back on his mattress and listen to the feeble cries. The sound gradually climbed to a higher pitch and became more hollow, and at some point it blended with the sound of the bamboo *klooee* that played its solitary morning tune.

The Cave of the Dead

M r. Geung woke in panic just as he had the previous two mornings. But whereas on those other occasions he'd found himself surrounded by soldiers, today he was wrapped in a canvas tarpaulin like pork in a Chinese spring roll. He struggled to get loose, kicked and punched and pushed, but could find no way to free himself. His mind was blank. All the details of where he was and why he was there were gone. And so, although it didn't help a bit, he started to cry.

"And what, tell me, do you think you're doing in me firewood cover?" It was the voice of an old woman, that much he could tell. But he couldn't see her through the opening at the top of his spring roll.

"I . . . I don't know," he said, and continued to cry. He felt a tug on his cocoon and was sent rolling across the ground and then flung loose from the tarpaulin onto the dry earth. An elderly woman and two giggling children were looking down at him.

"Grandma, he's a retard," the smallest girl said.

"So he is," the old lady agreed. "What do you want here, retard?"

"I d . . . don't know," Geung answered truthfully.

"Then I should call the police and have you arrested," she said.

"Yes, I th . . . I think so."

"Or maybe I should get my gun and chase you away."

Geung thought about that option. "Y . . . yes, that would be f . . . fine, too."

The old woman laughed. Her betel nut-stained mouth reminded him of a number of disasters he'd seen in the morgue. "Eeh. You really are crazy. How am I supposed to threaten you if you agree with all I say, boy? Where do you hail from?"

"Thangon."

"Never heard of it."

"Sorry. I have t . . . t . . . to go to Vientiane." He clambered to his sore feet, smiled at the children, and started walking.

"Wait. Wait there," the old woman said. "You think you're going to walk to Vientiane?"

"I p . . . promised."

"Is that so? You hungry, boy?"

"Yes."

"Well, you can't walk to Vientiane if you're hungry, seeing it's so far. And as . . ."

"Yes. I remember."

"What's that?"

"The mo . . . mo . . . mosquitoes. I wrapped up so the mo . . . mosquitoes didn't get me. D . . . d . . . dengue fever. Comrade Dtui s . . . said you have to wrap up against the mo . . . mo . . . mo . . . mo . . ."

"MOSQUITOES!" the two girls chorused.

"Yes." He smiled at the girls and they giggled back.

"All right," the old lady decided. "Come and eat and we'll see if we can get some sense out of you before you set out on your big march. And I think I can find you some homemade paste here, should keep the mosquitoes from your blood. It'll last for a week so long as you don't wash."

"Thank you, ma'am," he said and put his hands together in a polite *nop*.

"Well, I don't know where you're from or what you're about, but they taught you some nice manners." They went into her solid wooden hut. This was the home of the care-taker of the pine plantation through which Geung had trekked during the first day of his escape. "First thing you do is sit yourself down and take off them vinyl shoes. You wear them all the way to Vientiane and you'll be a cripple as well as a retard."

"Thank you, m . . . m . . ."

"MA'AM!" the children yelled as if the circus were in town.

"Mother," Geung said, and smiled again at the girls with his crazy-paving teeth.

Dtui's first day at Kilometer 8 Hospital was chaotic. It wasn't her fault. Chaos was the norm there. After only an hour she felt helpless. There was a staff of six, two of whom had no medical training whatsoever. The most senior medic had undergone six months of emergency field hospital training in Vietnam. Dtui, with a two-year nursing diploma, was their surgeon general. Each of them simply stopped making decisions and deferred to her judgment. She immediately mistrusted her ability to make the necessary decisions. Never had she been in a situation that was so desperate.

By far the largest population in the fifty-bed hospital was made up of *bombi* victims. Of all the wicked tools of war, the *bombi* was one of the cruelest. A shell packed with baseball-sized *bombis* was dropped from a plane. In midair the shell opened and the *bombis* rained over the selected target. On contact, two hundred and fifty white-hot ball bearings exploded in all directions from each one, ripping through buildings and people with equal detachment. Some of the *bombis* were on a short-delay timer to catch the survivors who went to care for their loved ones. But some just lay dor-mant for days, weeks, months, or years, to spring their deadly surprise on the innocent and ill informed. The *bombi* had no sense of who its victim should be. A buffalo, a hoe, a child, a young mother planting rice, it mattered not. It took them all.

Every day at Kilometer 8 new victims arrived with truncated limbs bound to stem the flow of blood. They came on ox carts, on ponies, on litters dragged by their relatives. The hospital staff gave them generous doses of opium to repress any sensations, good or bad, and did their best to clean the wounds. Many had lost too much blood or were too shredded to keep alive. Those who survived did so mainly of their own volition. Every few days, Dr. Santiago would come by to amputate whatever was unsavable and perform whatever miracles it took to give people another chance at life.

There were no shifts at Kilometer 8. Staff slept during the rare moments of quiet, day or night. They cooked for those patients whose relatives weren't camped in the wards. They kept them full of a painkiller they knew would leave them addicted, and they stretchered the deceased up the slope to the cave of the dead, a crematorium on the skirt of the mountain. At the end of her incredibly long first day, Dtui estimated she'd lost four kilograms. Singsai, the senior medic, told her if she stayed a month she'd be so skinny they'd be able to store her in the closet with the mops. She enjoyed that image.

It had been a comparatively good day. Only one lady had made the journey to the cave of the dead. Dtui had personally been able to save the life, perhaps temporarily, of a ten-year-old child, and at two in the morning the residents at Kilometer 8 were all stoned into a restful sleep. Dtui and Singsai sat in front of the long rectangular room that formed the main ward. They were too fatigued to sleep, so they gazed up at the stars that showed themselves so rarely in the northeastern sky that the medic saw their appearance now as an omen.

"Days like this make you realize how stupid you are," Dtui said.

"You aren't stupid at all, Nurse," Singsai assured her. He was such a brown-skinned little man his words seemed to come out of the darkness from a floating set of teeth. He reminded Dtui of the mummy in the president's house.

"OK, perhaps not stupid exactly, but . . . lacking."

"You've done a lot of good today."

"But there's so much more I didn't know how to do. It's so frustrating. It makes me appreciate your Dr. Santiago and my own boss that much more. They do this stuff day in, day out, year after year, saving lives as if it were as natural as breathing."

"I hope to be a surgeon someday," Singsai told her, looking at the sky as if that were the place such a hope might hang. He was in his fifties and unconnected so Dtui knew he had little chance.

She scrambled for a change of subject. "Do you ever have any cases here that aren't emergencies?"

"One or two malarials," he said. "We've a little boy with chronic diarrhea. They say that's the biggest killer of kids in the whole of Southeast Asia. Most of them don't make it, but we're fighting for this chap. He's been lucky. Oh, and then there's Mrs. Duaning."

"What's wrong with her?"

"Nobody knows. She's been in a coma for two weeks. We found her out on the road."

"Nobody's come to claim her?"

"No."

"Then how do you know her name?"

"We don't, but we can tell she's Hmong. One of our Hmong interns christened her 'Duaning.' It means 'nuts.'"

They went to visit Mrs. Nuts, who lay in a small block away from the others, where the non-life-threatening cases were billeted. She was on her back with her eyes wide open, staring at the ceiling and muttering.

"What's she saying?" Dtui asked.

"She only started speaking the day before yesterday. She says the same thing, over and over."

Dtui leaned over her and listened. The old lady's voice seemed less gravelly than one would have expected from such a battered old crone. The words came from her mouth on a breath that smelt musty. "Have to feed Panoy," she said. "Have to feed Panoy."

"You don't suppose Panoy's her name?"

"This woman's? No. It isn't a very Hmong-sounding name." He pulled up the single blanket to cover her and her feet were momentarily exposed. Both Dtui and Singsai looked at them in amazement. "What the . . . ?"

The soles of the woman's feet were caked in some maroon substance. "Has she been walking anywhere?" Dtui asked.

"No. As far as I know, she hasn't moved. And this doesn't look like clay."

Dtui scratched at one sole with her fingernail. She knew exactly what she was seeing. "It's congealed blood," she said.

"Why would she have . . . ? Are there any wounds?"

Dtui took a damp cloth from the basin beside the bed and carefully rubbed at one foot. "No."

"Then how . . . ?"

"It doesn't look random, Singsai. Look at this other foot. It's as if someone painted symbols onto her soles."

"With blood? Whatever for?"

"That Hmong intern might have some idea."

"Right. I don't want to wake him now, but in the morning I'll be very interested to see if he has an explanation."

"Me, too," Dtui said. "Me, too."

Two more emergencies during the night meant that Dtui didn't actually get to sleep until after seven. The breeze through the thin cotton curtains woke her at ten. Before heading for the main block, she stopped by to see Mrs. Nuts. She still lay staring at the ceiling but her tune had changed during the night.

"Panoy is weak now. Panoy is weak," she said.

"Who is Panoy?" Dtui asked.

"Panoy is weak."

Dtui pushed back the woman's white hair from her face and put her palm on the woman's cold brow. Her skin semed dull, as if she were covered in dust. Her pulse was slow. She wondered whether Mrs. Nuts would make it through the day. Before she left the room, Dtui pulled up the blanket to look at her feet. The left sole, the one she'd wiped clean earlier that morning, was once again covered in dried blood.

Dr. Siri was downstairs in the guesthouse dining room reading a month-old copy of *Pasason Lao*. There was a picture of his old friend Civilai shaking hands with a Mongolian diplomat. Both were smiling, neither convincingly. He could tell exactly what Comrade Civilai, his only ally on the politburo, was thinking. It reminded him of an earlier time and two more idealistic people.

For years, Siri and his wife, Boua, had been members of the Lao Issara, the Free Lao resistance. But Boua was working her way toward a more disciplined independence from the French than just being a nuisance to the colonists. She was the devout communist of the pair, and it was she who led Siri to Hanoi and into the Nguyen Ai Quoc college. There he learned his Vietnamese and attended classes in communist ideology. He was baptized in red paint, held under until he breathed Lenin and defecated Marx. And with this new vital system he'd gone out into the Vietnamese countryside and convinced the farmers that nothing but communism could free them from the yoke of French colonization. He'd worked in field hospitals throughout the north of the country, and even after eighteen straight hours of bloody surgery, he'd still find time to engage the villagers in ideological debates.

It was a period in his life he came to refer to as "the years they borrowed my mind." It wasn't until he met another enthusiastic cadre, a serious member of the Lao People's Party and lifelong communist named Civilai, that Siri was able to put everything into perspective. Although he'd been trained to report comrades who strayed from the axiomatic straight and narrow, Civilai was so experienced and so obviously intelligent that Siri had no choice but to listen and reevaluate his own clouded beliefs. Civilai loved communism. There was no question of his loyalty to the Party. But he believed that communism should work without scaring the daylights out of people. For his opinions he was labeled an eccentric. He was too senior and too well respected by the masses to be kicked off the central committee, but he was kept backstage.

Siri had immediately warmed to Civilai's middle path so he, too, had been ostracized by the top men of the Party. While Boua soldiered on in her attempts to educate a nation of proletariat, Siri hung up his red flag and became a full-time doctor. That was probably when his wife's love for him began to dim. In Siri's heart, the love light never went out. He loved her until her death, but he knew she'd already begun to consider her husband a disappointment. Through all that time, only his friendship with Civilai had kept him rational, and as the Party dumped more and more meaningless duties on Civilai, it was Siri who offered encouragement and hope to his friend.

The photograph before him showed one more symbolic handshake with one more foreign official. It was another snap for the diplomatic album. Civilai had told Siri he was becoming the Mickey Mouse of the new regime. He—

"Comrade?" Siri looked up to see the guard whose station was at the upstairs partition standing, drained of color, in the doorway. "You're a doctor, right?"

"That's right," said Siri.

"Come with me quick." He didn't wait for a response, but turned on his heel and ran back up the stairs four at a time. From his many years of experience, Siri knew that ten seconds saved by sprinting up a flight of stairs rather than walking rarely made a difference, apart from possibly killing the physician as well as the patient. So he took the stairs one at a time and was met by the flustered guard on his way back down.

"Hurry up," the guard said. "It's a life-and-death matter." Despite the urgency, he'd spared the time to relock the upstairs door before going for Siri. His hands shook now as he attempted to insert the key into the padlock. Siri reached the top landing just as the man burst through the first door and ran along the corridor to a second. That, too, was locked. Siri wondered what ferocious beast required such security measures. As he walked past the first room, he looked in through the open door. Three expensive-looking leather suitcases sat on one of the beds. On the floor was a large tray of seedlings and small pots containing cuttings.

"In here," shouted the guard. "He's not dead yet."

On the only bed in the next room, convulsed in pain, frothing at the mouth, was a middle-aged man with greased hair wearing simple but expensive pajamas. On the floor beside the bed, lying on its side, was a brown glass bottle. The label was in Russian but the universal skull and cross-bones left no doubt as to its contents. Siri prized open the

man's eyes and looked into his pupils. He then forced open
the man's mouth to see his tongue and sniffed at his breath.

"They was cleaning the rooms after them others left.
Stupid bitch must have left the cleanser in the sink. Don't
know how he got hold of it. Must've been on his way back
from the toilet and grabbed it without me seeing. Stupid
bastard. It'll be me that gets shot if anything happens."
The guard was ranting, pacing up and down the room.
"Hospital! Can we get him to the hospital? Can you fix him
up? Doc? Can you, Doc?"

"Listen, Comrade," Siri said, looking up at the frantic
guard. " I can't do anything with you stomping around like
a rampant capitalist. I want you to go down to the kitchen
and get the ladies to boil two liters of water. Stir in a hand-
ful of salt and about 30 cc's of cooking oil. Don't come
back till it's all ready."

"Right." The guard abandoned his charge and sped to
the kitchen. The poisoned man still squirmed in agony on
the bed.

"It's OK," Siri said. "He's gone. You can stop now."

The man flinched for a second but then began to growl
deep in his throat. "Hos-pital."

"You and I both know that isn't going to happen, don't
we now?"

"Dy-ing."

"Come on. You're no more dying than I am. In fact, I
probably look in worse condition than you do. Exactly what
did you think this little show would achieve?"

The man spat the remainder of the foam from his mouth
and looked up angrily at Siri. "Who in blazes are you?"

"Dr. Siri Paiboun."

"Egad. What are the odds of there being a bloody doctor
in a place like this?" He sat up and shook his head.

"It was a good show. I doubt anyone else would have

dared get close enough to smell the toothpaste. I imagine the staff would have thrown you in a truck and carted you off to the medical center in Xam Neua. But I still don't see what good that would have done you."

"No? Well, it's simple. There wouldn't have been security in a hospital. I could have sneaked out."

"And gone where?"

"I don't know, man. Stolen a car? Headed south?"

"You obviously don't realize where you are. There's one road in the direction of Vientiane, and there are some hundred PL and Vietnamese encampments you'd have to pass through on the way. Are you really that desperate to get killed?"

"Better to die fast from a bullet than after the slow torture your people have planned for me."

"How do you know what we've planned?"

"I'm not stupid. I know how you do it. Hard labor, primitive conditions, no access to medicines."

"I survived for thirty years in those conditions. Why couldn't you?"

"You obviously don't know who I am."

"Oh, I know very well. But that doesn't answer my question."

The man shook his head and looked out the window. "I've never had to fend for myself. Just the merest sniffle and I was pumped full of drugs. I have no natural immunity, no resistance, no stamina."

"You'd be surprised how quickly your body adapts."

"No. It will kill me. I'm certain. Listen. The guard will be back as soon as he completes the ridiculous mission you sent him on. How about you and I come to some . . . arrangement?"

"Surely you don't mean financial?"

"I have access to more money than you could ever imagine. If you could get me to Thailand, I c—"

"What would I do with money?"

"Do? What would anyone do? Live a comfortable life. Be free."

Siri laughed. "If you don't mind my saying so, in your present predicament you're hardly a glowing advertisement for the combination of wealth and freedom. But, good try, boy. You know, you're quite unlike your father."

"How would you know that?"

"We met. We spent a night together drinking rice whisky and sharing philosophy. I haven't spent a great deal of my life in the company of royalty, unless you count playing cards, but I was impressed. He was more resigned to fate than you seem to be."

"He's a defeatist."

"He's a realist. He was here, wasn't he? And the queen?"

"They took them away last night. Did you see the room they forced them to stay in? Disgraceful. Goodness knows what awaits them out there in the jungle."

"You're afraid."

"Don't be ridiculous."

"It's nothing to be ashamed of. Fear helps us survive. I've spent a larger portion of my life being afraid than I have being in control. But here I am. Forget this escape idea, son. It won't help you or your family. Play the game. Find a tall tree somewhere, a tree that's survived all the coups and massacres of history. Go to that tree and dig a hole near its roots and bury your pride there. Invest all your royal heritage into the majesty of that great tree, stash it there, and become the simple, humble person they'll ask you to be. Suffer the indignities they inflict on you and impress them with your will. Win them over with your humility. I know that's what the king and queen will attempt to do."

"I . . . I can't."

"You can. And it will have a deeper and longer-lasting

impact than any bravado, any heroics, any royal histrionics you have in mind. Show them you're a person of character. They won't know how to respond to that. There's nothing more disheartening to a bully than a man who doesn't get scared."

Siri picked up the bottle from the floor. The crown prince looked forlornly ahead of him. "Why did they separate us?"

"To break your will. You didn't actually drink any of this, did you?"

"It was empty."

Siri laughed. "You see? You're a very resourceful lad. You can survive a hundred reeducation camps."

The guard came running into the room. He held the handles of the steaming pot with rags wrapped around his fingers. The entire kitchen staff was behind him.

"It's done," the guard said. "What should I do with it?"

"Throw it down the toilet," Siri told him. "Better still, boil some decent vegetables for dinner."

"What? But you said . . ."

"I seem to have performed a medical miracle without it and brought the prince back to life. There won't be any more problems. We won't have to boil him in oil after all."

"Thank you. Thank you, Doc. Thank you." The guard mumbled the words a hundred times. The thanks, of course, were for the preservation of his own skin. He had no interest in the well-being of his royal charge.

Before Siri left the room, he saw the bamboo *klooee* on the desk. "Ah, so this is the weapon that's been inflicting pain on us since we got here. You only know the one tune?" he asked.

"And I can't even get that right."

"When I see you next, you'll have a thousand tunes of the jungle, and you'll be playing them to the envy of the birds in the trees. Mark my words." He gripped the prince's arm and smiled at him. "Give my regards to your father when next you meet him. He's an impressive man—with an impressive son."

Divine Impotence

Mr. Geung had left the forested mountain slopes and entered a valley that contained the first rice fields he'd seen on his walk. The rice stubble crunched under his feet. Everything seemed so dry, so dead. His country had been politicked into a drought. With every postrevolution month that passed, the Pathet Lao government was learning how much more difficult it was to run a country of warm bodies than it had appeared to be on paper. For ten years in the caves of Huaphan, the dream had always been to gain power. As few of the cadres honestly believed that dream would ever come true, no detailed plans were laid for the future. No practical policy of public appeasement was worked out. Nothing spoiled a good popular uprising more than the presence of people and the need to satisfy their unreasonable demands.

In Laos in 1977, the population was becoming more and more restless. The new leaders had been given over a year to show what they were capable of, but successes were rare. Some folks even dared to suggest that the communists were no better than the Royalists. The euphoria of victory was slowly giving way to politburo paranoia, and the resulting measures had caused even more dissent. In an effort to discourage large public gatherings, festivals were either cancelled completely or greatly restricted. They were

trimmed of religion, culture, and superstition, which naturally left very little to celebrate. Dr. Siri had compared this
with allowing the wearing of spectacles but banning the use
of glass lenses.

One such muted celebration had been the May Rocket
Festival. Obviously, the combination of disgruntled villagers
and large quantities of gunpowder was more than the
authorities could tolerate. The government banned gatherings in built-up areas and restricted all activities to remote
fields policed by both uniformed and quite obvious plain-
clothes soldiers. Female spirit mediums who normally gave
the festival its meaning were barred from attending. There
was to be no alcohol, no raucous music, and all activities had
to be completed before nightfall. The amount of powder
allowed for each bamboo shaft was so niggardly that many
of the homemade rockets barely left their launchpads. They
lurched a few meters into the air, then fizzled, and fell to
earth. There were spontaneous screams of panic from the
fleeing onlookers but few cheers of delight.

The consequences of this debacle reached far beyond
the disappointed villagers and their wasted day. The Rocket
Festival was a fertility rite. The noise and gaiety should have
awakened the gods of lust from their yearlong slumber.
The spirit mediums would remind the roused deities that
the time had come to send the rains and replenish the
paddies. The phallic rockets would stimulate a heavenly
orgy and the sexual juices would spill over onto the land.
Thus would a rich harvest result.

This was what the villagers believed. The new leaders
had no place in their soulless socialist hearts for such
mythology. Marxist-Leninist doctrine had no time for fairy
tales. Buddhism and animism were sins against rational
thought, and logic would always prevail in a communist
system. They'd see, these simple folk. The rains would come

in May as they always had, and the populace would begin to believe in socialist order.

The subdued May Day celebrations passed with the same lack of enthusiasm as had the Rocket Festival. May gave way to June and the gods of fertility still slumbered. The skies remained clear and the rice fields cracked and turned to dust. By July the people had no doubt that the new government was responsible for this unprecedented drought. Socialism was having a negative effect on the weather. This was clear to even the most simple of minds. The government's attempts at quelling dissent had only succeeded in exacerbating it.

All Mr. Geung knew of this was that the fields crunched under his feet, but his new boots made light of the terrain. They'd belonged to the old lady's husband, who had no use for them in his funeral pot. They were too small for her son but they fitted Geung to a T and made him feel proud to own them. She'd given him a large pack of dried food and smeared him with a foul-smelling ointment she promised would keep off even the vindictive dengue-bearing mosquitoes that plagued the land.

"W . . . we should f . . . f . . . follow the road," he told Dtui, who marched beside him. "But n . . . n . . . not be on it." The old lady had dragged his story from him over breakfast and was sure the soldiers from whom he had escaped would be searching for him.

"Stay close to the road but not on it," she'd told him. "If a car or truck comes from behind you that isn't the green of the army, beg them for a ride. Stay away from anything green. Got it?"

The words were embedded in his brain but some of the concepts hadn't taken root. "From behind you" was surely confusing, because if he turned around, anywhere could be behind him. And as he always looked out through the leaves of trees, it seemed that everything he saw passing along the road was green.

Geung had walked for the whole day. The urgency of returning to the morgue was his impetus. He ached. He wheezed. His anxiety rose and fell, as if he were riding to Vientiane on the back of a dragon. But when he heard a loud crack and saw a bloodstain appear on the front of his shirt, he was surprisingly calm.

"A . . . a . . . a bullet wound," he said as if assessing his state for observers at the morgue. He stood still and watched the red rose grow into a country, one of the countries in Dtui's atlas that she tried to convince him contained millions of people. What tiny, tiny people they must be. The stain grew to something like the USSR before Geung's eyes. He became pale and dropped like a fence post to the ground.

More panic. More emergencies and disasters. Soon, emergencies fell into a sort of natural ranking: drop-everything emergencies, do-what-you-can emergencies, and you'll-just-have-to-wait emergencies. Disasters, too, had their own ratings: unavoidable, did-the-best-we-could, my fault/your fault. Then there were godlike moments when a decision had to be made as to who most deserved to die. By the afternoon of her second day, Dtui wondered whether her heart had shrunk. She felt less. People had become less human. Death had become less of a tragedy. Her patients weren't blacksmiths or housewives, they were percentages. "With this little skill and this little pharmaceutical backup, this patient—let's call her number seven—has a forty percent chance of survival."

It amazed and saddened her that, in order to do her job properly, she had to stop caring. With all his years of battlefield surgery, she understood now that Dr. Siri must have been working the percentages for a long time. It hadn't made him cold, just philosophical. The burden was less if he lost patients when the odds were against him. Dtui had to play it that way, too, at Kilometer 8.

The lull came midafternoon. They'd sent two up the slope. They'd stabilized three. Dtui was on an adrenaline high that lifted her like a flying carpet. Tired though she was, a sledgehammer to the head couldn't have put her to sleep. She prowled the wards like a large unblinking polar bear. She bullied patients to stay alive, ordered medicines to work. At the end of the ward, the Hmong orderly, Meej, was searching without hope for a vein on the chopstick-thin arm of a patient. Meej was a stocky, good-looking man in his twenties. Like Dtui, his natural expression was a smile.

Dtui massaged the patient's arm until a faint bluish shadow appeared, which she speared with the hypodermic. Within seconds the patient was connected to his drip and she steered the intern outside.

"How are you feeling?" she asked.

"Drowned," he confessed.

"You and me both. Just keep a score of the ones you save. That's how I do it. Don't count the others. They would have gone anyway."

"All right. Thanks."

"I wanted to ask you about Mrs. Duaning."

"Is she dead yet?"

"Weak, but holding on. What I was curious about was the blood on her feet."

"Ah, that. It's an old superstition. If there's something seriously wrong, the relatives daub blood on the feet."

"Medically wrong?"

"Sometimes, or sometimes mentally. It keeps the evil spirits out."

"But this blood appears all by itself."

Meej laughed. "No, it doesn't."

"You know something I don't."

"The young girl's been here since the day before yesterday. I don't know if she's a relative or just someone from the village who was looking for the old lady. She'd wandered off one day. The girl found her here, spent a minute with her, then ran off home. She came back a few hours later with three pigs and a machete."

"How come I haven't seen her?"

"She isn't comfortable with white medicine. She stays hidden out back. Her role's just to keep the old woman's feet bathed in blood until it's all over."

"Does she know what's wrong with the woman?"

"She didn't say."

"Do you know where she is?"

"Yes."

"Can you bring her to me?"

"Well . . ."

"What's wrong?"

"Could you change out of your white uniform? She's quite certain you're a ghost."

Dtui looked down at the only uniform she'd thought to bring with her and smiled. It wasn't exactly white anymore. "They have ghosts this big up here? All right. Bring her into Mrs. Nuts's room and I'll change out of my ghost disguise." She covered her white uniform with green surgical scrubs.

Ten minutes later, Meej prodded a girl of about ten into the little ward block occupied only by three heavily drugged patients and Mrs. Nuts. The girl was carrying a jam jar in the bottom of which was a fresh batch of blood. Dtui smiled but the girl recoiled at the sight of her even white teeth. "Do you speak Lao?" Dtui asked.

The girl looked at Meej. "She doesn't," he said.

"Then can you ask her why she ran home to get the sacrificial pigs?"

He did. Dtui noticed that all the questions were long and the answers short. "She says the woman's possessed."

"How can she be so sure?"

The girl pointed to the woman's mouth, still repeating her weakening chorus. "That," she said.

"That what?"

Mrs. Nuts was still repeating the same words, over and over, in perfect northern Lao dialect.

"She said the old lady can't speak Lao. Not a word of it."

Dtui raised her eyebrows in surprise and whistled softly. "I see."

"And there's something else," Meej told her.

"I doubt it could get any weirder."

"It does, Nurse Dtui. She said this voice, the voice the old lady's using—it doesn't belong to Mrs. Duaning. Someone else is speaking through her mouth."

Comrade Lit arrived at the guesthouse in the middle of the afternoon and found Dr. Siri on the veranda. "Good health, Comrade Doctor." They shook hands. "I heard about your miracle cure of our . . . houseguest today."

"Nice to see that the grapevine is still up."

"I'd like to thank you. It would have been quite difficult if anything had happened."

"It was nothing, really."

"Nevertheless, the Party offers its sincere thanks, and . . ."

"Out with it."

"It would be greatly appreciated if the identity of our visitors remained confidential."

"Darn, and there I was just about to make an announcement over the national radio network. Who in blazes am I going to tell?"

"Particularly, I think it would be beneficial"—he lowered his voice—"to keep it from your nurse."

"She's already a security risk?"

"Not . . . no, she . . . Please."

"I'll see what I can do. Now, you have some news for me?"

"More than I expected to have," the tall man said, seating himself opposite the doctor. Siri poured him a cup of tea from the thermos and left it to cool.

"I've just been speaking to the Immigration Police in Hanoi. I called them yesterday and gave them the names of your Cuban interns. It's taken them all this time to go through the files. You know what it's like. It appears neither man left on the flight he was booked on. In fact, there's no record of their leaving at all."

"But they *were* shipped to Hanoi?"

"They made it that far. They had a military escort. I talked to the driver. He remembers it clearly."

"So may we assume they turned around and came back?"

"I don't know. If they did, someone must have noticed. I've got my men asking around."

"Anything about the Vietnamese colonel?"

"His name was Ha Hung. I'm afraid I've come to a dead end on that investigation—literally. The colonel was killed three months before the cement path was laid."

"What were the circumstances?"

"Hmong ambush."

"And what happened to his daughter?"

"I don't know. They told me his family went back to Vietnam after the old man's death. They won't be easy to trace."

"Could you try for me?"

"Certainly. Anything else?"

"Dr. Santiago will be dropping by here on his way to Kilometer 8 Hospital. I've asked him to take a look at our mummy. See if he recognizes him."

"Hmm. I doubt even the great Dr. Santiago could identify what's left. He'll probably be too busy chasing around

young girls barely old enough to be his granddaughters."
Siri noted his animosity but wasn't really interested enough
to dig down to its roots. Lit looked around. "I can't help but
notice the absence of Nurse Dtui at our last two meetings.
I hope it doesn't have anything to do with my setting her
straight the other day."

"Son, let me put it this way. You may very well be able to
domesticate a gibbon by repeatedly whacking it over the
head with a hammer, but people respond less kindly to
concussion."

"One of my duties is to educate."

"You don't beat people up with a philosophy, young fellow. You introduce them to it, gradually."

"You think I was a little too heavy-handed?"

"I'm sorry to say you're mired in the shattered cranium
school of mentoring. Take it a little easier in future and I'm
certain you'll have more success."

"Was Nurse Dtui upset? Is that why she isn't here?"

"Dtui's got a much thicker skin than that. No, she's help-
ing out at Kilometer 8 until the new Cuban doctors get here."

"She is quite remarkable."

The comment surprised Siri. "I thought you didn't
like her."

"On the contrary, Doctor. I've been more than impressed
from the very beginning. I admit she lacks discipline, but . . ."

Siri waited for the "but" to go somewhere but it just dangled. "I'll be sure to tell her when I see her this afternoon."

"You're going out there?"

"I'll go with Santiago. I'm interested to see where the
Cubans were billeted, and I'd like to ask around about them."

"And you'll be sure to let me know if you find anything?"

"Of course."

"The Central Administration was most distressed to learn
the victim might have been Cuban. Their delegation natu-

rally wants this cleared up as soon as possible. There's a
politburo member coming from Havana for the concert. I'd
like to have the culprit locked up by then. I think I should
come by and see you this evening so you can tell me what
you found out."

"Actually, I'm planning to stay out at the hospital
tonight."

"What on earth for?"

"Oh, I might be able to help a little bit, and it would be
nice to get some sleep. That confounded discotheque
dance has managed to wake me up every night since I got
here."

Lit laughed. "Doctor, this is Vieng Xai."

"So?"

"So there hasn't been a dance here since the senior
members all left for the capital. That's why next week's
concert is such a big deal."

"Comrade Lit. I hear it. I feel the vibration of the speakers."

"Perhaps it's a radio or someone's record player. What
type of music is it?"

"That annoying American rubbish. The type they used
to bounce up and down to in the hotel nightclubs in the
old days."

"Well, I'll look into it for you, Doctor. We certainly don't
want our youth polluting their minds with decadent Western pop. But, believe me, Dr. Siri, there never has been a discotheque in Vieng Xai, and as far as I'm concerned, there
never will be."

At the wheel of his yellow jeep, Santiago arrived at Kilometer 8, like every swashbuckling hero, with a screech of brakes
and in a cloud of dust. The beleaguered interns came out
to greet him, sighing with temporary relief. Only one person knew who the little white-haired man in the passenger

seat was. While the rest of the staff gathered around Santiago, Dtui strolled over to Dr. Siri.

He smiled at her ruffled look. "How's it going, Nurse?"

She laughed a sort of desperate laugh. "How many years did you do this?"

Siri climbed from the jeep and wiped the dust from his face with an old towel. "It gets easier after the seventeenth year."

"This is my second day and I'm a wreck."

They walked into the ward, and Siri briefly summarized the events of those two days from his point of view. "Santiago seems quite certain the body is that of Odon, the smaller of the two interns."

"Did you ask him about the parallel scars?"

"I pointed them out to him and I noticed a look of . . . I don't know, not fear exactly . . . but some darkness came over him. Don't forget, we can't speak to each other, so I'm looking forward to your translation later tonight. Meanwhile, what's to be done here?"

Siri and Santiago were a formidable team. Dtui followed them on their rounds and assisted them in the four operations they performed. Everything seemed so much more straightforward in their hands. By eight, the wards were settled and the staff was sitting around a table eating a dinner of baked lemur and sticky rice. Santiago preferred to save his comments until the three of them were alone, so Dtui entertained them with the story of Mrs. Nuts. Both surgeons were so fascinated by the tale they went to her ward the second they finished their meal. Dtui was saddened to see how pale the old lady had become. She still spoke in her stolen voice, although now the words issued painfully on labored breaths. They had to lean close to catch them, and her breathing was rank with decay.

Santiago asked what she was saying.

"She says, 'Almost too late,'" Dtui told him.

"What is?" Siri asked.

"I think she means she won't be around for much longer."

But Siri believed otherwise. The amulet around his neck was warm against his skin. It seemed to vibrate as if it were receiving an incoming call. The doctor was starting to recognize its signals. He took the old woman's hand in his and held the amulet in his other. Images fell into his mind that he knew weren't his own.

"Dtui, remember what I say," he called and began to describe what he saw. "Bushes, chest high. I'm falling. Water trickling. Concrete. All of this surrounded by darkness. A door, a very thick metal door, green, too heavy to budge. Hands. Small white hands. My own, as if I'm looking down at myself. There's blood on them."

And then, as if the line were suddenly cut, Siri saw nothing at all. He opened his eyes and the old woman was silent. He knew she was dead. "What did I say?" he asked Dtui.

"You don't know?"

"Not at all."

Dtui recited back his words as accurately as she could, then translated for Santiago, who seemed to have no idea what he'd just witnessed. She asked whether anything Siri had seen sounded familiar to him. He shrugged and opined that bushes and water could be anyplace.

"All right. Let's start with bushes." Siri took control. "Is there anyone on staff who's lived here all their life?" After a consultation they came up with Nang, a jittery nursing orderly who still fainted from time to time at the sight of blood. She seemed delighted to discuss something that wasn't related to surgery. What Siri wanted to know about was fruit. He didn't have the sample with him but he was able to describe the berry he'd crushed in his room at the guesthouse. The others looked on, bemused, as they tried to give it a name.

"Monkey ball plums," said the girl at last. "That's what you're talking about."

"And where can they be found?" Siri asked.

"All over if you know where to look. They grow on the karsts. At the market they pay well for this fruit, so a lot of village people go looking for it. More than a few people have been blown up while out scrounging for monkey ball plums."

"Can you find them around here?"

"Of course, at certain times of the year. All the mountains at Kilometer 8 have bushes where they grow."

"Do you want to share what this is all about, Doc?" Dtui asked.

"Clues," Siri told her. "We mustn't ignore any clues. Like the green door. Ask Santiago again if he remembers any green doors."

She did just that and watched the Cuban flick mentally through all the doors he'd known in his life. At last he asked her whether she was sure it was green and not blue. Siri had no recollection at all of his vision and could not confirm the color.

"If we say blue," Dtui asked, "would that make any difference?"

Santiago told her that indeed it would. The bomb doors at the old hospital were heavy metal, and they were blue.

"And where is the old hospital?"

He pointed through the window to the black shape of the mountain. It stood out from the indigo sky, looming over them like a giant raven.

She translated for Siri, who knew the hospital well. When they'd moved everything down from the original buildings, the old place was abandoned and closed up. There was no way in. The bombproof doors had been locked to keep out inquisitive children from the middle school down the hill. But in his mind all the pieces fit together: the berries, the doors, the water, and the concrete.

"Who has the key?" he asked.

Santiago took them to the administration office, unlocked the desk drawer, and rifled through the bunches of keys till he found the one that should have opened the old hospital main-door padlock. From the store cupboard he took a machete and three battery packs that powered headband-mounted lamps; their hands would be free. He led the way along the overgrown path that snaked up to the nearest entrance to the hospital. The door was nine inches thick and hadn't been opened for a few years. It took the combined effort of all three pulling on the handle to budge it enough to permit them to squeeze through the gap.

A sad, musty odor escaped as they entered. The hidden vents that brought air from above were clogged with weeds, and the air they walked into was old and stale. The histories of the hospital's victims still clung to the place. But Siri recognized something else deep inside its unrelenting blackness—the smell of a recent death. Dtui took a little longer to identify the scent. She and Siri switched on their batteries, and the three headlight beams swept back and forth across twelve hundred square meters of gray stone. The old doctors had spent many hours inside this hidden chamber, so the only thing that surprised them was the absence of sound—no scurrying of animals, no chirping of bats. It was as if nature had been too afraid to take over the vacated premises.

But Dtui stood open-mouthed at the sight before her, amazed that in wartime, under a barrage of bombing, such an incredible feat of construction had been achieved. Conduits in the cement floor allowed natural water from the surrounding mountains to pass through the cavern. There were operating rooms and offices off the main chamber and cleverly designed latrines that allowed effluent to flow away from the ward. Then the beam of her lamp caught a shape in the center of the vast concrete floor. It was a body. Its limbs were bent at impossible angles. As they walked toward it, they could see that she had been a woman in her early twenties. From her state they could tell she'd been dead more than twenty-four hours.

Directly above her, weeds dangled from one of the ventilation shafts, a perfectly round hole some two meters across. Siri knew the vent angled upward to a spot on the mountain slope, invisible from the sky, where fresh air would be drawn into the hospital by means of a pump. The pump was long gone, and all that remained was a hole, an almost invisible hole into which some unsuspecting woman collecting berries might drop.

Santiago bent over the body and looked at the dead woman. Dtui translated the words he spoke.

"The doctor's very impressed. He really wants to know how you were able to find her. But he's sorry that you were too late to help Miss Panoy."

"No," Siri said, strafing his beam across the cavern. "This isn't Panoy. The spirit of this woman spoke to us through the old Hmong, but she wasn't talking about herself. She had to be dead already to communicate in that way. There must be someone else here."

Dtui passed on the message to Santiago, who joined them in a continued search. The water in the old aqueduct had been diverted to the village at the foot of the mountain but the open drains still remained. Water still trickled through them. In some spots they were a meter deep, and that was where Santiago found Panoy. He called her name and dropped down into the channel beside her. She was about four years old. She was seriously injured and weak from hunger, but miraculously she was still alive.

Santiago called up to the others that he believed she could be saved. He climbed from the trench with the girl in his arms and walked quickly through the blue door. Dtui and Siri couldn't keep up with him. They stood at the entrance and watched the energetic old Cuban scurry down the slope to the new hospital. Dtui put her arm around Siri's shoulder and smiled at him.

"Nice one, Dr. Siri. How do we explain all this to Santiago?"

"Much as I appreciate the benefits of a good lie, I fear we may have to tell him the truth."

"You sure? Lying might be easier."

"Oh, I don't think that skinny old lion will have a problem with this. I get the feeling he's seen it all before."

She turned her head and her light beam drilled into the metal door beside them. "Tell me something. What color is this, Doc?"

"Green."

"You're color-blind, aren't you?"

"If this isn't green I suppose I must be. I dread to think what else Mrs. Nuts might have passed on to me."

Panoy was remarkably resilient. There wasn't much they could do about her cracked ribs but they reset both of her arms and an ankle, stitched a couple of large gashes, and put her on an intravenous drip that would slowly replenish her lost energy. Meej stayed with her to check her vital signs through the night.

Siri, Santiago, and Dtui sat beneath the night sky. It was cold enough for jackets but not so uncomfortable they needed to light a fire. The rice whisky worked well enough to keep the blood flowing. Siri was a bystander while Dtui, with her hard-worked dictionary and a flashlight, attempted to explain Siri's connection to the spirit world. She told Santiago about the thousand-year-old shaman called Yeh Ming he unwittingly hosted. She told him this spirit was patiently waiting for Siri's peaceful and natural death so he could retire from the shaman business. She told him about the teeth and the dreams and the white talisman he wore to keep away the evil spirits. During this explanation, Siri watched the reaction of his old friend. It was difficult to read, as if Santiago was organizing the information into compartments. At the end, the Cuban looked at Siri for a few seconds with an expression of pity. He pulled the perennial cigarette from between his lips and surrounded his head with a halo of smoke. Then there was a glint, perhaps of admiration, and finally, Santiago began to laugh. He refilled their glasses and patted his colleagues on the back as if this was the best news he'd heard in a long time.

Siri was once again sidelined while Santagio took his turn to tell another story. Dtui interrupted often to clarify points, looked shocked here, fascinated there, and at the end she sighed and raised her eyebrows. Then there was silence.

"What? What is it?" Siri said, flustered at being left in the dark.

"Oh, hello, Doc. You still there?" she smiled. "Look, I tell you what. I'm a bit tired . . ."

"Nurse Chundee Vongheuan, if you don't tell me right this minute . . ."

She giggled. "Only joking, Doc. Keep your toupee on." She took a sip of her whisky and settled back to begin Santiago's story. "Now that the old fellow knows how weird you are, he seems to feel confident enough to tell you what really happened here. It seems there was more to the two interns than met the eye. He was afraid if he told you everything you'd think he was out of his mind, so he's happy we can all be nuts together now."

Santiago smiled and looked at Dtui as if he was enjoying the story he had told her anew. He threw back another mouthful of whisky like a fire-eater about to blow forth a torrent of flames.

Dtui began, "In Cuba, it seems, they have their own shamans and strong connections to the spirit world. There are big cults and little cults. Many of the priests of these cults are phony. But there are some that really communicate with the spirits."

"Does Dr. Santiago actually believe this?" Siri asked.

Santiago laughed again when he understood the question.

"So he says. He strongly believes in the spirit world. He says he's seen too much in his life that has no scientific explanation. He says if you like, he could spend the next two weeks describing the rites of Palo and—what was it, Santeria?" She looked at Santiago, who nodded. "We don't want him to do that, do we?"

"I think not."

"Good. Then I'll just keep to the point: the reason that he sent the two Cuban orderlies home. It wasn't because Isandro was fooling around with the local girls. That was a good excuse, something he could write in a report to Havana. But there were other reasons. He was happy with the work they did, so obviously the things he found out about them had to be serious for him to sacrifice two valuable assistants."

She stopped.

"Well, what were they, these reasons?"

"He didn't tell me."

"What?"

"He says he'll take us to their cave in the morning so we can see for ourselves. Frustrating, isn't it?"

"Painfully so."

No amount of pleading and sulking would force the Cuban to change his plan.

They finished their nightcaps and retired to their allotted sleeping spaces in the nearby middle-school classrooms.

Earlier, Siri had been shown his spot, where several nylon quilts were laid out for him at the front of a year-two classroom. Someone had chalked WELCOME VISITOR on the blackboard. But as he approached the room now, he noticed that the door was open and he heard peculiar sounds from inside. Desks were being shifted. Something dropped to the floor and broke. Breaths, deep inhuman snorts. He considered going for help but realized he didn't know what he needed help for—or from. He grasped his amulet through his shirt and strode to the doorway.

In the light of a small orange candle someone had left burning for him on the teacher's desk, Siri saw a bizarre scene. Five buffalo in the small room were each apparently vying for a position at the front by the blackboard. One creature had leaned against the chalk and been branded with the message ɹoʇısıʌ ǝɯoɔןǝʍ Two had already claimed their places of honor and lay on the dirt floor on either side of Siri's quilt like enormous Dutch wives. All five looked up at him when he entered the classroom and, as far as creatures with no upper teeth are able, they smiled.

A Wart on the Hog

Mr. Geung's eyes opened slowly. There were no sharp edges anywhere. Colors seemed to bleed together. He knew it was morning because a cock was crowing; the sun was throwing out threads of light like a spider building the web of a new day. He'd awakened with the sunrise for most of the mornings of his life, but never here, never like this. This was—what?—not a house because there were no walls—but a roof. People were sleeping around him. He shifted, but one side of him was stiff. He ached numbly as if something heavy had slept on half of his chest. He looked down to see that he was fully dressed—boots and all—to the waist. His upper body was naked except for a long dirty pink bandage that wound tightly around his chest, his neck, and his upper arm. He touched the bandage tentatively, knowing it hadn't been there before and wondering what it was for. When his fingers reached a place by his left shoulder he winced. Something serious had happened there. He didn't remember the shot or the blood, only that he had to get to Vientiane to look after the morgue. He sat up.

"Hey, Kum," he heard. "He's up."

One of the bodies sleeping under the roof of the wall-less hut stirred from its place on the ground and came to Geung's side. It was a man of around Geung's own height with sun-darkened skin and short spiky hair. Across his shoulder was a belt of bullets. It must have been terribly uncomfortable to sleep on, Geung thought. The man's voice sounded bruised.

"How you feeling?"

"I . . . I'm good," Geung told him.

The man turned his back and yelled across to the colleague who'd spoken first. "He says he's all right. He can talk."

"Yeah, some of 'em do," came the reply.

Spiky Hair spoke slowly as if Geung were of another species. "I shot you. Do you understand?"

Geung looked at the pink bandage and nodded. His memory was slowly returning.

"I'm sorry," the man continued. "It was a mistake. I thought you were . . . Well, no. I didn't know what you were. I just shot. If I'd known you were . . . like you are, I would never . . ."

"Get him to forgive you," came the floor-bound voice. Slowly, other bodies were beginning to stir.

"I need you to forgive me," Spiky Hair said. "I can't afford to lose any more credits. You understand? You could really mess up my karma. Buddha's pissed enough already that I've resorted to thieving. But he was getting used to the idea till you come along. Now I'm back in the shits. You forgiving me would really help get me back in the good books."

Geung didn't have a clue as to what the man was talking about. "Who . . . o . . . o're you?" he asked.

Spiky Hair sat beside Geung and sighed. Forgiveness always came at a cost. "I used to be a soldier," he whispered. "Except I was on the wrong side. Now, I'm . . . now we're what they call opportunists. You know? We wait for trucks and convoys that aren't too seriously guarded and we sort of ask them if they can help us out with a few *kip*. We were lying in wait in the field when you crept up and spooked me. You know? I thought you were after us. I didn't know you were . . . how you are, honest."

"C . . . can I go?"

"Go? Go where?"

"Vientiane."

"That's a damned long way."

"I promised."

"Look, I'm not sure you're up to that journey, brother. Although there's no infection. The bullet wasn't that big and it went right through you. You hollered like a wild sow when we scrubbed at it with white spirit but I reckon we cleaned it up all right. But you're going to ache for a while."

"C . . . can I g . . . go?"

Spiky Hair shouted back over his shoulder, "He wants to go."

"Then let him go."

"What if he dies on the way?"

"Not your problem. Once he's out of here, you're off the hook."

"Why don't you just forget all that religious crap?" someone else said. "You're a bandit. You'll never get close enough to sniff Nirvana."

"No. Don't say that." Spiky Hair looked desperately at Geung and asked again, "Do you forgive me?"

"OK."

"Really? Thanks. That's big of you."

To show his gratitude, Spiky Hair put together some rations for Geung and walked a few kilometers with him. The effects of the opium Geung had been sedated with started to wear off and he grimaced with each step. Soon they were picking their way through thick vegetation that teemed with insects and wildlife. Lizards scurried out of their path, and squirrels climbed out of reach.

"Where's the r . . . road?" Geung asked.

"Road? You don't need a road. I thought you people were like dogs, just followed your noses."

Geung turned to him, bristling. "I . . . I'm no dog."

"OK, take it easy."

"No dog." His face turned pink with indignation.

"All right. Gee. I'm sorry. Listen. If you follow the road it'll add another sixty miles to your trip. Understand? The thing winds all over the place. Just keep the sun on your left shoulder blade in the morning and your right tit in the afternoon. That should put you on a straight line."

"I'm no dog."

"I get it. You aren't really paying attention, are you?"

"Well, I . . . I'm not."

They walked on but it was another twenty minutes before Geung forgave Spiky Hair for calling him a dog. Shooting him was one thing. Calling him a dog was another thing completely. By then his guide had come up with a plan to make the instructions clearer. The supplies he'd prepared for Geung were in a cloth shoulder bag on a long strap. As the gunshot wound was on the right, he hooked the bag over Geung's left shoulder to hang at his right hip. He explained that the sun should climb up the back of the strap in the morning and down the front in the afternoon. He made up a little song that just happened to rhyme: "The sun wakes up and climbs my back, / At evening drops into my sack."

They must have sung it a thousand times by the time they reached the foot of the Kuang Si waterfall. Spiky Hair still wasn't sure that Geung had grasped the idea, although he certainly knew the song well enough. He filled a canteen from the clear stream and put it in the pack with its stolen food and a supply of opium for when the shoulder started to act up. He made Geung promise not to take all the opium at the same time but Geung reminded him he wasn't stupid.

"No, of course not," said Spiky Hair as he turned back and left Geung to his own devices. "Keep to the footpaths," he said. He had little faith that Geung would make it to Vientiane but it didn't matter. The bandit had gained enough merit to compensate for that. Even a donkey would have more sense than to set off on a hundred and fifty-mile trek on a day as dry as a dead man's scrotum.

Panoy made it through the night. Her breath was shallow but her vital signs looked promising. Dtui felt confident enough to leave her for an hour and walk with the doctors to the complex that had once housed the Cuban workers. During the height of the bombing, some two hundred villagers had also spent their days in this network of caves that riddled the large limestone cliffs about a half mile from the hospital. Nowadays only the front section was used for storage and for keeping fodder dry in the rainy season. The rest was deserted.

As they neared the caves, Santiago told Dtui about the locals' resilience in the face of massive military offensives. The natives always seemed to have smiles on their faces during the air raids. He laughed as he told her how, early in the conflict, the American secretary of state had described Vietnam as a hog and Laos as no more than a wart on that hog. "But look how much trouble that little wart made for the great Americanos."

When they arrived at the front of the cave, Santiago introduced them to the Sheraton. It was even chalked there on the overhang: SHERATON DE LAOS. They'd brought their headlamps with them and they switched them on as they walked through Reception, a large, high-ceilinged cavern where most of the locals had stayed. Santiago led them to a smaller room that had once housed the Cuban contingent. It was empty now and there were no posters or mementos or signs of life other than a few scratched calendars here and there.

Santiago had stayed here when the work was going on at the hospital, he told them. It was a joint Vietnamese-Cuban project but the Viets had their own cave and they didn't mix much with the Cubans. It was on this project he'd first met and locked horns with Comrade Lit. Before he was promoted to head of security for the region, Lit had been the overseer of the Vietnamese engineers. The Cubans had skills and a good deal of knowledge, but from the beginning, Lit seemed to treat them like country bumpkins, no better than assistants. When his superiors informed Lit he was supposed to take orders from Dr. Santiago, that the doctor was to run the hospital project, Lit lost face. Santiago believed that Lit had never been able to forgive him for that.

Dtui was having trouble keeping up with him, so Santiago agreed to simplify both his language and his explanations. He told them that in the beginning, he'd considered the *negritos* to be friendly men, always in a happy mood. They worked hard and were good at their jobs. But Santiago had started to hear rumors, bad rumors from his staff. His country, as well as Haiti, had a tradition of black magic going all the way back to Africa. In Haiti it was known as Voudoun; in Cuba, Palo Mayombe. Cubans believed that Palo remedies could cure all ills. They could charm a lover and even change the ugly into the beautiful. Dr. Santiago joked that he obviously hadn't sampled that particular remedy.

In general the remedies did no harm. Many Cubans tried them just as the average person in Laos might read a horoscope. Some visited their shaman for counseling and a chance to have a chat. Some famous Palo Mayombe shamans were known to perform miracles. Most did only good for their communities. But there was a small cult, a branch of Palo, which was very dark. It was known as

Endoke, a word derived from the name of the darkest spirit, which utilized sacrifices and bloodletting to invoke the spirits. Santiago had known patients who had suffered as a result of Endoke.

They were standing in an eerie cave where the only light came from the lamps on their own foreheads. With the sound of water dripping echoing around them, Santiago's words were beginning to give Dtui the creeps.

"So," Siri summarized,"the rumors were that the two men, Odon and Isandro, were practicing this Endoke."

Dr. Santiago nodded. At first he'd done nothing; he knew that Cubans liked to make up stories, just like the Lao or the Vietnamese, to entertain their friends around a campfire or to scare the children to keep them from wandering off. But one day, a nurse came to Santiago and led him deep into the mountain in which they now stood. Asking Siri and Dtui to follow him, he walked off into the darkness.

The caves tunneled into the karst, narrowing as they proceeded. Dtui looked forlornly at Siri. Only a few months earlier, the pair had been involved in a horrific case that had taken them into tunnels such as these. Few sane people would knowingly set off down such dark passages again before that trauma had worked its way out of their systems. Siri paused and looked back at Dtui. "Are you up for this?"

"You know me, Doc. Anything for a laugh," she answered without convincing either of them. They scurried after Santiago's retreating light beam, Siri bringing up the rear. Fortunately, they didn't have to venture too deeply into the mountain. Santiago seemed to know his way around the caves and they soon found themselves at their destination.

The Cuban stopped and stood back, letting the light beam do the explaining for him. They were at a dead end that formed a natural altar with a ledge. Unreadable sym-

bols were chalked on the wall, and mud had been fashioned into an ornate frame around them. Siri took a step
forward and shone his light onto the ledge. He leaned over
and sniffed at the dark stain that began on the shelf and
dribbled down, in parallel lines, from its edge.

Santiago confirmed that it was blood: this was a sacrificial
altar. When he'd first seen it, there had been other objects
around it including a cauldron, he said, but someone had
removed everything.

Dtui scrunched up her nose. "Well, at least this ledge isn't
wide enough to sacrifice people on."

Santiago explained that most basic Endoke spells only
required the blood of chickens and pigs.

"So, apart from cruelty to animals and depletion of food
stocks," Dtui suggested, "Isandro and Odon weren't really
dangerous."

But when she translated her comment for the Cuban, he
became irate. He took Dtui's hand in his as he explained
just how dangerous they had been. The blood from the animals they sacrificed was intended to call down spells of
heavy black magic to satisfy the desire for revenge. Endoke
was a magic of vengeance. If you stole a man's wife, he
would curse you. If you killed a man's brother, he would
damn you to sufferings even worse than death. One should
never dare to cross an Endoke priest.

Dtui had just asked whether Santiago believed these two
men actually had such powers when, from the corner of her
eye, she noticed Siri's hand reach for the amulet beneath
his shirt as he stared back into the darkness. Santiago, however, was looking at the altar as he told her that he believed
the markings she'd found on their mummy were known as
"The Scratches," the symbol identifying those who practiced the dark arts. Once he'd discovered their altar, he had
confronted the two men in his office one day, forced them

to take off their shirts, and had discovered their ritual scars. That was when he had—

"How many?" Siri asked. He'd removed his flashlight headband and was squinting back in the direction from which they'd walked.

Dtui didn't even bother to translate the question. "Three on each side, Doc. Come on. Keep up. I've told . . ." She suddenly realized the question wasn't directed to her. Siri wasn't involved in their conversation at all. She shone her flashlight beam into the empty tunnel. The light seemed to snap Siri out of a trance.

"One of them is coming," he said to Dtui.

"One of whom?"

"The spirits of the *negritos.*"

She was reluctant to translate this but she owed it to Santiago. The old doctor seemed to take the news even worse than she did. He backed up against the altar, his black-olive colored eyes flitting back and forth across the darkness.

"Should we do anything?" Dtui whispered.

"No," Siri told her, still looking down the empty tunnel. "*She* says there's nothing for us to worry about."

Dtui didn't want to know who "she" was. She took hold of Siri's arm and held her breath. Behind her she could hear the Cuban muttering. She moved her head from side to side but her flashlight was useless. Only Siri could see the visitor.

He was naked and black as pitch. His face was a gathering of ill-matched features. He came loping urgently toward Siri and stood in front of him. Although Siri assumed this was the smaller of the two men, he still had to tilt his head upward to look into the man's empty eyes. And there they stood, neither seeming to know what to do next. The black man became frustrated and grew angry. He seemed to look over Siri's shoulder at Dtui with unconcealed fury. He raised his fist as if to strike her and bared his teeth.

"Dtui, step back. Stand next to Santiago," Siri shouted.

She did as she was told even though she could see no spirits. Siri stood with his neck craned upward and his arms out to his sides. He clenched his fists and shuddered slightly. The shudder grew in intensity, became more like the vibration of a silent truck engine. Dtui and Santiago looked on with astonishment as Siri started to shake with such violence they knew some external force was exerting itself. Fearing for his safety, Dtui threw her arms around the doctor. All the strength she could muster didn't stop his movement.

Then all at once, he went limp in her arms, and she lowered him to the ground. For several seconds there was no movement, no sound. Dtui put her hand in front of Siri's mouth but felt no breath. Then, just as suddenly as he had collapsed, his eyes opened and he gave her a friendly smile.

"Nurse Dtui, you really will have to resist these urges to throw yourself at me."

"I have a weakness for men who wobble," she said. Santiago, pale as marble, came over to take a look at his old friend. He checked first Siri's pulse, then his own. Siri looked as if he'd been in a fight. His face bore mysterious bruises that stood out against his drained white skin. Dtui looked into his pupils. As she held him, his strength gradually returned and, before her eyes, the bruises faded.

"Now that was an impressive recovery. I think you'll live, Dr. Siri," she said.

"Sorry about all that."

"You saw something, didn't you?"

"Yes, indeed I did."

"What did it say?"

"Nothing."

"But it did something to you."

"Dtui, I may be wrong about this, but I do believe one of our Cuban friends just took up residence in me."

That she didn't translate.

There were three things Spiky Hair had forgotten to mention when he sent Mr. Geung off on a beeline for Vientiane. One was that the reason the road took such a mammoth detour was to avoid the Kuang Si foothills, some of which had a gradient too steep even for goats. No sooner had Geung huffed and puffed his way over one than another loomed ahead of him.

Another thing Spiky had omitted was what to do if the sky became overcast, as Geung was orienting himself by the sun on his bag strap. In the beginning, he just stopped, sat, and waited till the cloud passed. But as he climbed higher, the clouds became thicker and his guiding sun made fewer and fewer appearances. His waits became longer so that by 3:00 PM he'd stopped completely. It was a dilemma. He knew he had to keep moving but not in which direction. Every hill looked the same. Any one of them could have been the one he'd just crossed. There were no landmarks. Every tree looked the same.

And then there was the third thing. It was a whopper. Despite the efforts of hungry villagers and traffickers and traders in animal pelts or exotic organs, these hills still teemed with wild beasts. If they should ever have met, most of them would have been more afraid of Mr. Geung than he was of them. But a tigress that had been stalking him since he'd passed the waterfall wasn't afraid at all. She had cubs to feed and she'd traveled far to find game. The human she was following was meaty enough, and he was heading almost directly toward her lair. It was as if she'd ordered room service and it was delivering itself.

The Million-Spider Elvis Suit

Siri returned to Guesthouse Number One. Santiago dropped him off and, as usual, said several things that Siri didn't understand. Siri replied equally incomprehensibly, and they parted company with a friendly handshake and a lot of laughter.

While they were still with Dtui at Kilometer 8, Santiago had submitted the circumstantial evidence that had convinced him Isandro and Odon were dabbling in ugly magic. It was quite compelling. Two cases were particularly hard to explain away. The first was that of a Vietnamese woman who had come to Vieng Xai with the Vietnamese engineers. She cooked for them and did their laundry. As it turned out, she was an incurable racist. She believed that black-skinned people were barely a rung above the ape on the ladder of evolution and had no qualms about voicing her opinions. Whenever she saw the two Cubans around the hospital area, she would quite proudly call them monkeys. As she believed they lacked the intellect to speak her language, she even went to the trouble of miming her views for them.

She was an average-looking woman with an unpleasant personality, but lonely men in a foreign country tended to overlook such flaws. So it transpired that the woman fell pregnant. She claimed it was a miracle, a divine conception, and as none of the men stepped forward voluntarily to claim paternity, one by one, the local people started to believe her. They realized this would be the perfect opportunity for her to finger some randy soldier and blackmail him into marriage. Yet she swore to the last she was still a virgin.

Santiago had been away on the early morning she was carried into the hospital. It was her seventh month and something had gone horribly wrong. The young Lao surgeon on duty that night believed the only way to stop her hemorrhaging was to remove the fetus. It was his call and nobody later questioned his judgment. But the woman had died on the operating table. When Santiago returned, the Lao surgeon was inconsolable. He found the boy drunk at midmorning and ranting. Nothing the old doctor did could calm him. He knew this was far more than a doctor's grief at losing a patient. There had to be something else. Santiago talked to the staff nurse. She told him the surgeon had ordered her out of the theatre before she could get a look at the fetus. He'd carried it himself up to the cave of the dead, where it was to be cremated the following night. Santiago, intrigued by the story, had gone up to the cave and there he found a burlap sack small enough to contain the Vietnamese woman's baby. What he discovered inside was not human. In the sack was the incomplete fetus of an ape.

Both Siri and Dtui felt they'd been spun a campfire horror yarn, but the teller was impressively calm and sincere. His second tale was no less peculiar. A Party cadre had come from Havana to make an official appraisal of how Cuban aid was being spent at one of the country's few humanitarian projects overseas. He was due to stay for a week, check the books, and return. It was quite straightforward, but he was an observant man and not without some experience of Palo ways. Yet he was committed to the Cuban Communist Party and had no desire to complicate his life with magic. The Party had taught him that shamanism was one more opiate for a people who would be better off drunk on socialism.

In Vieng Xai, the bookkeeper saw something that concerned him, and he decided to discuss it with Santiago. They had an appointment to meet one evening at eight, but an hour before that time, Isandro came to Santiago's office to tell him the accountant had been struck down by some affliction and was clutching his throat, unable to speak. The director went to the man's bedside and could see he was in agony. They rushed him immediately to the theatre, where Santiago performed an emergency tracheotomy. There was no evidence of disease or trauma to the respiratory tract, so the surgeon concluded the man's labored breathing resulted from intense pain. After several more exploratory incisions, Santiago found the cause of his problem. The accountant's epiglottis had turned to wood— more accurately, to a hard substance like the pit of a small peach. The surgeon had no choice but to remove it. They sent the bookkeeper home in a deep coma. When they were putting together his belongings to ship back to Havana, they found a slip of paper in his bag. On it were the names of the two interns, and beside them the man had doodled various Endoke symbols.

Although the monkey fetus story had been secondhand and, to some extent, conjecture, the doctor had seen this bizarre manifestation for himself. Soon after, Santiago discovered the altar, confronted Isandro and Odon, and insisted they return to Cuba.

Siri had asked why, if the two men were so powerful, Santiago hadn't been afraid of retribution. The Cuban had smiled broadly and had slowly begun to unbutton his shirt. Siri and Dtui were astounded by what they saw. A necklace of talismans hung like a mayoral chain of office against his undershirt. This esteemed man of science was adorned with a lei of talismans, dried flowers, nuggets of metal, miscellaneous teeth, and carefully placed knots. It was a wonder he could stand upright under its weight. Siri's single white amulet paled by comparison. Santiago admitted openly his fear of the two Endoke priests Siri felt oddly comforted that he wasn't the only man of learning forced to use magic to stay alive.

In his room, Siri began to undress before heading down to the shower. Since his experience at the altar he had felt peculiar. Strange desires were welling up in him. Normally, he spent as little time out of his clothes as he could, but today he felt an odd hankering to look at himself in the closet mirror. This was something he'd avoided doing for a number of years. He was no oil painting. They wouldn't ever cast a statue of him. But for some reason he felt a surge of pride as he looked at his solid frame. If he dyed his hair he could pass for, what—sixty? Fifty-five? He was strong, virile even. Today, for some reason, he believed he could break rocks with his bare fists, rip the husks off coconuts with his fingers.

He let his gray PL-issue undershorts drop to the floor, and he strode up and down the room, straight backed and buck naked. He let his penis swing from side to side, flexed his biceps, bared his teeth at . . .

"Can I get you some more tea?" The kitchen lady was standing in the doorway. He hadn't heard the door open. In her hand she held a fresh thermos. She looked at him sadly as if he were a dementia victim who had lost track of his trousers. "Are you all right, uncle?"

Siri grabbed the quilt from the spare bed and wrapped it around himself. "I'm fine. Thank you."

An hour later, respectably dressed now but no less embarrassed, he was back at the president's house. Once more he was standing over the dissected mummy. He'd never revisited a body so many times, but this particular victim kept changing personality the more Siri learned about him. Two things still worried Siri. If the two Cubans had been sent home, what had Odon been doing back at the president's cave a month later? And if he was being violently beaten and held under cement, what possessed him to hang on to a key? Surely he would have wished to use both hands to defend himself.

Siri fished the key from his pocket and went out onto the balcony of the new house. First he enjoyed the splendid view across the valley. Then he went to the back of the building and strained his neck to look at the very top of the karst cliff. It was from there the boulder had fallen that had led to the discovery of the body. Odd that it should land exactly where it did ten days before the concert. He went to the start of the pathway that led up to the old cave. The broken sections and the boulder were halfway between the house and the cave entrance. *What were you doing there, señor?* he wondered.

Once the former cave dwellers' houses had been completed and all their documents and personal belongings moved into them, there had been no reason, none at all, for the senior cadres to go back into the caves. Such a visit would have been no more likely that the Count of Monte Cristo popping back to the Chateau d'If to reminisce over the happy times he'd spent there. So the caves were locked to keep out animals and preserve what someday might become historic sites for tourists. *What better place?* Siri realized. *What more unlikely hideout could there be than the vacated caves of the president himself?*

He walked up the concrete path, around the removed section, then onto the path again, which brought him to the front door. There was an actual door in a rectangular frame set back from the rock face. Siri had a delightful sense of the absurd, so he visualized ringing a bell, peeking through a mail slot, and wiping his feet on a donkey-hair doormat. But the door was barred and locked, and it would have taken a small brigade of very persistent firemen to break through it. He walked around the rocks to the right of the door heading upward but quickly came to a dead end. He passed the door again heading south, rounded a small outcrop, and came to what must have been a back door.

At first glance, this, too, seemed locked and barred. The cursory inspection of a night watchman would have ascertained as much. But Siri stepped up to the door and looked at the wooden planks that were nailed across it. A thick metal chain with a padlock was wound around two links connecting the door to the frame. It looked impenetrable. He stood back and stared at it like a puzzle.Once he'd taken in the whole scene, he smiled. Before him, he knew, was an optical illusion. He took hold of the handle and tugged at it. The door, complete with its nailed planks and its frame and its metal chain, swung open on oiled hinges.

Before going inside, Siri reached into his cloth bag for his flashlight. He paused briefly to admire the brilliance of the faux-locked door, then let it shut silently behind him. PL caves were part natural, part sculpted. Where alcoves didn't exist, rooms were constructed of plywood to give the feeling of a rather claustrophobic motel. Each cave had an airtight room with a pump and fallout-shelter doors in case of chemical weapon attacks. For some reason, perhaps because the Americans really didn't know they were there, the Pathet Lao in their Vieng Xai caves had escaped such vulgar onslaughts.

He followed his flashlight beam through the Stone Age apartment. He'd only visited it once before when one of the president's sons had been ill. It had been more homey then. There had been pictures and carpets and ornaments. With the generator lights and a good imagination you could have been in a bungalow on the Black Sea. Now, it was just a cave. Siri opened the last door off the old meeting room, expecting to find it just as empty as all the others, but the door nudged something. He shone his light inside and took a look. It was crammed with all kinds of ill-matching objects like a jackdaw's cache.

Somehow he knew. This was where Odon had stayed after his return from Hanoi. Siri imagined him holed up here under the noses of the LPLA. The stone grate in the corner, directly under the air vent, still had a sooty black pot standing on it. The long straw nest must have been his bed. A green plastic pail with a broken handle still contained drinking water, and, standing against the wall, was the only piece of furniture in the entire place: a tall wooden wardrobe. Even before he approached it and tried the door, he knew it would be locked and that the key in his hand would open it. Even so, he tugged at the handle first and thought he heard a sound from inside. The key turned easily in the lock and he pulled open the door. Although it appeared empty at first glance, something fled past his ear from out of the darkness. He was too slow to catch it in the beam of his light but he sensed rather than heard the soft flapping of wings. He assumed it was a bat but it was already out of the room. He looked into the closet again—a simple rectangle with a shelf at the top and a rail for hangers. That was it— no clothes, nothing. There wasn't even a mirror on the inside of the door. He wondered why a man would lock an empty cupboard and hang on to the key even when he was under attack. Even when he knew his life was about to end.

Siri ran his hand around the back edges and corners inside the old wardrobe to find the hole or gap through which the bat had entered. Failing, he started again, more carefully this time, pushing at the wood to find a spot that might give way. He tapped the solid teak of the sturdy old structure and stood back, scratching his head. There was nothing. There was no possible way for the bat to have entered that closet. None at all. Of course, that made no sense. The key was in the hand of a man who'd been buried in cement five months ago. For the bat to have survived for that length of time, there would have to have been large amounts of food in there with it. Even if it had managed to eat all that food, it would have done an awful lot of shitting in five months. There was no sign, visual or olfactory, of that. Siri was flummoxed.

"All right," he said aloud, his words bouncing around the inside of the cave. "Then there had to be another key in someone else's possession. Whoever that was—and let's, for argument's sake, say it was Isandro—must have taken out whatever was in the cupboard and put a bat in its place. Perhaps it was an accident and he didn't see the creature fly in. But why would he bother to relock an empty wardrobe?" Siri was no expert on the eating habits of bats. All he knew was that they tasted like duck and were very good for your health. But he assumed a bat could live no longer than two weeks without food or drink. That would suggest Isandro had still been in the cave for several months after his friend was killed.

He knew there were more holes in his hypothesis than there were pots in the Plain of Jars. But at least now he had one; it gave him something to work from. He spent the next half hour searching through the contents of the room. Everything was veiled in a shimmering layer of spiderwebs that reflected the torchlight like frost. There was one knapsack; small piles of clothing; a shaving and washing kit; some Spanish language books; candles; two Soviet-issue Makarov Pistolets, both unloaded; small packets of dried rations—tea, coffee, powdered milk; a tray of what had once been vegetables—now fossils; matches; and an old flashlight whose batteries had leaked and left a crusty white layer on everything around it.

If the sacrificial items had been removed from Kilometer 8, there was no sign of them in this room or anywhere in the president's cave. If Odon had continued to practice black magic upon his return, he'd practiced it somewhere else.

Siri was surprised to find the passports of both men inside an old tin can standing on a makeshift shelf. With them were bundles of Lao *kip* rolled in rubber bands. They were beautifully printed with a broad-jawed, crew-cut king glaring defiantly, but, as a result of two devastating devaluations and a switch to the watery liberation *kip*, they presently had no value beyond the aesthetic.

Siri had seen enough and he was feeling claustrophobic. He went back to the side door and stepped into the glaring daylight. As his eyes became used to the dazzle, he looked down to see that his dark blue safari shirt and black trousers had picked up a thick layer of white dust. He was about to slap at himself to shake it off when he noticed the dust was moving. He scooped the side of his hand against his sleeve and looked more closely. He was surprised but not startled to find that he was covered from collar to cuff in tiny white spiders. As he'd cleared away their webs in order to search the room, the owners had one by one attached themselves to his clothing. He looked admiringly at himself—millions of tiny spiders reflected the sunlight like a slowly shifting Elvis Presley suit.

Siri arrived back at Guesthouse Number One to find Lit's jeep parked out front. He wondered why it was that he was doing most of the work on this murder inquiry himself while the head of the security division made brief guest appearances and took a lot of notes. As he was climbing the front steps, an answer of sorts came to him. Lit, just as Santiago had suggested, was an administrator. He was faithful to the Party and was being promoted vertically—this month, head of security; next month, head of sanitation. It had very little to do with ability and everything to do with trust. He'd never been a policeman, had no investigative training, and didn't have a clue how to handle this, his most serious high-profile crime. He had men under him who might have been competent police officers, but he couldn't be seen relinquishing control over anything so important. So Siri was his solution.

"Dr. Siri, I didn't think you'd ever return," the chief said, rising from his seat to shake the doctor's hand.

"Comrade Lit, you could have come by Kilometer 8 at any time. You knew where I was."

"Didn't want to disturb you all. I know how hectic it can get out there. Come to the dining room. I brought us some Vietnamese beer. I can't wait to hear how our investigation's going."

The beer turned out to be a mistake. It was warm and slightly flat, and Siri knew from experience he'd have a thumping headache the following morning. But the debriefing was pleasant enough. Omitting only the encounter with the spirit of Odon and the bat, he told Lit everything exactly as it had happened—the altar, the sacrifices, the secret hideout in the president's cave. Lit took notes and looked impressed. That seemed to be the sum total of his contribution. He'd had no luck locating Colonel Ha Hung's family and hadn't found anyone who'd seen the two Cubans returning from Hanoi. Siri wondered whether the man was actually trying.

One thing that had been niggling at Siri was why the powers-that-be would spend a lot of money constructing a nice pathway from the president's house to his cave, as the cave was deserted and nobody had shown a moment's interest in it since it fell vacant. Lit reminded him that this was a historic site like Lincoln's cabin or Hitler's bunker and that, in the not too distant future, large parties of tourists would be making pilgrimages to Vieng Xai to see where the proud and glorious republic had taken shape.

That reason satisfied Siri, although he had trouble imagining bus tours to Vieng Xai. They drank their beer from teacups, and Lit drove off into a mist that had arrived along with the night.

Now Siri found himself sitting on the veranda with a strong coffee. He missed the sound of the *klooee* playing its single tune. The upstairs guard was gone, the plywood partition disassembled, and the rooms empty. None of the staff seemed to know, or was prepared to say, where the royal family had been moved to, but he doubted he'd ever see them again. The kitchen people had gone to bed and made Siri promise to take his cup to his room when he retired. The cups, like the plates and cutlery, were numbered and had to be accounted for at the end of each month.

After two days at the busy hospital, he was enjoying the late-night peace of Vieng Xai. Despite having the makings of a city, it was still inhabited by country people who went to bed early and rose with the sun. He enjoyed the feeling of cold and a damp sky so low he felt he could stand on a chair and reach into it. He enjoyed the distant crowing of badly tuned cockerels and the barking of lemurs high on the karsts. He felt a marvelous peace. And then, as if the god of unhappiness had caught him enjoying himself, the blasted discotheque started up. It was no record player, no radio broadcast. The ground beneath him trembled from the bass. He heard youths whooping along to a chorus they didn't know the words to.

He hadn't yet had the opportunity to go to his room, so

his bag with its flashlight was still beside him on the seat. Something urged him to go and see for himself—to follow the beat and see where it led. An echo in a valley littered with stone outcrops can be deceptive, but he guessed the sounds were coming from the direction of the military cave complex. It was about half a mile away, beyond the football field. He emptied the grounds of his coffee and put the cup in his bag. The walk would have proven difficult without the flashlight. There were no stars, no moon, and with all the guesthouse staff in bed, no lights from anywhere to guide his way. Only the throbbing of the ground beneath his feet and the increased volume of the music gave him direction. But something odd began to happen as he pursued the sound. He got rhythm.

Siri and Boua had slow danced in little student cafés in Paris during their years of study. When they'd returned to Laos, they'd enjoyed the drunken *lumwong* circle dances, a slow-motion swatting of mosquitoes to music. But none of these demanded a great sense of rhythm, which was just as well because Siri didn't have one to speak of. He wasn't a natural head nodder or foot tapper, yet here he was, amazingly, walking in time to the beat. His hips were actually swaying. The middle finger of his right hand began to strike repeatedly against its thumb like a match on a damp box. It was a bizarre but not totally unpleasant experience. He felt some inexplicable connection to the music that he wouldn't previously have believed possible.

He crossed the potholed football field and headed along the dirt track that led to the general's house and the army caves behind it. He'd been to them a number of times. Above were the cave apartments of the military hierarchy. Below was an enormous natural cavern that had been converted into an auditorium. There was a concrete stage at one end with a deep orchestra pit in front of it. The ground rose in gentle tiers to the rear wall where the mouth of the cave was wide enough to let in natural light during the day and a current of cool air at night. It had a flow of spring-water to quench the thirst of concertgoers and acoustics to shame La Scala.

This was to be the site of the following week's Friendship and Cooperation Concert, an all-star event to mark the signing of the Lao-Vietnamese Twenty-Five-Year Treaty of Cooperation and Friendship. All the old cave dwellers would return for a nostalgic weekend. They'd entertain their foreign guests in the smart new houses, and on Sunday night, bring them to this underground marvel to watch the top Vietnamese dancers and musicians perform. Then, they would *lumwong* themselves to rice-whisky oblivion before being carried back to their lodgings. Siri had asked Lit why all the entertainment was Vietnamese. Huaphan province protruded geographically into its neighbor like a large lady's bottom sticking out of a bathroom window, but as far as the doctor knew, it was still Laos. Lit recited all the appropriate propaganda—"showing respect to its Viet-namese guests," "learning from more experienced per-formers," but he hadn't been able to explain why Laos couldn't produce one act to impress its visitors.

These thoughts were going through Siri's left-right bob-bing head as he reached the vortex of the noise. He told himself this must be a rehearsal. They were testing the sound system, checking the acoustics for the microphone. Disco music was all they had on tape. It was a logical expla-nation and he could probably bring himself to forgive them. He'd spent his last thirty years around soldiers for whom the phrase "following orders" overrode all social and moral considerations.

The thick gooseberry bushes that had once disguised the mouth of the cavern had been cleared, so Siri walked

unhindered up to the entrance. There was a high stile fashioned out of stone that he had to climb over before reaching the steps that led down into the hall. But from the top
of the rock he was able to see all the way to the stage. His
breath left him. He sat on the stile with a bump. A second
later and his legs would have given way. The concert hall was
full—full to overflowing—full to rib-crushing, joint-jumping
insanity. He had no idea where the music was coming from.
There was no deejay on the stage, no visible sound system,
but the music was loud and throbbing. He tapped his foot
to the beat and scanned the assembled throng in disbelief.
These weren't trendy young kids in wide-collared shirts and
flared trousers. They were common folk. They were farmers, mothers with babies strapped to their backs, old men.
The only teenagers he saw wore stained uniforms and confused expressions as if they'd stumbled in by mistake. Rarely
in Huaphan had such a diverse crowd assembled in one
place to share an experience so enthusiastically.

Apart from a fondness for jazz, Siri had no interest in
American music and would have failed the simplest quiz on
its origins and genres. But either from Dtui or the other
nurses at Mahosot, he'd heard the word disco. He'd been
amazed at how it had managed to squeeze through the
gaps in anti-American feeling. After he'd learned what it was
called, he heard it often on Thai radio broadcasts. It was for
sale on the black market for commandeered U.S. belongings. Lao bands sneaked numbers into their repertoires
and fooled the government spies into thinking it was ethnic
tribal music. And here it was now in the concert cave in
Huaphan.

Circulation had returned to Siri's legs and they were
swaying like windshield wipers to the music. His brief feeling of panic had turned to excitement. He'd known immediately what these enthusiastic partygoers had in common.

They'd all been deprived the opportunity to enjoy life without fear. They were the innocent victims of the endless war. All they asked was to live their simple lives, but they'd made one mistake. They'd been born in a province that had become a political front line. For reasons they didn't really understand, they were the enemy, and what good is war, what is its point, if nobody suffers? The dancers at the disco-cave concert had all suffered to varying degrees, then the suffering had stopped. They had died. Siri had never been exposed to anything like this magnitude of spiritual boogie. He was a relative novice. He'd heard voices but never seen such a sight as this. Three ghosts were a crowd to him.

A week earlier, he would have smiled and gone home at this point. There would have been nothing to be gained by staying. But tonight he found himself walking down the steps to join the dancers. He knew he was hosting a spirit with rhythm and who was he to begrudge the man his final bop? No one showed any hostility toward the old doctor. Nobody paid attention to him. It was as if he were the only one who wasn't there. He pushed his way politely through the crowd without actually making contact and began moving in ways he'd never before moved.

A half hour later he was still there, still dancing. He was exhausted but he couldn't stop. He knew the anatomy of the human body intimately and could account for aches in every one of his muscles, but he was just a vehicle tonight. His failing breath wheezed like a Bulgarian air-conditioning unit. The music seemed louder, thumping against his ears. People crowded in on all sides. Flashing lights from nowhere blinded him. One spotlight seemed to pick him out—spot prize—top dancer—crowd recedes—he struts his stuff alone—the microphone: "Hey!"

He said, "Hey."

"Hey, Comrade."

He said, "Hey, Comrade."

"What do you think you're doing?"

He said, "Wha . . ." Siri looked into the bright spot and then beyond it. There was now just the one light. It was being held by a man in an army jacket several sizes too big for him and a knitted hat. He was directing his flashlight directly into Siri's face. The doctor looked around at the cold, deserted limestone cavern.

"You got no right to be here. What are you playing at alone in the dark?" the old watchman asked. "You drunk or something?"

Siri stood bent forward with his hands on his knees, struggling for breath. His body had just completed the Alpine section of the Tour de France. He knew he wouldn't be able to get out of bed in the morning. But as soon as he had the breath and the strength, he started to laugh. The watchman was sure Siri was crazy and took a step back.

"Sorry, Comrade," Siri said at last. "Rehearsing for next week's show."

"You don't say. That doesn't seem right to me, making an old fella like you perform. They should be ashamed of themselves."

"I'm a lot younger than I look, brother."

"Well, I suppose you must know what you're doing. Don't you stay here all night, now."

"I won't. Thanks."

The beam swung around and the watchman followed it into an ominous tunnel on the far side of the auditorium. Siri remained standing in the center of the huge, people-less discotheque feeling more than a little silly, but somehow invigorated.

A Thoroughly Decent Proposal

M r. Geung had been in the tree for eighteen hours. He could tell the time quite well but his watch was hidden safely under a loose tile beneath his bed at Mahosot. So eighteen hours was a guess. It could have been three hours or a week. He still had food and some water, but he was missing sleep. He hadn't been able to work out how to catch a little shut-eye without falling to the ground. His shoulder ached but he'd changed the dressing as instructed and the wound looked free of infection. He was something of an authority on the look of wounds but only now realized how much they hurt. Climbing up the tree hadn't helped in that regard. He was quite proud that he'd been able to get as high as he had with one arm. He'd never been much of a tree climber, but then again he'd never had such an incentive.

The tiger hadn't chased him up the tree, not in the sense that the animal runs, is about to pounce, and its prey is forced to scurry up to a high branch in panic. That hadn't been the way it was. Geung had been sitting waiting for the sun to return to his shoulder strap when he first noticed the tiger at the edge of the clearing. The only time he'd ever seen anything like it had been at the last New Year show. It had been apparent then, from the reaction of the audience, that large cats with fangs were fearsome creatures. By the end of the show, he'd been as nervous as all the other onlookers. The sense of danger is contagious, and that is just as well, for, without it, he might very well have gone over to the animal to make friends. If the tiger had been of a mind, she could have attacked and devoured Mr. Geung during any one of his eleven attempts to get up the tree. It was, however, daylight, and her prey was still strong. She had him cornered and weakness would finally overcome him.

Dtui and Geung sat there in the tree exchanging jokes and laughing at their predicament. They kept each other awake. Once, when the tiger attempted to climb up after them, Dtui egged on her champion as he poked at the drooling mouth of the cat with a dry twig. It was fun having his friend there. Only fatigue and discomfort stopped it from being a most enjoyable adventure.

Dtui was in the sleeping ward. Again the image of Geung came into her head. If only there had been a telephone in the morgue she might have phoned to see if everything was fine. The bed vacated by Mrs. Nuts was now being used by little Panoy. She still hadn't regained consciousness but her pulse was as strong as a horse's. Dtui could recognize the signs of a fighter. She'd already made up her mind to do all she could to reunite the girl with her relatives and see her settled into some semblance of a normal life.

She stroked Panoy's hair from her forehead and turned from the bed. To her surprise, Comrade Lit was standing in the doorway. With the sun at his back, he looked positively godlike. The new epaulets on the shoulders of his uniform glinted like wings. For a second she almost forgot she didn't like him.

"Nurse Dtui." He nodded stiffly.

"Comrade Lit. Can I help you?"

"I'd be grateful if you could spare me a few moments."

"Shoot," she said.

"I was thinking perhaps outside."

"Comrade, these patients are so drugged you could drive a truck over them and they'd smile at you."

"Even so . . ."

"Look, it's hot out there. This room's twenty degrees cooler . . . and I'm on duty." He annoyed her. She wanted him to get whatever it was over with and get the blazes out.

"Very well," he said and walked into the room. Dtui stood with her arm crooked against her waist waiting for some lecture. But she noticed now that the head of security had apparently forgotten to put on his armor of arrogance. He seemed rather frail; almost, one could say, timid. He continued to hold himself upright but it wasn't without effort: he seemed more like a wall hanging than a signpost. Dtui found his silence disconcerting.

"The sooner you start, the sooner I can get back to work," she said. She was confused by the look of uncertainty on his face. He was gazing over her shoulder at some point on the wall beyond her.

"Yes," he said. "That's quite right. The plight of the downtrodden and oppressed takes precedence over the personal issues of us servants. The patients should quite rightly be our priority."

"Good," she said. "In that case I'll go and look after the downtrodden. If you'll excuse me." She walked past him and headed for the door. There was something unnatural about the situation.

"But . . ."

She turned to him. "But?"

It was at this point he began his speech. It had obviously been written beforehand and memorized. But there was no doubt in Dtui's mind that Comrade Lit had spent many hours composing, decomposing, rewriting, and practicing this recitation. Even with occasional lapses into engineering analogy, it was unquestionably the most beautiful thing anyone had ever said to her.

At school, she'd had what might possibly be termed *boyfriends*. At least there had been a culture of pairing up and going out. But the boys that she'd paired with had been well down the pecking order. They'd been more interested in her breasts than her soul. Thinking back on those disastrous dates, it had occurred to her once that her boys had all been the shades of fruit—the pale pink of lychee, the tan of sapodilla, the orange of sweet mango—and, like fruit, they'd all gone off in the hot season. As she listened to Lit make his presentation, like a fifth grader reciting the national creed, she plummeted instantly and hopelessly in love with his words. Once he'd finished, she could recall very few of them because she'd been too stunned to record any in her memory. But she knew there had been mention of his first impression of her on the day they'd unearthed the mummy. He'd confessed to thinking about her constantly and made some comparison between her eyes and stars. It might have been a line from a well-known song but she could forgive him for plagiarism. The fact that he'd even noticed she had eyes was enough for her. He had summarized his financial status and prospects, and, almost in the same breath, came straight out with his atomic bomb blast. He'd said he would be delighted if Nurse Dtui would be kind enough to be his wife—just like that, straight to the temple, without even a hint that he might like to sample the goods beforehand.

Something like that can have a profound effect on a woman, particularly one to whom such a proposition has never been made. A man—fully sighted and with a complete set of limbs—liked her sufficiently to commit his life to her. It was enough to momentarily erase all her negative thoughts of him. It was enough to make her knees wobble so violently she had to sit on the edge of a bed. She couldn't bring herself to speak. He, for his part, had come to the end of his script, so the two of them remained, mute, in the dark room, with only the clicking of one old man's unconscious tongue against his palate as an accompaniment.

At last, Dtui found her voice. "I—"

"You'll probably need time to think about all this," he interrupted. "So, I'll leave it with you. If it helps, the regional Social Relations Committee has already given us the go-ahead for our engagement. It's all signed and stamped. Right, then. I'll see you later." He didn't actually salute before leaving, but it was a very military nod that he gave her before marching triumphantly out into the sunshine.

Few things in life could stop Nurse Dtui from speaking. It was her forte. She had smart responses for every situation—a witty comment to brighten even the most difficult of times. But for a full five minutes, she sat in the ward of the unconscious, and could think of nothing at all to say. She was as delirious as all the patients around her. She might have remained in that state for a good deal longer if Panoy hadn't chosen that moment to come out of her coma. Dtui jumped up when she heard a sound. She turned to see Panoy sitting upright with her eyes staring directly at Dtui. Slowly, the little girl's voice uttered a stream of Hmong language Dtui couldn't understand. What was clear, however, was that her voice was not that of a child.

Once all the guests had vacated Guesthouse Number One and their belongings had been successfully pilfered, there was no longer a role for the guesthouse truck. The staff didn't see any harm—as long as he put his own gasoline in the tank—if Siri borrowed it for the day. He'd heard there was a Vietnamese unit stationed up near Sop Hao, at the border. That same unit had been in Laos before the well-publicized but temporary Vietnamese troop pullout. It was the same unit to which Colonel Ha Hung had been attached. Siri decided it wouldn't do any harm to visit the place.

He was enjoying the drive. Whereas the rest of the country was dying of thirst, the northeast still had enough rain to replenish the water in the hillside paddies. The late-morning sun reflected from them like broken pieces of a mirror stacked in jagged pyramids. Little girls, straight from their bath at the local pond, too young to feel shame, walked naked along the dusty roadside, wearing their sarongs as hats. A truck overtook his, carrying small pigs in light cane cages on their way to the abattoir. Their beady eyes streamed with tears.

The rice fields on either side were neatly laid out and well tended. Big spoon blossoms and itchy fruit lined the hedgerows. He passed a single temple, its doors padlocked. Hill tribe people carried baskets of twigs high on their backs and suspended from straps around their foreheads. Ponies with bells warned nobody in particular of their coming. A young man in the middle of nowhere hoisted a guitar over his shoulder. Without exception, every buffalo he passed looked up from its munching and watched the doctor's progress. He felt happy to be surrounded by this unprecedented peace. He smiled to himself and his shoulders rocked to some unheard disco tune.

At one point he found himself driving along a newly laid road that suddenly stopped at a river. The bridge was five yards to the right. He had to leave the road to get to it. Once across, he had to drive along another dirt track to get back on the road. It was a fine bridge and the road was straight and level so this lack of coordination troubled him.

He stopped to talk to the owner of the nearest shack, who explained that in Huaphan province, the Soviets were now responsible for bridge building. The Vietnamese had the road portfolio. Each resented the other. The Vietnamese weren't the fastest of road builders, whereas the Russians had their bridges in place at exactly the contracted-for time. On roads that were merely being upgraded, this wasn't a problem. But on new roads, the Vietnamese engineers sometimes arrived at a river with their road trailing behind them, only to find they'd missed the bridge by several yards. The Vietnamese refused to reroute the roads; the Russians had no intention of rebuilding the bridges. As Civilai often said, "The monk is in no position to return the alms if he doesn't find them to his taste."

By the time Siri had found the discreet, unsignposted unit of Vietnamese infantry it was already midafternoon. The Lao sentry at the turnoff swore on his grandmother's grave there was nothing but trees at the end of the dirt drive he protected. Siri had the unit number and the exact kilometer marker, both provided by Central Command in Xam Neua, so he ignored the man and his shouldered rifle and turned into the drive. It was unlikely a solitary old doctor would be shot for attempting to invade a compound of militia.

A mile farther on, he found the camp: a well-organized, tented expanse that clearly housed more than just the one unit. He was stopped by a real guard in uniform at a weighted red-and-white barrier. The soldier was sharp with the doctor and within a minute was yelling Siri's ID information into his walkie-talkie. As he waited, Siri took in the sight in front of him: foreign troops on his native soil. He felt resentful. The war was over, won. Why were these Vietnamese still here? He'd trained in Vietnam and done most of his doctoring there. Yes, Laos had a debt of gratitude to repay. Yes, it was true, she probably wouldn't have defeated the Royalists without Vietnamese help and the present administration wouldn't be sitting where it was. But enough!

A reply crackled over the wireless. The guard pointed out the officers' tent and raised the barrier to let him pass. He drove down a slope and then up the rise upon which the foreigners were billeted and noticed permanent buildings here and there in various stages of construction. As soon as he skidded to a stop on the loose gravel in front of the main tent, a captain strode out to meet him. Siri recognized him.

"Dr. Siri." The soldier smiled and shook his hand warmly.

As always, Siri's Vietnamese took a while to warm up. "Captain Vo Chi. They didn't tell me you were here. How have you been?"

"Alive and well, thanks to you, my good friend. I thought you'd have been put out to pasture a long time ago."

"I was there, Comrade. I smelled the daisies. I could almost taste the grass. Then I felt the lariat around my neck and I was hauled back to the knacker's yard."

In the mess tent, they ate and reminisced over the year or so Siri had traveled with Vo Chi's division as its head field surgeon. But Siri wasn't there to indulge in nostalgia. He had a long drive back and a lot of information to gather before he started. Siri gave Vo the name of the man he was interested in. Vo confessed he'd only vaguely heard of the colonel but recalled there was an old sergeant major at the base who had been with the commander for much of the campaign. Vo sent an officer to find him and bring him to the mess tent.

Although Siri was unable to place the face of Sergeant Major Giap, the old warrior recognized the doctor as soon as he entered the tent. He even remembered his name. There had been many battles, many units, many transfers, and so many men. Siri could hardly be expected to recall all of them. He got straight to the point.

"How did the colonel die?"

"In a Hmong ambush, Doctor." The sergeant major replied directly but Siri noticed him cast a glance toward his captain. He wondered whether this was the official account of the colonel's demise.

"When Colonel Ha Hung was stationed in Vieng Xai," Siri continued, "I believe his family was with him."

The sergeant major seemed much more relaxed about answering this second question. "Yes, Comrade. His wife and daughter."

"No one else?"

"No. Well . . . they had a *moi* maid who came over with them." Moi was the derogatory term for the montagnards. They were to the Vietnamese what the Hmong were to the Lao: minority, ill treated, unloved. Siri noted in the timbre of the sergeant major's voice that he had no respect for them.

"And you met the wife and daughter?" Siri asked.

"Oh, yes. Certainly. It was a long-term posting. We had the option of bringing our families along. My old lady was here at the time, too."

"What was the daughter like?"

"Gorgeous. Hong Lan, her name was—Pink Orchid. She must have been about, I don't know, seventeen at the time. She had more troops after her than the Hmong did. A little cracker."

Siri's fingertips tingled. "And did anyone catch her?"

Again, Giap glanced at his captain. "The colonel and his wife were very strict with her. Very possessive, the colonel was. He made it clear early on that he'd shoot any man who laid a hand on her. And he was scary when he got mad. He frightened me lots of times, I don't mind admitting."

"And do you believe he would actually have killed anyone who touched her?"

"How can you tell a thing like that, Doctor?" He turned and smiled at the captain, whose face remained blank.

"Right," Siri said. "Of course. So, as far as you know, nobody made any official—I mean, appropriate—advances directly to the colonel?"

"I don't think anyone dared, except for . . ."

"For whom?"

"Well, there were rumors. But I'm sure you aren't interested in camp gossip, are you, sir?"

"I'll take anything I can get right now."

"All right. There was a time when the girl got very sick. I mean, *very* sick. Some woman's thing, I heard it was, and they had her in the hospital for a couple of months. A Vietnamese doctor operated on her. The colonel wouldn't let any of them foreign doctors anywhere near h—Oh, sorry. No offense to you, Doctor."

"That's all right. Not every day you get the chance to be called an alien in your own country. So, she was in the hospital at Kilometer 8?"

"Correct. And she pulled through, much to the relief of her parents. But she had to have—what do you call it?—convalescence. They couldn't move her for quite a time. And while she was up there in the caves—and this is where the rumor starts—she got friendly with one of them interns. Cuban fellow he was. Don't know whether he stuck his old fellow in her there in the hospital or—"

To his own amazement, Siri lunged across the table in the direction of the sergeant major and sent cups and plates flying. He seemed intent on striking the old soldier. Both soldiers jumped to their feet and stood looking down at the doctor in shock. It was no less a surprise to Siri.

"I . . . I'm terribly sorry," he said, groping for an explanation.

"I . . . I have this nervous tic. It does that sometimes. Please forgive me." He began to gather the Bakelite cups from the floor.

The sergeant major laughed. "That's all right. Frightened the life out of me, though. Thought you must be squeamish about sex or something."

"Are you all right?" Vo asked.

"Just fine," Siri told him, weaving his fingers together on his lap. Odon had to be controlled. "Please go on, Sergeant Major."

"Right, then. Where was I? Oh, yeah. So, this 'thing' happened with the intern and I suppose the guy thinks all his birthdays have come at once. He meets a pretty Vietnamese girl, knows they make the best wives in the world, so he decides he wants her. He goes up to the colonel—had to have balls like coconuts to do that—and he asks for the colonel's permission to go out with his daughter. The colonel couldn't believe his ears."

"Why not? It sounds like the correct thing to do."

"Why not? I'll tell you why not, Doctor. This intern was black, wasn't he? Black as a monkey's asshole"—Siri fought down his hands—"black as a . . ."

"Yes, I get it. He was black."

"You know how it is. One of them fair-weather communists from the Caribbean. Natives that join whatever army pays best. And the way the story goes, the colonel laughed in his face. But the blackie just sat there. Colonel told him to get out but he didn't budge. So the colonel took a switch of bamboo to him. He still couldn't get the bastard out of his office. It took a dozen men with coshes in the end."

Siri was developing a strong dislike for Giap and his tale. "And what happened?"

Giap hesitated. "I guess that was it. They took the girl away from the caves and put her in a place where the nurses were women and wouldn't do any twiddling about while she was unconscious. I hear she got better."

"And she didn't see the Cuban again?"

"Don't imagine so. If she had, he'd be dead by now."

Siri wondered whether that might indeed be the case. "How did they communicate?"

"Say what?"

"The intern and the girl. What language did they use?"

"No idea, Doctor. But she was a smart girl. I know she understood Russian. She might have spoken African for all I know."

The interview continued for another half hour. There were several other things the sergeant major was ignorant about. But, most important, he didn't know what had happened to the mother and daughter after the colonel's death. Siri began asking a series of mundane, unnecessary questions and waited for Vo to lose interest. But the only time Vo left them alone was when he paid a brief visit to the latrine. Then Siri pounced.

"Listen, brother. I promise you this information will never get back to your superiors. Please trust me. I need to know exactly what happened at the ambush. How did Colonel Ha Hung die?"

Giap looked at the tent flap, considered the question for a few seconds, then leaned across the table toward Siri. "He went instantaneously insane, Doctor. Really. We were there in a valley. Our outriders were butchered but we were in armored trucks. We could have held out for days. What usually happened was, the Hmong would pin a convoy down for a few hours, pick off whoever they could, then run off into the jungle to boast about it. The Yanks had deserted them by then so they didn't have unlimited ammo to throw at us. We could have waited them out."

"But?"

"But"—he lowered his voice—"something came over the colonel that I'd never seen in him before. He was always Colonel Cool in battle. Never saw him lose it. But this particular day he says something like, 'You deserve this!' A deep scary voice he used. He takes out his handgun and jumps down off the armored car. Just leaps out, like a cowboy. And he shouts 'Charge!' Now, I tell you, there wasn't one of us dumb enough to charge in a situation like that. But he wasn't really expecting us to. He headed off across the clearing by himself. He hadn't gone but ten steps before they got him. He swatted off the first couple of hits but I bet them Hmong were singing up there in the trees. A uniformed officer? I bet that got 'em some points. They peppered him."

Siri was astounded. "So, in your professional opinion, that wasn't the action of a man in control of his own faculties?"

"Every surviving man of us agreed the devil had got into him that day, Doctor. Every single man of us."

Behind the Teak Wardrobe

Mr. Geung rejoined Route 13 at Kasi. He didn't know it was the same road he'd left four days earlier. All roads looked alike. But the sun was prodding him south and he knew this road was now heading in the right direction.

In his hand he held a pointed stick. It was a weapon against wild beasts. It had been a much larger stick that killed the tiger, but that branch had been too heavy to carry. A stick was a stick. A dead tiger was a dead tiger.

It had been getting close to morning and he still hadn't slept. The tiger was resting directly below him, waiting for him to tire, to drop from the tree like a ripe mango. Several times she'd tried to climb up after him and failed. On one occasion, Geung had kicked out at her. The impact of his boot against her teeth caused her to lose her balance and fall to the ground. He felt guilty about that. From then on, frustrated but ever patient, she slept with one ear pricked up. Whether she heard the crack before he felt the branch give way was something he pondered later. All he could be sure of was that he and the branch suddenly dropped, very quickly. There was a second crack and a thump that sent a bolt of pain from his bottom to his shoulder and back again several times. He was thrown into the thick grass where he lay hurting, waiting for the tiger to come and eat him. But she hadn't come.

He looked to his side and saw her close, and dead. She was such a beautiful creature. Her eyes were mascaraed like those of the girls behind the Hanoi Road market. (He'd only looked, not touched.) Her fur was thick and prettily patterned. He reached over and ran his hand through the soft coat. He cupped her sad face on its twisted neck. Then he put his cold nose against her warm one, and he wept.

Apart from the cockroaches in the morgue and several million mosquitoes (Dr. Siri had assured him they were unfeeling and certainly unworthy of pity), Mr. Geung had never been directly responsible for the death of another living creature. He was truly ashamed of his first murder. He understood death. He worked with it every day. He knew it was the end of people. They wouldn't come back. This lovely animal wouldn't come back either and it was because of him. He also knew what happened after death. He'd been to temples with the nurses and watched dead people being readied for their trip to Nirvana. Although he never actually saw any of them leave, he was certain that's where they were going. The nurses said.

He had to honor the tiger in the same way. It was the least he could do. Despite his own injuries, he spent much of the morning collecting kindling from the forest to build a pyre. The animal was incredibly heavy—so heavy he hadn't been able to lift her onto the sticks. He had no choice but to rebuild the rude structure on top of her. He doubted Buddha would mind too much if a body arrived upside down. With the matches from his bag he lit the dry twigs and sat beside the fire as it quickly engulfed the pyre, which collapsed onto his victim. The cooking meat smelled delicious and Geung's stomach rumbled, but his mind didn't let him know how inappropriate such a connection might be.

He didn't have the words the monks used, but he knew it was appropriate to chant. There was a song in his head and, in a deep voice, he sang it over and over the way the monks would have.

"The sun wakes up and climbs my back / At evening drops into my sack."

Mr. Geung didn't know just how long ago all that had been. But knowing the sun would always be at the tiger's back certainly made him feel better. And besides, it was her destiny.

He'd tramped over endless hills since then on his flat feet. Whenever he came across a stream, he'd taken drinks but resisted the temptation to bathe. "Don't you dare wash it off," the old lady had told him while coating him with her mosquito balm. He didn't dare. So, in all this time, he hadn't washed and he knew he was starting to smell bad. But he'd promised the old lady. His skin was flaking, not only on his neck where the sun baked him, but inside his clothes, too; he was itchy and uncomfortable.

If things weren't bad enough, he found that he was going deaf. It had happened before in his life. He'd been told it was common for people like him because of a buildup of fluid in his ears. But here in Nowhere Land he had no nurse to help him hear again. Of course he had Dtui, but she was only in his head.

"Never mind. To Vientiane," she told him, and he started to march down the center of the potholed road at approximately three miles an hour. He was still 120 miles from home.

Dtui needed Siri more than she'd ever needed him. It wasn't about the medical problems that she faced. She could just about keep on top of those. No. She needed Siri to help her with two absolutely baffling emergencies that weren't likely to be explained in a medical textbook. In the once-quiet sleeping ward, a four-year-old child sat wide awake, babbling in the voice of a seventy-year-old woman. Meej had listened to her for an hour. The language was certainly Hmong, although the child was Lao. According to the intern, she was reeling through an oral history of the life of the seventy-year-old. He said it was like listening to a recording of everything she'd ever said, starting around 1940— played fast-forward, too quick to catch. Dtui was in no position to doubt Meej's appraisal.

And, as if that mystery wasn't confusing enough, there was the proposal. It sat heavily on her mind like the carcass of an overweight sloth. She had developed infinite respect for the underpaid staff toiling around her at Kilometer 8, but, no matter how much she liked them, she wasn't about to discuss her intimate feelings with them. She needed a cynic. She needed someone to put her thoughts into perspective. Comrade Lit was tall and gangly, but certainly worthy of a hug. He had a kind, strong—at a stretch—handsome face that would be nice to wake up beside every morning for the rest of her life.

Indeed, it was only the being-an-ass issue that presented any obstacle to her falling into his arms and cooing, "Yes, yes, my love. Take me." Was being obnoxious really that much of a stumbling block to being a good husband? Would it take much of a change on her part to fit into his two-dimensional, brainwashed, personality-deficient life? Surely, if a pig could mate with a dog, Dtui could become a good Party wife: the wife of a man who does the paperwork for marrying a woman before he asks her. There was no doubt about it. She needed Siri to slap her a few times to help her see sense.

Siri was in the president's cave sitting cross-legged in the Cuban's hideout. Something didn't feel right about this story of the relationship between Isandro and the girl. If the two Cubans actually had the magical power to kill her father, to make monkey babies and peach-pit larynxes, then surely they could enchant the hospital-bound girl and have their wicked way with her. Why would Isandro go through the humiliation and loss of face of asking her father for permission to woo her? The sergeant major's rumor didn't make any sense at all.

Siri decided, spiders or not, he had to go through Odon's things once more. He had to be sure he hadn't missed anything. He burrowed deep into the knapsack, felt below the straw mat, flipped through a shelf load of books whose titles meant nothing to him. But there wasn't a thing—no further evidence that Hong Lan, the Pink Orchid, had touched the lives of the Cubans. Yet, they'd come back. Why? They'd given up their tickets home and put themselves in a dangerous situation as conspicuous outsiders in a hostile land. For what?

Siri was a champion at asking himself questions. All he needed was another voice that could answer them. There was never a helpful spirit around when he most needed one. The ghost of Odon, assuming it was still inside him, hadn't done a damned thing of any use. Dancing and swaying weren't going to get them anywhere. Siri didn't need rhythm at this moment; he needed solutions.

He shone his flashlight around the cave for the umpteenth time, illuminating the humps of clothes, the fireplace, the bed, the big teak closet that stood ominously against one wall. He thought back to his brief visit here ten years earlier. What had this room been then? He closed his eyes and retraced his previous steps through the cave. The son and mother had been visiting from China. The boy had picked up hepatitis somewhere on the journey. It wasn't serious. He was strong and the right diet and rest would see him through it. They isolated him.

That had been in one of the plywood rooms. The living room was down from it, the bedrooms were—that was it. This armoire had been in the president's bedroom then, all the way at the other end of the complex. This had been the business end, where meetings were held and plots hatched. What on earth would possess anybody to go to the trouble of lugging a heavy old wardrobe to the other end of a cave? It had obviously been so heavy they hadn't bothered to drag it down to the new house. It had been left behind. But to Siri it seemed likely that it would have been abandoned in the place in which it usually stood. The Cubans must have manhandled it here themselves. Now why would they have done that?

He walked to the beast and stood in front of it. He'd already given it a thorough internal examination and found nothing. He closed the doors and scanned the front in the beam of his light. He looked to its right side and found nothing. He was walking around to the left when he stepped on something that sent him skidding forward; he almost fell. He heard whatever it was ping against the wall in front of him, then roll back in his direction. He slowly regained his composure and waited for his breathing to return to normal.

He shone his flashlight at the floor. There he saw the cause of his skid. The floor was dotted with ball bearings—the type used in truck or tractor wheels. Hundreds of them sat on the ground in no particular pattern. When he'd visited the room earlier, he hadn't noticed them. Nobody would have, unless they'd bothered to go around the wardrobe. But, once he saw them, he knew immediately what their function was. It was a simple but brilliant idea. He knew it had been conceived by the same mind that had created the optical-illusion back door. He returned to the right side of the closet and pushed. It didn't take a great deal of effort. The massive wooden cupboard glided majestically on the ball bearings beneath it as if it were on ice.

Siri stood back to admire his discovery. In the wall of the cave an aperture large enough for a man to climb through had appeared. His heart was beating fast. It was like discovering a Pharoah's secret chamber in an ancient pyramid. He shone his light inside the opening. Here it was. This was the Cubans' temple—a room no bigger than an air-raid shelter. Here was their sacrificial altar, their cauldron, their paraphernalia. A feeling of foreboding came over him. He had little doubt that this was the center of their black magic.

He removed the white talisman from inside his shirt and allowed it to hang openly around his neck. He breathed deeply and clambered inside the chamber to get a better look. There were two more beds in there, woven more carefully than the bed in the first room; one was covered in a stained cloth. There were various pots and jars of unidentifiable pastes and powders. In one corner there was a stack of dried fudge from tapped opium plants. In that state, the drug would maintain its potency for years. He recognized the unmistakable odor of dried blood and went over to the sacrificial altar. It was broad, easily wide enough for a body. Behind it was displayed what looked like photographs, but as he reached out to touch them, the talisman began to tremble against his chest.

He wondered what wickedness had been conjured up here, what evil spirits had been awakened inside these walls. He sensed something lurking, pressed high in the shadows against the cool stone. But it was nothing you could use a flashlight to see. His instincts told him to leave. He knew that he now hosted a dark Cuban spirit and that made him susceptible, open to attack. Panic took hold of him, but even so, he willed himself to reach out again for the photographs that were taped behind the altar. As he ripped them free, a high-pitched scream seemed to emanate from the rocks all around him.

He hurried for the aperture and flung himself through it. On the other side he lay on the ground, trying to catch his breath. His lungs were weak and useless now in times of crisis. Once more he'd ignored the advice of the shaman— "Do not subject the spirit of Yeh Ming to danger. Protect your ancestor and yourself at all costs."

Siri wondered what there was about his character that impelled him toward dreadful danger. He was a terrible disappointment to himself. When his breathing was almost normal once more, he rolled the wardrobe into place to conceal the secret chamber, sat with his back against its doors, and shone his light onto the pictures. One was slightly larger than passport size. It showed a handsome black man in a humorless photo studio portrait pose. The other was larger, about six by eight inches. It was also a studio picture but the girl, whom Siri took to be the colonel's daughter, Hong Lan, had been posed to look above and to the left of the photographer. She was a long-necked beauty with a shy, Mona Lisa smile. In her hair she wore a pink lotus.

Siri could certainly see how Isandro had fallen for her. Any red-blooded man would have. But this was wrong. The pictures as the centerpiece of a sacrificial altar pointed Siri to one unavoidable conclusion. The Cubans had used their magic to bewitch the girl. Her heart had been hijacked and she had been forced to love this man against her will. Odon must be dead. The living didn't have the facility to haunt. Siri didn't know why the man had chosen to use him as a vehicle but he could imagine a reason. Siri was afraid the Endoke priest needed his body to complete whatever process had been set in motion in this temple. He knew he had to find Hong Lan, but was afraid that this was exactly what Odon wanted him to do. By making contact with the girl, would he be bringing danger into her life once more? If Odon had been killed by the girl's family to protect her, would it not be better to leave these skeletons in their cupboards in order to keep her safe?

The Small Blue Peugeot

In July 1977, the average yearly income in Laos was a little over eighty dollars. In Laos, some things people in the West considered necessities were unattainable luxuries one might read about in foreign magazines. Gasoline was one of these. Most people who owned a car and hadn't been quick enough to flee to Thailand considered their vehicles to be permanently immobile; now they were small wheeled sheds or outside cupboards. On the roads, the majority of transport had some government connection or was owned by foreigners. Anyone who could afford to run a private car and claimed not to fit in one or the other of these categories had to be viewed with some suspicion.

Mr. Geung had made every effort to leave the road whenever he heard an engine approach. He was exhausted. His feet were blistered and the muscles in his legs were screaming for him to stop and rest. But he had to get to the morgue. Dtui had helped him fashion a hat from banana leaves that kept off the sun and made him look quite decorative. She was with him most of the time now, giving advice, urging him on. He couldn't have made it this far without her, however far this far might be.

As his hearing slowly faded, he found he was catching the sounds of approaching trucks later and later. But for the last hour or so, nothing at all had passed him on the highway.

It was almost as if the road were running out of strength, along with Geung. The asphalt had gradually turned to gravel, which had now become sand. The sun was on his shoulder so he knew he was still heading in the right direction, but the road beneath him seemed to have lost faith that it could make it to Vientiane.

A car—a small blue Peugeot—suddenly darted out of a side track a hundred yards ahead of him. Mr. Geung was in the center of the road and there was nothing but open clearing on either side. There was nowhere to run, so he continued walking. There was nothing to worry about. Only army trucks had to be avoided. One thing he was sure of was that the army didn't drive little blue cars. He expected the driver to ignore him and go past but the car stopped beside him. The driver obviously expected Geung to stop also and talk to him, but Geung continued on his journey. After a few seconds of silence, the car dropped into reverse and rolled backward till it was traveling parallel to him.

The driver was a middle-aged man with dyed black hair and a cigarette hanging from his mouth. "Good afternoon, Comrade," he shouted above the sound of the whiny engine.

"I . . . I'm walking," Geung told him.

"That, brother, I can see. Are you walking because you like to or because you have no choice?"

"Yes."

"Yes, which?"

"I . . . I'm w . . . walking to the morgue."

"Oho. Don't be so negative, brother. Nobody died from walking. Where you headed?"

Mr. Geung thought it was funny that the car could go backward along the road. It made him laugh. It was the first time he'd laughed all week. "Vientiane," he said.

"Well, then, maybe it *will* kill you. Especially seeing as you're on the wrong road. Route 13 took a left turn some ten miles back. You missed it."

"I have to go . . . go straight."

"You'll end up in Thailand if you do that. Listen, Comrade, I'm on my way to Vang Vieng. That's halfway to Vientiane. It'll take a big chunk out of your journey."

Vang Vieng. Geung had heard of that place. He didn't know where it was but people in his village used to talk about it a lot. If it was near his village, it couldn't be that far from Vientiane.

"All right," he said, and stopped walking. The driver opened the passenger door. Geung noticed a pistol on the spare seat; the man hurriedly put it into the glove compartment.

"Nothing to worry about," the man told him. He watched Geung climb painfully into the front seat. When he was in, the driver leaned over and slammed the door shut. His passenger smelt like a latrine. The man introduced himself as Woot. Geung introduced himself as Comrade Geung, and they shook hands. Woot's fingers were sticky, as if he'd just eaten glutinous rice and had not bothered to wash them. That thought reminded Geung that his supplies were gone and he was hungry.

The little blue Peugeot went back along the old road, then—just as Woot had promised—they turned right onto Route 13. Geung had seen the sign earlier but ignored it because the sun had wanted him to go straight. A few miles farther on, there was a tall signpost listing the names of the places the road would take them. The driver slowed down as they approached it.

"See, brother?" he said. "That there, halfway down. That says Vang Vieng. Can you read that?"

But Geung was more excited about the final name on the

list. He recognized the characters for that one. He smiled at Woot, then looked back at the sign.

"Vvvv . . . ien-tiane," he said. "Vvvvientiane."

It was the happiest word he'd ever spelled. He couldn't get the smile off his face. When the car sped up, he looked out at the passing rice fields and bared his teeth to the warm air that blew in through the window. He was joyful. He thought how great it would be if Comrade Woot could go all the way to Vientiane. But what he didn't know was that Comrade Woot didn't even plan to go to Vang Vieng.

Siri sat alone in the guesthouse restaurant and stared into a mug of coffee so thick you could lose an anchor in it. It was his second mug. He missed Vientiane baguettes and omelets and fresh-caught river fish. In this part of the country there was no drought. Things grew readily in the northeast. Civilai had once said you could drop a lemon-flavored lozenge up here and within a week you'd find a lemon tree. So Siri couldn't understand why the only dish on the Guesthouse Number One menu was *feu* rice noodles and cabbage.

The coffee was intended to take away the taste of the cabbage and stimulate his leaden mind. He had lots of little clues but he couldn't seem to put them together in an appropriate order. The previous night, the disco had kept him awake till two. Some infernal bongo drum had tried to lure him back there, but he'd fought off the temptation. He'd been hoping for a dream, but when sleep finally came, there had been nothing to see. At least, there was nothing he could remember.

He'd awakened again later when it was still dark. He had an urge to go to the bathroom. It was an annoying urge because the bathroom was downstairs and dark. But he'd arrived at the age when a man's bladder has risen through the hierarchy of bodily organs to become all-powerful. It made the rules. He slipped on his sandals and walked down to the communal lavatory. The air was still and cold. Smelly water squelched under his feet. He left the flashlight on top of the partition wall. His memory was good enough to have no need for a spotlight on his business. The beam was directed into the shower booths.

The sound of water dripping behind him gradually became a spurt, as if someone had turned on a shower. He lowered his sarong and turned. The water beneath his feet had risen drastically. The shower opposite was gushing, throwing forth impossible torrents of water—far more than could ever logically pass through a lead pipe. Siri had learned how to overcome fear during moments such as this. It was his reverse twilight, the time before sunrise when he was neither awake nor asleep. It was a time to observe and learn. There was no need to panic.

The water poured now from the ceiling of the shower stall like a mountain waterfall. It continued to rise past his knees. It had no temperature, no substance. He was vaguely able to make out a shape beneath the surface two yards away. He took up his light and directed the beam down into the water. There, lying flat on the bathroom tiles, was Isandro. He reclined like a cadaver prepared for burial with his large hands spread, one on top of the other on his chest. He looked serene, peaceful—complete.

The next thing Siri knew, he was being roused from sleep by a banging on his door. It was an angry banging. His door didn't have a lock but he'd wedged the chair under the handle, and it appeared the maid, who walked in ten times a day without warning, was taking it personally.

"Who is it?" he asked sweetly, knowing the answer full well.

"Your breakfast," she snapped, "is in the bowl. If you aren't down in five minutes it'll be cold."

"You are an angel in brown burlap dungarees, Comrade," he shouted through the door. "The Party extends its gratitude for your keeping me in sustenance."

He'd learned from experience, if he took five or fifty-five minutes, breakfast would still be cold. So he took his time going down, picked at the tepid noodles, and continued considering the mystery. And still, an hour later, here he sat with his second mug of sea mud, still contemplating the vision he'd had in the bathroom. If Isandro had died peacefully, why was Odon's spirit this restless? What was the connection with water? Had he drowned? Why couldn't Siri's spirit colleagues just put up a blackboard with all the answers chalked on it? Why did it all have to be so cryptic?

"Good morning, Doc."

Siri looked up in surprise to see Dtui walking into the dining room. Her once-white uniform looked like she'd offered it up as a canvas to an abstract painter from an Eastern Bloc country. In her arms she carried little Panoy who, despite her splints and bandages, was looking quite rosy. The sight of them erased the puzzles from the doctor's mind.

"Morning, Panoy. Morning, Nurse Dtui. What are you doing here?"

"The Cubans have landed. They got in last night. I've been relieved."

"How did you get here?"

"The truck that brought the new doctors gave me a ride back."

"And should I assume you've become a foster parent?"

"I found out what village her mother was from. As soon as she's back to normal I'd like to take her there."

"That's nice of you. I doubt the fractures will take long to heal. I imagine we could take her anytime."

"Er . . ."

"Yes?"

"It isn't really the fractures we need to worry about."

He felt the child's forehead and looked into her eyes. "Has there been some complication?"

"You could say that. The truck ride quietened her down a bit, but I reckon she could start up any time now."

"Start up what?"

The spirit of Mrs. Nuts had a marvelous sense of timing. Even as Siri stared at the girl, she seemed to change to a different gear. She smiled and giggled once as a four-year-old, then continued where she'd left off in the voice of a grandmother.

"Oh, I say." Siri raised his bushy old eyebrows and watched in surprise. "We seem to have a few wires crossed here."

"Tell me about it."

"I'm not sure I can. If she were a radio we could just twiddle with the antenna a bit. But this isn't going to be easy. Not easy at all."

Mr. Woot—the spy, the bounty hunter, the chicken counting Khon Khouay representative for the region—was sitting in the office of the local Insurgency Intelligence Unit five miles from Vang Vieng. He still had that Darkie toothpaste smile on his face, just like the minstrel on the tube, but it was beginning to fade. Woot's capture of the day was safely in his cell, and all Woot wanted now was his bounty money. Once he was paid, he could return to the streets to hunt down insurgents, discover double agents, and weed out Royalist sympathizers. But the unit director still hadn't handed over the reward.

"Woot," he said. "You know? I don't think I can sell this tale to Vientiane."

"What are you talking about?" Woot said indignantly. "I caught him red-handed taking notes at the airfield."

"You didn't bring me any evidence."

"Ooy, I told you. Before I could get to him, he'd swallowed the paper. I wasn't about to reach down his throat and fish it out, was I now?"

Captain Bounyasith was an old drinking buddy of Woot's and he got a percentage of all the bounty money he handed out to his field agents. He was trying very hard to make the story fly, but it was still too heavy to get off the ground. "Plus," he said, "there's the fact that the airfield down there hasn't been used since Air America left."

"Reconnaissance, Comrade. Reconnaissance. The insurgents have obviously got it earmarked as a future invasion site. Come on. Work with me on this, brother."

"I'm just telling you what Vientiane's going to say to me. That's all." The tired old captain sighed and dipped his Vietnamese biscuit into his tea. All but the pinch between his fingers broke off and sank beneath the surface. He swore under his breath. It was a crumbly, soggy type of day all around.

"OK," Woot conceded. "But we do have the actual insurgent locked up."

The captain fished around in the tea with his pen. He could find no evidence at all that the biscuit ever existed. "Have you not noticed what he is?" he asked. "Don't you think they'll notice that at the interrogation?"

"It's a front."

"A front? You mean he's pretending to look the way he does? You mean he doesn't actually have speech and hearing problems? You mean he doesn't have flaky skin and flat feet and stink like a field latrine?"

There were a few seconds of silence.

"He's good, I'll give him that."

Captain Bounyasith leaned back and emptied his tea out of the open window into the yard. They heard the chickens cluck toward it in a frenzy. "No, Woot. It isn't going to work. Nobody's going to believe it."

"Shit!" The spy, who everyone in the province knew without any doubt was a spy, stood up and cursed his luck. "What are you going to do with him?"

"Give him a bite to eat and let him go."

"Did he have any money on him?"

"Not a brass kip."

"Shit. I can't even get my petrol money back. What a day."

Mrs. Nuts Goes Home

Mrs. Nuts's village was only three miles from Vieng Xai but there was no road to it. To get there, Siri, Dtui, and Panoy had followed their guide along a narrow track that wound slowly through a gentle valley, past rocky outcrops that poked up like fingers making rude signs. The village itself sat ridiculously on top of a high knoll as if, one day in its distant history, it had fled there to escape a flood. The final fifty yards of pathway seemed to climb vertically. Panoy weighed no more than a wish, but Dtui had carried her all the way and she was certain this final stretch would be the death of her. Fortunately, the girl who had daubed Mrs. Nuts's feet with blood recognized the big nurse and came running down to relieve her of her burden.

They were welcomed with some confusion by the villagers and led to the hut of the shaman, where they discovered him swaying in one corner. He flapped his arm slowly as a gesture for the strangers to come in. He was a man of around forty, muscular and kindly. But he was so laid-back, Siri and Dtui almost fell asleep listening to him. He had apparently invented a cocktail of local herbs that, he claimed, dispensed with the need for food if taken three times a day. It also left him in a state of perpetual bliss, one which he was reluctant to disturb with work.

"You see?" he said in a slow drawl. "Organizing an exorcism

takes many, many, many days. Weeks sometimes. Years." He obviously didn't know to whom he was speaking. Dr. Siri understood only too well that given the right frame of mind, an exorcism could be patched together in an hour or so. He just had to elicit that frame of mind from the stoned shaman.

"Great and respected witch doctor," Siri said. "Of course, you're right. But here in your village you have a poor unfortunate lady wrapped in betel-nut leaves who can't be cremated until her soul has been reunited with her body. And we have brought that soul to you in the body of this little girl. It's barely an exorcism—more like replanting a yam in a different garden. It couldn't be any easier."

Of course, it wouldn't be quite that easy, but all Siri needed was for the shaman to bring together the tools of his trade and Yeh Ming would probably oblige with the rest. The shaman sighed long and deep and started to list the difficulties. Siri didn't really have time to hear them. He decided it was necessary to give the man a small prod. He reached for his hand and gripped it firmly. All those present noticed a change come over the shaman. He seemed to be witnessing events nobody else could see. It was as if he were being filled with information like a tire slowly pumped full of air. But, before he could burst, Siri released his grip.

"Well, why didn't you say so?" The shaman smiled. "Welcome."

Within an hour, the paraphernalia was ready. The shaman was dressed in red and had a hood pulled back from his face. It was a humble affair. Apart from the two main participants, the shaman, Siri, and Dtui, there were three witnesses. One of these appeared to be the shaman's wife, who played various percussion instruments, making them all sound like kitchen utensils rattling together in a drawer. Ordinarily he would not have cared but now something within Siri bemoaned this lack of rhythm.

Siri had seen this all before on a much grander scale, but it was Dtui's first paranormal ceremony and she wished she'd had the presence of mind to bring the morgue camera. She studied the tray of assorted stones and ornaments, the dagger, the offering of food and cigarettes. The cone of banana-leaf origami she'd seen often at weddings and funerals, but never decorated as lavishly as this. Threads of unspun white cotton looped down from the display and were long enough to drape across the supine bodies of Panoy and Mrs. Nuts. For everyone's sake, the village women had treated the old lady's body with musky oils and scents. These had the effect of dulling the putrid stink of death for long enough for the ceremony to take place.

For twenty minutes, the shaman sat cross-legged in front of the display, chanting a well-worn series of mantras. A ceremonial dagger jutted from the lightly packed earth at his feet. Siri held his amulet lightly. A tingle of nervous apprehension climbed the back of his neck. At his last exorcism, the *Phibob* had killed the shaman and all but drained the life out of Siri. He was better prepared now, but still hoped the malevolent spirits weren't tuned in at such an early hour.

The shaman, already one or two paces closer to Nirvana than most, was quick to enter his trance. His wife lowered the hood over his head and Dtui wondered how he was going to see what he was doing. But he didn't need his eyes. For the next few moments, all his movements would be guided by some nonbeing. Siri had seen mediums thrown across the room by the spirits that possessed them at this stage. He'd seen shamans hit themselves violently with their own fists or rise into the air. But there were no such histrionics for this gentleman. His visiting spirit seemed as lethargic as its host.

He rose to his feet as smoothly as smoke rising from a mosquito coil and walked once around the spectators. His feet seemed barely to touch the ground. He sighed and knelt by the body of Panoy, who still muttered in a stranger's voice. She lay on a straw litter parallel to that of Mrs. Nuts. He leaned down at her head, cupped his hand around her ear, and began to whisper. Siri knew by this stage that the shaman would need no help. All was under control. After two or three minutes, the little girl's body jerked slightly. Only one person in the audience saw what happened next. The spirit of Mrs. Nuts rose from the girl's body, looked around the room, then crossed over to her own. She woke the spirit of the little girl, who slept in her place and watched as she stumbled sleepily back to her own body. Mrs. Nuts then curled up in her old carcass, oblivious of the smell. It was that simple. Like changing beds in the middle of the night.

Little Panoy's eyes opened. She looked at the threads that lay across her body like spiders' webs, then noticed the red-hooded shape beside her. She jerked away and, like any normal four-year-old, began to wail. Dtui rushed to comfort her, but none of this noise or movement had any effect on the shaman, who was by now in a deep sleep.

Later, Dtui and Siri and their guide took tea beneath a straw canopy. The sun was harsh but a breeze skimmed across the top of the knoll. Siri stared at the pretty girl who'd brought them the cups and was now sitting beneath the leaves of a banana tree. There was something about her that drew him to her.

Dtui's voice pulled him from his reverie. "Of course, it was interesting. I'm not saying it wasn't. But I have to say I was expecting something more—more violent. You know? Blood and screaming and people going crazy."

"That does occasionally happen," Siri told her. "This was the soporific version."

"When will the shaman fellow wake up?"

"Judging from his normal relationship with consciousness, I'd say sometime around November."

"So we should get going."

"Hold on a while."

"What for?"

"There's something else here."

"What?"

"I don't know. But there's a connection. There's always a connection. I feel we shouldn't leave just yet."

"You're the boss. I'll go see how Panoy's doing." Dtui clambered to her feet and walked over to the hut where the little girl was sleeping off her ordeal. Siri sipped his tea and smiled at the teenager. Her features were finer than those of the other women of the village and her skin darker.

"Little sister," he called over to her. She smiled shyly. "Where are you from?"

"From Vietnam, uncle."

"You're montagnard, aren't you?"

She seemed pleased that he'd not used the derogatory word moi. "My mother's Hmong; my father's montagnard. He came here with his family when the Vietminh started to . . ." She stopped herself.

"I'm Lao, not Vietnamese," he told her.

"My father's people had sided with the French colonists against the communists. When the war was lost, the Vietnamese made them suffer for it."

"There can't be many montagnards here in Huaphan."

"There are a few."

"Tell me about them."

She appeared to be delighted that the old Lao doctor was showing an interest in her people. She sat beside Siri and told him about one young man who was portering for the military and about a family she knew who were working on the Vietnamese roads, and on she went. There was an amazing grapevine. In spite of her isolation here, she could reel off the details of dozens of the expatriates from the Central Highlands. At last she got to one that pricked Siri's interest.

"Then there's H'Loi," she continued. "She's married to a Lao. She used to be the maid of a big Vietnamese soldier who died. Then there's . . ."

There it was: the connection. Siri interrupted her gossip. "Do you know what happened to the family H'Loi worked for?"

"The soldier's family, you mean? No, uncle. All I know is she found herself stuck here without a job. But she got lucky and caught a local chap."

"Do you have any idea where they live?"

"Of course."

"Is it far?"

"About half an hour. Do you want to go there? I can show you."

Siri sent Dtui back to the guesthouse with Panoy and the guide. She had been anxious to talk to him about another pressing issue, but she decided it could wait. He had a feeling it was something serious and promised he'd return as soon as he could. He set off across the rolling hills at the montagnard girl's heels. Very few hikers in Huaphan strayed from well-trodden paths for good reason. In fact, even the well-trodden paths were known to explode from time to time.

At a village so simple it made the previous hamlet look like Manhattan, they met H'Loi. She was a plain, jolly girl in her thirties who lived with an extremely ugly Lao man much older than she was. The marriage had given her legal status. Necessity, for the victimized montagnards, was the mother of invention. The woman had already been fluent in French and Vietnamese as well as two local dialects. Since her marriage, she'd mastered Lao. In any other society she'd be a highly sought-after personal assistant or interpreter. In this village she made babies and cooked. She knew there was no point in arguing with her fate.

She sat in her simple house with Siri and was happy to discuss her time with the colonel and his family. She'd been recruited by the colonel's wife when they were at their previous posting in Ban Methuot in Vietnam's central highlands. It wasn't as if she'd had any choice. She was lucky to have any kind of work at all. She'd made the thousand-mile journey to Huaphan with them for their next posting. Although the wife could be something of an ogre, the daughter, Hong Lan, was sweet and, in H'Loi's charming phraseology, as smart as a bath full of judges. Apart from being maid, cook, and tutor, H'Loi had also been the girl's companion. They became close.

When Hong Lan fell sick, H'Loi had gone to the hospital every day. Often she stayed overnight. Hong Lan said it was just a little stomach pain, but the doctor had confided once that it was more serious than that. She had to have two operations to make things right. The girl was in the Kilometer 8 Hospital for over a month, recovering. Then, one day, the mother turned up out of the blue and had her transferred to a military hospital just outside Xam Dtai. That had been too far for H'Loi to travel every day so she hadn't seen Hong Lan until the girl returned home.

Hong Lan hadn't been herself after that. She was still very weak, but everyone said the operation had been a success and it wouldn't be long before she was well again. But H'Loi wasn't so sure. All those positive words didn't seem to change Hong Lan's condition one little bit. They talked a lot in those days. Once, the girl confided that she'd fallen in love during her stay at Kilometer 8. That came as something of a shock to H'Loi because she'd never suspected anything of the sort.

Although Hong Lan didn't tell her who the man was, she talked about him as if she knew him intimately. She said there was good reason why she couldn't mention his name.

But, by then, H'Loi had already started hearing rumors. She knew about the black magicians and their love potions and their hypnotism and their sacrifices. H'Loi's people had their own share of occult practices so she knew how dangerous they could all be. In spite of her love for the girl she'd nannied for nine years, H'Loi feared she didn't know what she was saying. She'd been bewitched. She'd never before talked of love, never shown an interest in men. Then, suddenly, after six weeks in a cave hospital, she'd fallen head over heels in love with a man, someone she hardly knew; a man who was totally wrong for her.

When she finally confronted Hong Lan with her suspicions, H'Loi didn't pretend to mask the hatred she felt for the Cubans. It didn't matter to her whether they were black, pink, or cobalt blue. They were bad. She told Hong Lan they were devils, and her relationship with the girl soured.

The colonel's death had been so unexpected it left them all stunned. The war was over and the family had dreamed of a normal, happy life. As a military family under the Vietminh, they'd never had a permanent home. So close to their dream and suddenly the old soldier had managed to get himself killed. After the funeral, the mother started preparations for their journey back to Vietnam. They had a small army pension, enough for a little house. Perhaps Hong Lan could even go to college.

But, just before the departure, the girl was kidnapped. She was taken right from their wooden shack in broad daylight. At the time, the mother had been away making final arrangements for transport. H'Loi was out picking fruit for the journey. When she got back to the house, Hong Lan was gone. There were signs of a struggle. A strongbox had been broken into and the housekeeping money was missing. According to H'Loi, everyone knew who was responsible. There was a huge search. The colonel's old regiment was mobilized. They scoured the whole province. After two weeks, when there was still no sign of the girl or the Cubans, everyone assumed they'd taken her out of Laos. The mother had returned to Vietnam, leaving H'Loi to fend for herself.

Siri had so many questions about this amazing story he didn't know where to begin.

"Why didn't you return with the mother?" he asked.

"She didn't ask me to. She blamed me for not watching her daughter that day. She vanished with all their belongings and my wages, what little there was owing to me. I didn't have any money at all. The regional command sympathized and they kindly found me a husband."

"Very nice of them," Siri said. "And you didn't hear anything else of Hong Lan?"

"Oh, there were stories. This is the world capital for rumors. I'm sure you know that, uncle."

"Were there any credible ones?"

"Not really. There was one that they'd murdered her and buried the body. Another was that the blacks had smuggled her to Cuba to use as a sex slave."

"And what do you think happened?"

She gave him a look as if it had been a very long time since anyone had sought out her opinion on anything. "I really have no idea, uncle. I'd like to think, spell or no spell, that she enjoyed this love she thought she'd found, and that she's still living in blissful ignorance somewhere."

"How was Hong Lan's relationship with her mother?" Siri asked, again catching the woman by surprise.

"I suppose there's no harm in telling you. I doubt I'll ever see the old witch again. You know? If they were close, they wouldn't have needed me. It was as if she'd done her national duty, produced the child the colonel expected, then left it to grow by itself. The mother was politically active. She ran seminars and organized this and that. But I never once saw her hold her daughter. I wasn't the first nanny. The girl had had half a dozen before I came along."

"Yet she turned out OK?"

"She turned out lovely. See what happens when you have a montagnard looking after your children?"

"I'll keep it in mind when I have my next." They both laughed, and the husband poked his ugly head in through the window to see what was happening.

H'Loi ignored him. "I often wonder whether she would have been so susceptible to the magic if she'd had a little more love from her family."

"The day of the kidnap, whose decision was it for you to go and pick fruit?"

H'Loi laughed again. "Do you really expect me to remember such a thing? I'm just a simple housewife, remember?"

"Madam," Siri said in all sincerity, "I have met many simple housewives in my life, and, believe me, you are not one of them. You are a very astute, intelligent woman." She looked at him with her mouth open, astounded. Never in her life had she received such a compliment. The fact that it had come from a man of letters, a physician no less, made it all the more incredible. All the more profound. A solitary tear gathered momentum in the corner of her eye and rolled down her cheek.

"I suppose it had to be Hong Lan," she said, wiping it hurriedly away.

"What did?"

"Who suggested I pick fruit. She was the only one who ate the stuff. I'd never seen anyone get through so much fruit without spending the day in the toilet. Her mother lived on a diet of rice and pork rind for years. That was probably the root of her nastiness."

"Do you believe Hong Lan might still be alive?"

"Doctor . . . honestly, I don't feel her presence anymore."

Siri got lost three times on his walk down from the hills, but as any way down would lead him to the only road, he was never in a state of panic. He arrived at the guesthouse just as the day ended. He found himself mesmerized by the setting sun. He saw it as a huge bullet puncturing the horizon in slow motion. The horizon bled, red seeping from the entry wound, and oozing across the landscape. It occurred to him that forensic pathology might be damaging his appreciation of nature.

Before he reached the front steps of the building, he saw Dtui and Panoy under a *don soak*, the sad tree. He walked over to them.

"Hello," he said. "Having a picnic?"

"They won't let us in," Dtui told him.

"In what?"

"In Guesthouse Number One."

"Why on earth not?"

"They say this little girl here"—Panoy looked up and smiled and tried to reach for Siri's eyebrows—"is illegal. They say they can't allow guests who are not on the official Party register."

"But she stayed here last night."

Dtui put on the strict tone of the guesthouse manageress. "'That was an absolute infringement of regulations for which somebody will be punished.' If they'd known we'd smuggled her in, they'd probably have shot us on the spot."

"I take it you've already argued the point?"

She smiled. "Isn't my face still blue?"

"Then let us once more attempt to champion our opposition to silly rules."

The manageress, still in her apron and army fatigues, stood at the top of the steps with her arms folded. It appeared she'd anticipated this second foray. Siri took a moment to size up the enemy. She'd never formally introduced herself, though Siri had noticed her lurking in the background of every meeting, meal, and melee. She was fortyish and formidable, but Siri had battled worse.

"Good evening, Comrade," Siri smiled.

The woman responded with a line she'd obviously been rehearsing. "I'm sorry, Doctor. She can't come in. There are rules. I've already reported last night's infringement."

"She doesn't need a room," he tried.

"She isn't registered. She can't come in."

"This is a guesthouse."

"Not that kind of guesthouse, it isn't."

"You mean, the kind that admits guests?"

"Only guests that are on the list." She was an immovable object. "Rules are rules. Where would we be if we all went around bending them?"

"Quite right. And what is your stance with regard to evidence?" said the irresistible force known as Dr. Siri.

"I . . . you what?"

"Evidence, Comrade. I'm the national coroner. I've come north to collect evidence for the president."

"Evidence is things."

"It certainly can be things, as you rightly say. It could be photographs or even the spoken word. Or it could be a person who bears evidence."

"I'm not sure I understand what you're getting at."

"This little girl"—he dragged Dtui forward with Panoy in her arms—"is covered in fingerprints."

"She . . . ? There aren't fingerprints on people."

"Obviously you haven't been keeping abreast of world developments in forensics. Why do you think we didn't let her shower last evening? According to the law—and I'm also an attorney, so I know what I'm talking about—this little girl is not technically a person. She's a *corpus delicti*. In short, she's my evidence. Naturally, if there were some way to remove the fingerprints from her and take those to the Justice Department, I would do so. But I'm sure you realize how nasty that would be. She is the evidence that carries the prints. So you don't have to worry about her being registered, do you?"

"I . . . I don't?"

"No. Because by the letter of the law, as she isn't a person, she can't be a guest." He winked at her and smiled. He doubted she was silly enough to believe such rubbish but he had given her a way around her rules.

"I . . . I suppose."

"I'm sure Comrade Lit of the Security Division will confirm this when he gets here."

The woman's left eye looked first at Siri, then at the child. The right eye did so a split second later. Both eyes eventually settled on Dtui. "Why didn't you tell me this?"

Dtui shrugged. "I'm in medicine. Law's way above my head. I wouldn't have known where to start. I was sure, as legal adviser to the president, Comrade Siri here would be able to clear things up for you."

"Well, yes. I mean. If only I'd known."

Panoy slept soundly on the spare bed in Dtui's room. Siri and Dtui sat out front with their feet up on the balcony wall. Dtui had just finished explaining her dilemma. Siri grunted.

"I mean, it is a marvelous compliment," she said, looking up at the cliff that towered over them like a purgatorial mother-in-law. "I mean to say, it isn't as if he doesn't have choices. He's somebody. He'll probably keep climbing till he's—what?—Prime Minister or something. Women like men with power. But if he got that far, I doubt he'd want me gabbling on about his politics. It would be sure to annoy him. Perhaps I'd be able to tone it down a little. I could run the house and leave the country to him."

Siri took a sip of his tea and smiled.

"I mean," she went on, "he'd have to make changes, too. That's what a good marriage is—compromise. Right? I'm sure you and Boua had to make compromises. And look, you were together for a hundred and some years. It just takes a little work." She sipped her tea also.

They watched an egret, caught in the light from the balcony, swoop down from a ledge and perform an almost perfect loop-de-loop before continuing its gliding descent. It was worth a comment but Dtui was preoccupied. "I mean, how many offers like this is someone like me going to get? Perhaps I should think about that. If I pass this up, there I'll be, an old maid with varicose veins and a moustache, always ruing this lost opportunity."

A little girlish sigh escaped from Panoy, dreaming in the room. Dtui let it fade away then continued. "I suppose the question is which would I regret more, marrying him or not marrying him? My ma says a man is never going to be sweeter than he was on the day he proposed to you. She said that's the best you get. Once you're deposited in the wife bank, he never has to make that effort again. He really knocked me flat with his speech, but I wouldn't be surprised if he got a subcommittee to write it for him. I didn't see any emotion. He recited it like he was making a presentation to the grand assembly."

She swung her feet down from the wall and stood with her hands on the balcony railing as if she were about to address a large gathering. "And the damned permission form." She almost spat out the words. "What arrogance. What spineless-ness. Would he have to get Party permission before every decision he made? Everyone at the regional office knew he was going to propose before I did. Is that how he'd run his personal life? 'Dtui, darling. I think it would be nice if we made love tonight. I'll just pop down to the Social Relations Committee suboffice and fill out an F27b.'" She blushed. "Ooh, sorry, Doc." He raised his eyebrows in forgiveness.

"I mean"—she appeared to be on the last lap now— "what kind of creep wouldn't have the backbone to stand up to a room full of bureaucrats? And who does he think he is—negotiating me into a marriage without any flirting or wooing? Surely a girl deserves that? Perhaps he knew I wouldn't have any of it. I'd have knocked him back at the first glimmer of a come-on. The shock marriage card was the only one he had to play.

"But this is all academic, Doc." She looked over her shoulder to see if he was still there. "You know why? Because when I get married, it's not going to be to somebody who's suitable or well-off or looks good in a uniform. I'm going to marry someone who turns my insides to soy paste. I'm going to marry someone I hate to leave when I go to work in the morning: someone I miss all day. I'm going to marry some-one I love and I'm not going to settle for anything less. I could no sooner love Comrade Lit than I could learn to like this horrible creepy building. No, you self-assured Party machine—go find yourself another 'suitable' woman to appoint to the wife position. I'm out."

She heaved a sigh of relief and sat heavily back onto her chair. Siri put his hand on hers.

"Thanks, Doc," she said. "I knew you'd sort it all out for me."

"Glad to have been of service," he told her.

Laoness

Mr. Geung had followed the coastline of the Num Ngum reservoir for twelve miles. He'd spent the night in an abandoned fishing hut on the bank. The first thing he noticed when he woke was his own smell. He could hardly remember why he was coated in this dark brown gunk that had hardened to a shell, and the clear water was right there in front of his door. He walked, fully dressed, apart from his boots, into the reservoir. It was a wonderful feeling. Not till he was in up to his neck did he undress. His shoulder stung a little but the cool water soothed his aching muscles, soaked his flaky skin, and washed away his only protection against insects.

What makes the dengue mosquito so deadly is its dishonest use of time. Once the sun dips below the horizon, people know that it's mosquito frenzy time. They wear long sleeves, put on repellent, and light their coils. At night they sleep under nets. It's a type of unspoken contract between man and his bloodsucking foe. But the dengue mosquito is a contract breaker. She strikes in broad daylight when you're sweating in the fields, when you're swinging on your hammock in the shade, even when you're sitting stark naked beside Num Ngum reservoir, waiting for your clothes to dry.

The incubation period for the disease is five to seven

days. A little after that, you'll know whether the strain is one that will make you violently ill but not kill you, or whether you've contracted the bleeding fever, which will usually finish you off painfully but quickly. Even in the absence of the rains, tens of thousands of lives had been claimed by the wicked daytime blood thieves in a single year. This year's epidemic originated in the north of Vientiane province, probably in the area around the dam.

Geung slapped at his arm a fraction of a second too late. He picked his attacker from his skin. She was a tiny thing, black-and-white-striped and bloody. He wondered how such a small thing could bleed so much.

People had been incredibly kind to the odd man who passed through village after village on his long march down the western shore of the reservoir. Before the days of political deception and fragmentation, this had always been the Lao way. If a stranger came to your house, you would offer him what you had to help him on his way. Even families with barely enough food for their own children would break off some of their sticky rice and prepare a separate bowl of spicy vegetable sauce for a visitor. There had always been trust and respect.

In the large cities, that feeling was all but gone. But in the small villages, the elders still held out hope that Laoness wouldn't be destroyed by politics. They fed Geung, gave him balm for his skin, dressed his blisters, and offered him a bed for the night. They had to shout loudly now to be heard because all sounds had become an underwater buzz to him. Although they all tried, no one could dissuade him from his foolish desire to complete his walk to the capital. They yelled, "Good luck" and watched him limp his way south. Everyone doubted he'd live long enough to complete the trip.

Mr. Geung was getting a bad, bad feeling, too. He'd walked more than he ever had in his life. Already he could feel his strength draining away. He couldn't count how many daybreaks he'd woken to or how many flat footsteps he'd trodden. Strange things had begun to happen in his head. He felt sure he was becoming a moth. The only thing in his mind was the electric lightbulb of Vientiane. It dazzled him, casting his actual surroundings into a fog, and filled his head so completely he often didn't know where he was or who he was talking to. Every woman he met, he called Dtui. Every man he addressed as Comrade Doctor.

Siri and Dtui sat silently on the concrete path not far from the broken slabs. The "evidence" continued to sleep off the trauma she had undergone beneath the watchful eyes of the guesthouse maid. There was no sun and the sky promised a depressing period of rain—not a good old central plains monsoon, but a slow, drizzly rain that could soak into a man's mind and dampen his mood. A line of red ants had found Siri on their proposed parade route. Before heading back in the direction from which they'd come, each ant stepped forward to take a look at the doctor like visitors at a mausoleum.

"Perhaps we're looking in the wrong places," Dtui said at last. Siri had taken her to see the Cuban hideout and the eerie altar room. They'd found no new clues at either.

"Or not looking in enough right places. I feel perhaps we aren't talking to the right people."

"You're right. Let's start talking," Dtui agreed.

"Any suggestion as to where we might start?"

"Right here under our backsides." Siri raised an eyebrow. "Look at all this concrete. How long do you suppose it took to build this path?"

"A couple of men? One or two weeks."

"And the Cubans were right here in the cave behind them all that time? Don't you wonder if they might have seen something?"

"Excellent. Yes, indeed. That's the kind of . . . concrete thinking that will get you to the Eastern Bloc."

"Doc . . ."

"I'm sorry."

The guesthouse truck arrived in Xam Neua an hour later. Tracing the contractors had been comparatively simple. One main team did most of the cement work on government projects. They were presently working on the new police station down by the bridge. The foreman of the team was an old soldier whom Siri knew from several campaigns. The cement layer's name was Bui, and he had the type of face and build that doesn't undergo any drastic changes between sixteen and sixty. In Laos, the odds of bumping into people one knew were far from astronomical. In fact, it happened all the time. Dtui was impressed that, excluding high-ranking bureaucrats, everyone was truly delighted to be reunited with their old friend Dr. Siri.

They sat together on the newly dried concrete floor of a room that would soon house a police lieutenant. Bui wished he had whisky to welcome the doctor, but they had to settle for warmish water that smelled vaguely of paint thinner. Once they'd caught up with one another's news, Siri told the old man why he was in the northeast and asked whether Bui might have any information that could help them. He never expected the response that he got. Dtui's instincts had, as they say, hit the water buffalo right in the balls.

As they sipped their water, a light drizzle floated down from the clouds, and Bui told them the story of what had happened one day in January.

"It was a Tuesday if I remember rightly," he began. "The

reason I know that is because the president's footpath was the last one we did and some inspector was due in on the Wednesday flight to check that we'd got it all done. There were only two flights a week then. Well, we were only just on schedule. We found ourselves working late into Tuesday evening to get it done. So it turned out we were walking back down to our huts in the dark.

"There were three of us and we were all tuckered out, looking forward to a good meal and our beds. We'd just got to the football field. As usual, there was a mist, one of those that makes you shudder just walking through it. That was when we saw them."

"The Cubans?" Siri asked.

"And the girl."

"Hong Lan? The Vietnamese?"

"Can't be sure it was her, but we'd all heard the stories about black magic and the kidnapping and all. The bigger of the two, he had the girl in his arms, you know? The way you carry an old person. She looked drugged."

"Or dead?" Dtui asked.

"Could have been. Her arms were dangling down, and her head was hanging. They walked out of the mist about thirty yards ahead of us. Me and the boys froze. It was like something out of one of them Hong Kong ghost films. The big guy was in front with the girl, walking slow. About five paces back was the little one, and he had this knife, more like a sword, really. Whatever it was, it looked like it could do a lot of damage."

"Did they see you?"

"If they did, they didn't let on. But, to tell the truth, it was as if they couldn't see much of anything—like they were in a trance."

"Where were they heading?" Siri asked.

"Straight for the military complex."

"The concert hall cave?"

"In that direction. So we waited till they were gone, long gone, before we said anything. Even then we whispered. Sound carries on the mist. We got into a huddle and decided what we ought to do. We knew the Vietnamese had been looking for the girl, but the mother had left already—gone back to Hanoi, I heard. So one of the boys rode his bicycle over to the army post—the one that used to be up at the Xam Neua intersection. You remember it?"

"It was still there? I thought all the Vietminh pulled out at the end of '75."

The old soldier laughed but didn't bother to explain away that particular piece of PL trickery.

"And what happened?" Dtui asked.

"Well, that was it."

"What was it?"

"We didn't hear anything else about it."

"Didn't you ask?"

"We went back to Xam Neua the next day and were busy with the inspector. He wanted this and that changed. You know what they're like. Afterward, nobody seemed to know anything. We sort of forgot all about it."

"Hell! If it had been me, I would have exploded with curiosity," Dtui told him.

"It's true," Siri agreed. "I've seen Nurse Dtui explode with curiosity, and I have to tell you, Bui, it isn't a sight you'd want to witness twice."

There were still a couple of hours of daylight when Siri and Dtui reached Vieng Xai. They stopped at the guesthouse only long enough to check on Panoy and pick up two flashlights and a kit of assorted tools. Three messages from Lit awaited them. Each asked that they get in touch. Siri and Dtui ignored them and headed off to the caves.

Dtui was amazed to see the concert hall hidden within the karst. It seemed even larger now to Siri without its midnight crowds.

"Something's been drawing me here since we arrived in Huaphan," Siri confessed. "I should have paid more attention."

"It's enormous," Dtui said. "Where do we start looking?"

"Up top are the chambers and the general's quarters. Down below we have this space, then there are various alcoves, and there's a long tunnel that leads to the other end of the mountain, where we should find the dining and kitchen area. I suppose we should just poke around till something sparks our instincts."

"Doc?" Dtui looked around at the high, arching walls, her flashlight making ominous shadows behind the irregular overhangs. "We are . . . you know . . . alone here, aren't we?"

"We should be," he told her honestly. "Until about midnight."

"What happens then?"

"The disco starts."

He walked toward the stage, leaving her wondering whether that was a Dr. Siri joke or whether she should perhaps keep an eye on her watch. Together they scoured the walls for any icons or symbols similar to those they'd seen at the altar. They saw none and the question remained: why would Isandro and Odon bring Hong Lan here as a sacrifice when they had a bloodstained shrine set up inside the president's cave?

They went through the auditorium inch by inch without result, then began working through the alcoves. Here the military had plotted its strategies, learned the arts of bomb making and guerrilla warfare, and played ping-pong by candlelight. There was one small room where male nurses, trained by Dr. Siri, had administered medicines, and one more that had served as an armory. But none of them yielded any secrets.

"So, I suppose we should go through to the kitchen," Siri decided as they neared the narrow tunnel drilled fifty yards through solid rock. They stepped over an underground stream that had been steered into a concrete conduit. Once it had been used as a collection point for drinking water. Siri led the way into the tunnel, then abruptly stopped. Dtui stumbled into him.

"Hey," she said.

"Dtui, back up."

She did so. "What is it?"

Two things had caused Siri to stop. The first was a feeling as if someone else's legs were inside his own, walking in the opposite direction. The second was a recollection—the vision he'd seen in the guesthouse bathroom—of Isandro lying serenely under water. He turned back to look at the trough through which the water flowed. It was no more than two yards long, designed to gather the naturally flowing water together at one side of the walkway, then release it on the other side. Once free to find its own level, the stream spread out rapidly before disappearing beneath the rock face.

"Shine your light down here, Dtui." The ground sloped gently downward for three or four yards. The earth was a mixture of clay, sand, and fine gravel. It was one of the few sections of floor, presumably because of the running water, that hadn't been banked in concrete. Without taking off his old leather sandals, Siri squatted in two inches of water.

"You see something?" Dtui asked.

"I'm not sure. Would you mind going back a few yards and shining your lamp from a different angle?" She did what he asked. "A little higher, perhaps. Splendid. Can you see anything?"

She tried to. She squinted and jiggled the light, and willed herself to see something, but apart from the uneven ruts, there was nothing unusual. Unless, the ruts . . . She raised the light even higher, then walked slowly back toward Siri. At last she'd seen what he'd seen. It could merely have been the different quality of the soil, or the packing of it, or the slight ridge, but there were two distinct shapes. They were oval, side by side, too neat and regimented to have been caused naturally.

"Dr. Siri. I see them. You don't think . . . ?"

"Only one way to find out." He went to the concreted area and swung his old army pack from his shoulders. It contained the tools they'd brought with them from Vientiane. As they hadn't known what to expect, they had an interesting collection. He gave a short-handled garden spade to Dtui and took a cement trowel himself.

First they confirmed that the area around the ovals was more tightly packed than that within them. This increased their belief that something might have been buried there. They dug at the center of the first oval, a more sensible and less tiring method than attempting to empty the entire space. At a depth of about two hands, they began to dig with more care. If a body had been buried there, it wasn't likely to be very deep.

Down they went—three, four, five hands—and still they encountered nothing. Clear water filled their hole and caused small avalanches to frustrate their work. Before they realized it, both of them were sopping wet and getting colder as the night mist enfolded the looming cliff.

Suddenly, Dtui stopped digging and sat back. "Dr. Siri . . ."

"I know," he said.

They were seven hands deep and had hit tightly packed mud. What they'd expected to be a grave was, in fact, empty. Dtui felt an odd sensation. She was aware that something had happened to her sense of decency over the previous year. Before this, she would never have dreamed of digging into wet earth, hoping—yes, she had actually been *hoping*—to find a body. She knew Siri had been hoping also. What kind of person had she become? She was a ghoul.

"I suppose we shouldn't be disappointed," Siri said, mirroring her own feeling.

"Hardly worth trying the other one," she added.

"Not much point."

"It's getting late. We really should take a look through the other chambers before . . ."

"The disco?"

"Right."

But they both looked at the second oval the way children, already full, might stare longingly at one more sweet goat's-milk *roti*, wondering if they could perhaps make a space for it. Without a word, they were soon on their damp knees, scraping away at the top layer of gravel. At three hands, Dtui's fork was met by something solid.

"Doc?"

Immediately the water filled the hole they were digging, and something floated up to the surface. It was a wooden shirt button. Without a word, they pulled back to broaden their excavation site. For another hour they worked carefully to exhume the body that lay beneath the stream. They scraped away the gravelly sand and piled it behind them so it wouldn't collapse back into the grave. When at last the body was completely exposed, lying in a bath of crystal-clear water, Siri and Dtui stood on either side, shivering in the dank cave. Their flashlight batteries had almost expired, and faint beams of light shimmered onto the weird scene before them.

"Dtui," Siri said at last. "I doubt you or I will see anything like this again as long as we live."

People still spoke to Geung but he no longer heard them. They looked at him kindly but he hadn't the ability to return their smiles. He concentrated, and with the last of his strength, put one foot in front of the other, one foot—in front—of the other. Left, and then right. Left, and then right. His aching head dipped low, watching his boots. Responsibility. The morgue. Left—right—food from somewhere—water from somewhere. Insects biting. Left— left, no, that wasn't it.

One town, then another, then one more. How many more towns could there be? How many miles of road? Was the sun at his back? He no longer had his bag straps. Where did they go? Was the sun somewhere, dropping into his sack? In the morning . . . strap . . . what was the song? Then, the road . . . just stopped. One minute it was there—then it wasn't. Instead, a wide, slow-moving river. A group of people, their mouths moving at each other, moving at him, laughing. A ferry comes, a flat slab of metal, so heavy, so unlike a boat, you could never imagine it staying on top of the water. Under it, yes. But not floating. Something . . . was . . . familiar.

The group, like one big crab with many heads, steps onto the slab of metal. So familiar. Amazingly they float, the crab, the car, the dozen motorbikes. A boy comes. He prods Mr. Geung in the chest and holds out his hand. He prods again. Geung looks into the boy's eyes and sees himself reflected there.

The slab of metal runs into the far bank as if it isn't expecting it to be there. The crab lurches forward but keeps its feet. Geung is thrown to the deck. Hands collect him, shuffle him forward. The road reemerges. People come to stand in front of him, around him. So many mouths moving, so many teeth. They steer him like a bicycle piled high with sugarcane. They steer him off the road, and the sun is off his shoulder, onto his nose, in his eyes. A face eclipses it, blocks the sun, switches off the electric light over Vientiane. It is a face without features that leans into his, a ping-pong bat all in black. Mr. Geung blinks. Why is this bat holding his shoulders, brushing the hair from his forehead?

They turn, he and the bat, in an odd tango. And by some miracle, the bat acquires a familiar face—the face of Mr. Watajak, the man who'd gone to all that trouble to sire seven children, only one of whom was a moron.

The White Negro

In the kitchen of the military cave complex, an area once covered in camouflage netting but now open, Comrade Lit, Dr. Siri, and Nurse Dtui stood around a trestle table upon which lay the almost complete cadaver of Isandro Jesus Montano. Comrade Lit wasn't feeling his best. In fact, he'd already thrown up once and was planning to do so again. It's true he was nervous because in less than four days, the entire politburo would be attending a concert not thirty yards from where the body had been found. It's true he was nervous because the woman whose name he'd already submitted to the Social Relations Committee to become his betrothed, the women who still hadn't displayed any gratitude for this proposal, was standing no more than a yard from his side. Yet, daunting as these two facts may have been, it was undoubtedly the sight of the body that was causing his stomach to churn.

He had seen the other Cuban, of course, even handled his mummified cadaver. But it had been inhuman, more like a knotted tree branch. This . . . thing, this was obscene. So alive it might almost rise from the table and take hold of his throat. And how could a man who had been black all his life become so white? There were tints of green and yellow, but much of the bloated skin was ashen, like the flesh of the Chinese Buddha. The doctor had given the condition a name, *adipish . . . adipoch*, something like that. But there was no translation for it in Lao. The doctor had remarked on how uncommon it was, but that submerging the body in damp earth in such cold conditions had changed the chemistry of the fat and turned it into a thick, soapy substance that maintained the shape of the original body. According to the doctor, Lit was very lucky to see such a sight in his lifetime.

Lit didn't feel at all lucky. He just felt sick. The cheesy smell was crawling through the cloth that covered his lower face, and he knew his stomach couldn't take what the doctor was about to do.

"I'm going in," Siri said innocently. "Hold on to your breakfast."

He held a scalpel that glistened in the morning light.

Lit began to sway.

The night officer had awakened the security chief at midnight to tell him the doctor had found the second Cuban. According to the message, there was nothing to be done but guard the body until morning. Lit had arrived at six with two aides and was met in front of the concert cave by a smiling Siri. Without any attempt at disguising their disgust, the aides had manhandled the body from its bath and onto a stretcher. Then they had carried it through the long tunnel to where it now lay.

As they worked, Siri had updated Comrade Lit on everything he'd learned since they'd last met. Lit applauded the coroner's skill in the art of detection and made copious notes in his book. But now, with the scalpel hovering above the abdomen of the cadaver, he volunteered to make himself scarce and return later when he was feeling better. At that time, and no sooner, he would be happy to hear the results of the autopsy.

Obviously, a rickety table in an open-air kitchen amidst a cloud of curious flies was not the ideal setting for a postmortem examination. The relative wholeness of the body made everything just a little bit less unpleasant. The only sign of disfigurement was an eight-inch incision at the top of the abdomen. The fact that the body had been sub-merged in damp earth for all this time might have affected the wound's appearance, but it seemed to Siri that there was no scar tissue or tumor, suggesting that this surgery had taken place after Isandro's death.

As they worked through the standard autopsy proce-dures, it was hard to believe this was a five-month-old corpse. Almost immediately, the reason for the hole in the abdomen became apparent. Someone had created the aperture in order to hack through the half inch of tough diaphragm muscle and break into the heart cavity. Once there, they'd carefully cut loose and taken the heart. All of this had occurred after Isandro's death.

"Can I say, 'That's weird' yet?" Dtui asked.

"Go ahead," Siri told her.

"That's definitely weird."

"And do you know what else is odd?"

"Give me a clue."

"Do you see any evidence of parallel scars on the chest?"

"You're right. Not a one. That's weird, too."

And they were still left with the dilemma of finding out what actually had killed the Cuban. There were no other wounds, no internal traumas they could find, and without a lab, they weren't in a position to analyze the stomach contents. Everything pointed to the big man dying peace-fully, despite his sparkling good health.

Although they could ascertain what hadn't happened, rather than what had, Dr. Siri and Dtui were left with a quandary. As they bagged their samples, they went over the scenario of what had taken place that night: The Cubans are seen carrying a comatose, possibly dead Vietnamese beauty to these caves. Isandro dies peacefully and is buried in a watery grave. Later that same night, Odon is killed in horrific fashion, buried alive in concrete. But their lovely victim vanishes without a trace, in some manner avoiding the second grave that may have been intended for her.

They put Isandro, in some semblance of order, into a body bag that the Security Division had left for them, and returned to the guesthouse to get cleaned up. They were still confused, yet strangely invigorated, by the puzzle they had been presented with. It wasn't yet ten. Panoy knelt with them at the coffee table, playing cards with her good hand. She'd worked her way into the hearts of the guesthouse staff, even that of the frightening manageress who usually waited for Siri and Dtui to leave before coming to play with the girl.

The intake of misguided capitalist lackeys had dried up until after the concert. In two days the first delegates would be arriving in Vieng Xai. Those not invited to stay as honored guests of the Lao politburo members in their houses would be put up here in the guesthouse. It was hoped that Guesthouse Number Two, under construction at a frenzied pace at the far side of town, would be ready to accept the overflow. But, until all this happened, the workers at Guesthouse Number One had nothing much to do other than fall in love with a four-year-old orphan.

Yet, despite their free time, the staff still didn't allow any flexibility when it came to the guests' timetable. Siri and Dtui had left before breakfast time, yet still had two hours before they'd be allowed lunch. They sat on the veranda drinking tea and nibbling sunflower seeds, watching Panoy talking happily to the two-dimensional royal family. Fortunately, Lit turned up at ten thirty with two slabs of peanut brittle that the three of them devoured with relish. Putting considerable effort into making eye contact with his intended, Lit told them what he had discovered when he completed the task Siri had entrusted to him earlier.

Before giving up his information, he wanted to firmly establish that what he was about to tell them was absolutely confidential, as it concerned a mission that was still classified. This information could go no further than the veranda upon which they sat. It was, he informed them, a national security issue. Siri reminded him that nobody at the table, including Panoy, was likely to pass anything on to the Americans, so he should get on with it.

"Very well," Lit began. "The unit—and it was only a unit—that was stationed at the Xam Neua intersection the night Isandro was killed, was a guerilla outfit whose mission was to conduct clandestine operations inside Hmong-occupied territory. It was set up shortly after the ambush of Colonel Ha Hung's men, two months earlier. A number of its members had been in Ha Hung's battalion, and most had been involved in the earlier search for their commander's kidnapped daughter."

The unit had since been disbanded and the men dispatched to other sections, but Lit proudly produced a carbon copy of the names of its original members. He handed it to Siri, who ran his finger down the list. Although he doubted a list of the names of Vietnamese soldiers would have much meaning to him, one name leaped from the paper. Siri took a pencil from his top pocket and encircled it. He smiled at Dtui and Lit, but didn't bother to explain.

"Are you free, Comrade Lit?" Siri asked.

"Dr. Siri, in two days, I have to ensure the safety of sixty foreign dignitaries, almost our entire cabinet and forty odd generals. Before then, I have to solve a murder mystery to the satisfaction of the president. If you could do anything to make that possible, I would gladly give up sleeping for the next seventy-two hours."

"Good. Then let's go for a drive."

As Lit drove and Dtui sat silent in the backseat, Siri described, perhaps in too great detail for his auditor's comprehension, the findings of the autopsy. The young man nodded at the right times, but Siri could see that he was out of his depth. He was doing a job he saw as temporary but knew he had to do to the best of his ability in order to leave it. Thus he was willing to afford Siri every ounce of cooperation he had to offer. Often, Lit looked in his rearview mirror, not to check whether they were being followed, but in order to establish the day's first eye contact with Dtui. In spite of the width of his mirror and the breadth of his fiancée, she always managed to be somehow just outside the frame. In fact, the journey almost ended in disaster at one point. Lit, with his eyes on the mirror, failed to notice that the road led directly into the river. Siri had awakened from his catnap just in time to yell a warning.

Siri knew the route well. When they turned off at the appropriate kilometer marker, the same ragamuffin Lao guard was there beneath his straw shelter. They didn't even stop to be lied to by him. The poor man slowly got his hunting rifle from his shoulder and eventually maneuvered it into a firing position, but by then the jeep was long gone. Not a problem as he didn't actually have any bullets.

Ten minutes later, Siri, Lit, and Dtui were sitting around a table in a tent that contained nothing else. Siri had pulled his old friend, Captain Vo, to one side to explain the situation. This was no longer just an informal chat. Events had reached an official level that involved military protocol and records and witnesses. So while the Vietnamese were setting up all the official rigmarole, Siri had nothing to do but sit between Dtui and Lit like an Italian grandmother chaperoning a date. Dtui was grateful; Lit, annoyed.

The silence was relieved by a procession of serious men

in dress uniform who filled up all but one of the remaining seats around the table. It occurred to Siri that this was probably not the most likely atmosphere in which to induce a career soldier to admit to premeditated murder. In his head, he went through a number of strategies for eliciting a confession, but even as Sergeant Major Giap walked escorted into the tent, saluted, and sat in the final seat, Siri still hadn't the vaguest idea of how he could get the man to talk. As it turned out, he had nothing to worry about. Captain Vo took the lead.

"Sergeant. Major Giap . . . ?"

"Yes, sir?"

"In January of this year, you were a member of a unit of Vietminh troops stationed twenty miles from Xam Neua."

Giap looked around at the faces of the strangers and realized the army expected him to tell what he knew, secret operation or not. "That's right, sir."

"One night," Vo continued, "a tradesman working in Vieng Xai came to your camp and reported that he'd seen the two missing Cubans. Is that correct?"

Siri supposed that if the sergeant major had said no at this point, the matter might be dropped. But once again the old soldier looked around at the expressionless faces of his accusers and seemed to know instinctively that these were all questions to which there were already answers.

"Yes."

The captain looked harshly into his eyes. Siri saw that this was no longer the laughing man with whom he'd played chess deep in nameless jungles. Captain Vo had hardened into a leader who demanded unswerving loyalty and total honesty from the men under him.

"When Dr. Siri was here before," he continued, "you apparently found it unnecessary to mention this rather important fact. Could you explain to us why that was?"

"He didn't ask, sir."

The captain quickly produced a smile that covered a lot of fury. "He's asking now, Sergeant Major."

There was no halfway for the old soldier: he could be silent and get shot, lie and get shot, or spill the beans and get court-martialed and then get shot. It wasn't a great choice. This was the Vietnamese army. There was nowhere to appeal. If you screwed up, justice was swift.

"We were picked individually by our lieutenant," he began. As he spoke, one of the uniformed officers recorded his words in shorthand. "He rushed around and only selected those of us who'd served directly under the colonel. Some of us had been involved in the search for his daughter. We were given the choice to join in or not. Of course, we all did. There were seven of us, I suppose eight, if you include the old Hmong scout. It all had to be discreet—no guns. We had no authority to do what we planned to do. We made a vow not to talk to anyone about it, whatever happened.

"We set out as quick as we could. We weren't sure how long the Cubans were going to be around. We went in one truck, parked half a mile from the cave, and ran in."

"What did you take as weapons?" the captain asked.

"We all had knives. A couple of the men had crossbows for long distance."

Siri mentally slapped himself for not thinking of this. Of course there was no bullet in Odon's wound. It hadn't been caused by a gun at all. If he'd been hit by a crossbow bolt, the attacker would have pulled it out, leaving a wound identical to that of a bullet. He looked at Dtui to see if she'd also worked it out, then realized she was sitting in ignorance, listening to a language she'd never had cause to learn.

Lai continued. "We went into the military caves from both ends. The lead man in each team had a lamp with a red filter. The team that entered through the auditorium saw her first. After all the searching, it was heartbreaking. I can't begin to tell you how infuriated we were at that sight. She was dead, sir."

"Miss Hong Lan?" Siri asked, although he was an outsider at this military tribunal.

"Not just dead, Doctor. Gutted. She was lying there in a wet grave with her insides hanging out. Carved up, by the look of it. But you'd have to stick in the knife and move it around to get the size of wound she had on her. It was sick, really sick. It had to be the damned Cubans who did it."

"You only saw the one body?" Siri asked.

"One was enough."

"Sergeant Major, this is important." Siri knew he was hijacking the inquiry but there were a number of questions that had to be asked in a hurry. "Where exactly was the body?"

"In a grave. There was that little stream running through the cave and the hole was just beside it."

"But there was only the one grave."

"Yes, sir."

"And was it completely uncovered?"

"Not exactly, Doctor. Her legs were covered in sand, and there was a little spade there, like we'd disturbed the Cubans before they could finish the job."

"And the water had washed the blood from the body?"

"That's right."

"Was there any blood anywhere else? Any suggestion there'd been a fight of some kind?"

"Didn't notice any. But don't forget we were using torches with red filters."

"What happened next?" the captain asked.

"We went looking for the bastards. We didn't think it was just that they should get away with it. We figured if they'd heard us coming and run off, they couldn't be that far away. The Hmong scout picked up a track outside the concert cave, running feet."

"Just the one track?"

"Yes, sir. We figured the Cubans had escaped in different directions. We searched I don't know how long. An hour? Two? Then we found one of them up there in front of the president's old cave. He was singing, sir. I swear he was singing. He was wearing just this pair of old football shorts and dancing and goddamned singing. Sir, people like that don't deserve a fair trial. We got him with a crossbow, but it didn't finish him off. He was still staggering around. We were on him, all of us. I tell you, he was strong, strong as an ox. But we hadn't planned on the cement thing."

"But you had planned to kill him," the captain said.

"Not really, sir."

"You took knives and crossbows."

"Just for self-defense, sir."

"I don't believe you. Go on."

"Sir. Well, the cement was there and it was still wet. When we pushed him under, he sort of came out of a trance and realized what was happening. He fought like a tiger—scratching, kicking. Then he went quiet. The archer pulled out his bolt, we smoothed the cement, and got the hell out before anyone could come and see what all the singing and screaming were about."

The men around the table sighed audibly when he stopped talking.

"Sergeant Major," the captain asked, "did you find the second man?"

"No, sir. We went back the next night but there was no trace."

"And what did you do with the girl?"

"We filled in the grave, took her out to the truck, and

brought her back to the camp. The lieutenant got in touch with the mother in Hanoi and explained what had happened. We thought she'd travel back or ask for her daughter's body to be shipped there for a funeral, but she didn't. She just told us to give the girl a decent burial and send her a lock of her hair."

"Where did you bury her?" Siri asked.

Thangon was a small enough village for everyone to know everyone else and their business. Even the people on the ferry had recognized young Geung. He'd been a celebrity, after all, one of the town crazies, for eighteen years of his life. Mr. Watajak hadn't exactly been delighted to see his son, but he put on a show for all the neighbors. Geung's father was alone now and getting old. His wife had left her drunken husband long ago. All the kids had grown up and gone to the city. Apart from his monthly trips to Vientiane to coerce money from his offspring, he stayed in or around his little hut. This was the same hovel in which Geung had been born and lived before his move to Mahosot.

When Geung had emerged from his exhausted sleep that first morning, and seen everything as he remembered it, it was as if everything he'd experienced—Vientiane, the morgue, Dr. Siri, Dtui, the trip to Luang Prabang—had all been part of his coma. None of the dream had really happened, and he was still a teenager in Thangon. He called to his brothers and sisters, called to his mother, but only his father came. Except his father was much older than he should have been—and the house was dusty and empty.

The neighbors came by regularly to bring food and drink and put balm on Geung's dry skin. He remembered their faces. He remembered the old midwife, who had been old when she birthed Geung and was still old today. She used a syringe to drain the fluid from Geung's ears, a duty she'd performed regularly while he was growing up, and as ever, hers was the first voice to enter his head when his hearing returned.

"It's lovely to see you back, young Geung."

Hearing brought him back to reality. He could make out questions now from the curious visitors and answer them. In a place with no electricity and no other entertainment, people came by to listen to his memories of the hospital and Dr. Siri's morgue—the cases they'd worked on. Of course, his version was simplified and left out some rather vital details, but for the simple people of Thangon, that was probably not a bad thing.

There was no way he could know what was slowly happening there in his old home. His father, the wise seer, in order to feather his own financial nest, had turned out children with the same regularity as a factory producing meatballs. The people of Tnangan had said, "How clever he is, that Watajak. Seven kids and he'll never have to work again." And here he was today sitting in the shadows like a fool. Who respected him now? Who listened to him? He watched as people came to hear the wise words of his son. The moron had become a genius.

Autopsy of the Pink Orchid

The people from Vientiane had already arrived in Vieng Xai to set up for the concert. The following day, the flight from Hanoi would bring the entertainers. There'd be a day for rehearsals, then, on the Sunday morning, the delegates and Party chiefs would start to arrive. Comrade Khong was therefore most insistent that Dr. Siri should move the body out of the concert hall kitchen immediately.

Comrade Khong was a severe man with a large chest and menacing eyes. No earthquake, no invasion, and certainly no autopsy would stand in the way of his carefully charted preparations for the Friendship and Cooperation Concert. The housekeepers were equally indignant about the slices of dismembered mummy littering the president's meeting room. They, too, had to go. Absolutely barred from Guesthouse Number One, which was undergoing a top-to-bottom spring clean, the two Cubans were returned to the scene of the first act, the Kilometer 8 Hospital.

Lit had spent the night writing and copying his detailed report. It lacked only one final paragraph outlining the findings of the last autopsy, that of Hong Lan, the pink orchid. Now he sat on the bench in front of the same middle-school classroom where Siri had spent his night with the buffaloes. None of the patients in the other buildings who looked out at him through their windows could work out why he was wearing a gas mask.

If they'd sat beside him they would have known. Inside the classroom, sweating and confused, Siri and Dtui sat on either side of the skeleton that had once been a beautiful Vietnamese girl. They wore three surgical masks apiece over their mouths and noses. The middle mask had been liberally spread with aromatic Tiger Balm. But nothing could possibly take away the awful smell that permeated the room and everything in it. They'd laughed at Comrade Lit when he'd arrived in his mask. They'd told him their noses were used to the smell of death. But if the glass hadn't been so restrictive, they would now have been wearing the extra two he'd brought along for them. In all their time in the morgue, they'd never smelled anything like this.

One mummy; one body preserved as adipocere, but now reacting to the air; and one more, interred in a plastic body bag and subjected to the natural ravages of bacteria—each rotted at its own pace, each with its own unique scent of death. The combination was overwhelming, but the doctor wanted all three together to make comparisons and provide inspiration. During the autopsy of Hong Lan, they found their first similarity. Just as in the case of Isandro, what traces remained of the diaphragm suggested that it had been punctured. The body bag had slowed the process of decomposition sufficiently to leave a number of clues that might otherwise have been erased by vermin. Although there were no organs left within the carcass, score marks on the inside of the rib cage suggested that some amateur surgery had been conducted. Those two items combined pointed to the possibility that Hong Lan's heart had also been removed.

The tendons and ligaments had so far resisted decomposition, and, the uterus was still partly intact.

"My goodness, take a look at this," Siri said to Dtui.

"What is that?"

"Why don't you tell me?"

"Well, they look like fibroids, but she was only—what?—eighteen?"

"Unusual, isn't it? I wonder whether this is the reason for her hospitalization."

"I thought fibroids were benign."

"Not always. And don't forget, there may have been cysts as well. But even if that was the case, there wouldn't be any trace by now."

"Is there some way we can find out?"

Siri cleared an area behind the cervix to get a better look at the spinal column. "Oh, my."

"What?"

"Can you see?"

"What is that? What's happened to her spine?"

"It's been eaten, Dtui. The cancer spread from her uterus and infected her bone marrow. It started to destroy her spine. She must have been in terrible pain at the end."

"Could it have killed her?"

"If it didn't, there's no doubt it soon would have."

"So what does this all mean?"

Siri pulled down his masks, needing air more than he needed to be protected from the smell. He gasped in a few deep breaths and swallowed back the nausea in his throat.

"It means she was in great distress for the last few months of her life. We can only hope her jailers were giving her painkillers." The memory of the dried opium in the president's cave came to his mind.

"Surely they couldn't have been so heartless . . ."

"You know? I think . . ." He was too slow to choke back the second arrival of bile and Dtui watched with amusement as he turned away from the table and vomited. She'd outlasted the great surgeon.

* * *

Half an hour later they were presenting Lit with their findings. They'd walked away from the room and were sitting in the shadow of the hospital cliff but the smell was still in their noses. They admitted they couldn't prove the cancer had killed Hong Lan. In order to get to her diaphragm, an attacker would first have to puncture the abdomen. That could have caused enough bleeding to kill the girl, but there was no evidence to prove or disprove whether this had happened. And, as with Isandro, they could find no other obvious cause of death. Comrade Lit was happy to write in the final paragraph of his report that there had been "evidence of foul play in both instances." He closed with "The hearts of both bodies had been removed, and given that there was only one other suspect present, it has to be assumed that Odon was responsible for these two deaths."

As Lit's major criminal responsibility—the body found in the cement path—had been accounted for, he was more than pleased to leave the other two cases pending. He was sure his superiors wouldn't expect him to interview a dead suspect. He knew the army would have to decide for itself how to punish Giap and the other members of the lynch party. Given the ugliness of the crime they were avenging, he guessed it would take the form of a rebuke and a demotion rather than a firing squad. But it was no longer his concern. He was off the hook.

Before he left to file the report, he announced to Dtui that he would be back later to complete the "unification arrangements." This she took to mean the wedding, and she wasn't at all surprised that he was able to make an engagement sound like a merger. She walked with Siri along the skirt of the mountain and breathed in the scents of the tiny wild bladderwort that grew in abundance there. They'd become accustomed now to keeping to well-worn tracks. She doubted she'd have the courage to stroll over unmarked fields or through virgin forest ever again.

Both she and her boss were troubled, and neither had spoken since they'd parted company from Lit. The man had been so elated. It was as if one more barrier had been lifted between him and his next promotion. Siri noticed her glum look.

"Are you thinking about what to say to Comrade Lit?"

"No. Not really. That can take care of itself."

"Then what is it?"

She stopped walking and put her hands on her hips. "I've got a bad feeling about this case."

"Me, too."

"All right. You go first. What's worrying you?"

"Probably all the things that are worrying you. Let's go over it." They went to a shaded boulder and sat side by side. "I know it looks like we've reached the end of the story, but I keep thinking we've missed an essential part of the plot."

"That's exactly it. I'm having a lot of those women's intuition twinges. The mother worries me. You know? They still hadn't found her daughter but she waltzed back to Vietnam as if it didn't matter. Then, when they did find the body, she couldn't even be bothered to come back for the funeral. Her only daughter. That doesn't sound like a very warm mother-daughter relationship to me."

"Perhaps she was unbalanced by the death of her husband."

"So you'd hold on even tighter to the relationship that remained. No. Something happened between them. I'm sure of it. Are you still hosting Odon?"

It was a surprise question. Siri had forgotten all about the wayward spirit. "I don't think so. I don't know. I haven't felt anything since we found the body. I haven't shimmied once

in the past twenty-four hours. It was never really a possession, more like a presence—an influence. And that's
another thing that didn't ever sit right. If Odon and Isandro were as evil as everyone's painting them, I wonder why
I didn't feel that? Why didn't I ever sense their power? I
don't know. I wonder . . ."

"What?"

"I wonder if we're not seeing what we've been told to see."

"What should we do?"

"We could go back to Vientiane, tell everyone Inspector
Maigret and his faithful lieutenant have solved yet another
dastardly crime, and know deep down that we haven't. . . ."

"I like the second alternative."

"I thought you might."

Dr. Sounsak, the young physician who had purportedly
aborted the monkey's fetus from the Vietnamese maid, was
one of the few Lao involved in the shady dealings of the
Cubans. Although Dr. Sounsak had since been transferred
to a hospital in Savanaketh province, Miss Bong, the lady
he'd been dating at the time, was still living in the village at
Kilometer 8. This gossip had been provided enthusiastically by the kitchen staff at the guesthouse.

Siri and Dtui had put together a hypothesis—an alternative scenario for the mysterious events in Huaphan the
previous year. Working along this shadow plotline, they
were going back over events, reexamining issues. Miss Bong
was a sturdy, sunburned woman with a back already crooked
from a lifetime of stooping in paddy fields. They found her
planting young rice shoots, apparently too busy to stop her
work to talk. This was obviously a subject she wasn't particularly happy to discuss.

Dtui wasn't too happy either. "Is this field safe to walk
around in?" she asked.

"No safer than any other, auntie," Miss Bong told her. Dtui was prematurely exploded by the reply. Her pieces flew in a million directions. "Auntie?" The woman was a good ten years older than she. Had she aged that much over the past week? But once she'd collected her parts into a semblance of decorum, she noticed neither Siri nor the woman had spotted her detonation. It was a wound she'd have to bear alone.

"Couldn't you stop for a moment and talk to us?" Siri was saying. "I'm getting a stiff neck."

"We have to get these in before the big rains come," Miss Bong said. "Can't be wasting my time with idle chat." It was clear she hoped her rudeness would make the city folk leave her alone.

"All right." Siri sat on the bank of the field. "Then tell us about Comrade Sounsak."

"Nothing to tell."

"You were going out with him when—"

"We were engaged," she interrupted.

"Sorry. You were engaged to Comrade Sounsak at the time he had a strange and rather disheartening experience at the hospital."

"Yeah? What was that then?"

"Something involving the fetus of a monkey?"

She looked at Siri the way you would a lizard attempting to open a can of corned beef. "Eh?"

"He didn't tell you about it?"

"We didn't talk a lot about monkeys."

"About a pregnant Vietnamese woman who produced a stillborn ape? He didn't mention that to you?"

The woman looked at Dtui. "Is your granddad all right?"

Dtui sighed, then spoke slowly to her because she obviously wasn't very bright. "There was a Vietnamese housekeeper," she said. "She used to cook for the engineers working on the hospital here." The woman began to positively punch the poor little shoots into the mud. "Did you know her?"

Siri saw that the woman's body answered yes. "What can you tell us about her?"

Comrade Sounsak's erstwhile fiancée stopped her work and lifted her head to the intruders. "What can I tell you? What can I not tell you? I can tell you she was a whore, and a gobbler-upper of other women's men, and a devil. Is that enough for you?"

Siri cast a look at Dtui that suggested the next question would be better coming from her. She picked up on it.

"What did the bitch do to you, sweetie?" she asked.

Miss Bong turned her back on Siri and directed her venomous eyes at Dtui. "She preyed on them—men who were in happy, loving relationships. She flashed her well-used Vietnamese titties at them and swished her squashy hips and lured our men away."

"The whore," Dtui agreed. "And your man . . . ?"

"Was swept away like the rest of 'em. And when she fell pregnant, what fool was it dumb enough to front up and take responsibility for being the father? She was the inkwell on the paymaster's desk. Every man in the village had dipped his pen there at the end of the month, but my stupid Sounsak was the only one to own up."

"And?"

"And she had it. He even birthed it himself."

"And it survived?" Siri asked.

"I wish it hadn't."

"What happened to them?"

"Ran off that same night. Acting like they were in love or something. Never saw him again." Her eyes were starting to dampen.

"That's terrible," Siri nodded, although his expression

was more one of fascination. "Did you ever hear anything about the woman and the two black Cubans?"

"Oh, yes. She had a special grievance against those two."

"She didn't like blacks?"

"She would have done, given a chance. They were the only two with enough sense to leave the devil alone. She tried all her tricks, but she couldn't get those two boys into her bed. We heard her boasting that it wouldn't be long before she got that big one between her legs. Then, when her sex wiggles didn't work on him, she tried the little one, but he wasn't having none of her either. So she went around telling everyone they was—you know—together."

"That's the kind of thing she was saying?" Siri asked.

"She was the sort that couldn't believe a man could resist her if he was a real man."

As they drove back to the guesthouse, Dtui looked at her boss. He had a glazed look on his face that she'd seen a few times before. "So, do we now have a complete understanding of what happened?" she asked.

"We're getting there, dear nurse."

"She could have been lying."

"Possible."

"Or her fiancé didn't tell her what really happened up there. He could have been trying to protect her."

"That's possible, too. But there's one more possibility that I want to ride with."

"Good, I'll eventually work it all out, too, once I get over the trauma of suddenly becoming middle-aged. What's next?"

"Sleep. We should turn in for the night. I have several phone calls to make to Vientiane, then I'm hoping for a dream or two. I'm sure your fiancé has given up waiting for us tonight. In the morning, we'll go for a little drive. If everything works out the way I hope, things should make themselves crystal clear before the end of the day. I think we could even stick around for the concert the following evening without feeling too guilty about leaving our Mr. Geung alone in the morgue all this time. I bet the poor chap's bored out of his mind."

"Hello?"

"Hello?"

"Civilai?"

"Yes. Who's that?"

"The empress dowager of China."

"Siri? Is that you? Awful line. God, you sound like you're standing in a tub of lard."

"Yes. It's my new hobby. Have you missed me?"

"Have you gone somewhere?"

"I'm in Huaphan."

"Really? I'm off there myself, for the concert."

"I hope they aren't letting you sing."

"No, I'll just be doing my exotic dance. You know, the one with the feathers?"

"I'll make sure not to eat anything greasy before it starts. Look, I need a favor."

"You surprise me."

"Do you have anyone there who can speak Spanish?"

"Yes. Why?"

"What time is it in Cuba?"

The crow and the sparrow lay in the paddy mud, barely breathing. Their eyes were glazed. Two men knelt over them: the teacher and the acolyte. Behind them stood an elderly couple, darker than the night around them. The woman put her hand on the young man's shoulder and told him to go ahead. The teacher nodded and the dark-skinned novice took the birds gently in his hands and held them together as if in a prayer. He pressed his palms together, softly at first, then, as the birds became one, he clasped his fingers shut and squeezed till a slither of smoke escaped from his grasp and wafted upward. He opened his palms, and the birds, and the old couple, and the teacher were gone. But the novice remained. He smiled at the observer of this dream, and slowly, without the aid of language, set about explaining to Siri what he had just witnessed. Before the morning sun rose, the old doctor understood everything.

M r. Watajak had once been an early riser. Out in the boondocks the sun dictated when to sleep and when to wake. But farmers had even more sensitive clocks in their brains that told them when the dawn sun was rising over the Irrawaddy Delta, an hour before it reached Laos. So, when it finally clambered over the horizon, the farmers were already out tending their crops. But rice whisky can rust the cogs of those old brain clocks something horrible. When Mr. Watajak awoke in a sweat that morning, the sun was already baking the east wall of his old hut. He was alone. The solitude threw him into a drunk's "what happened?" panic.

He'd been getting used to having the moron there, attracting neighbors, being smart, getting better, making him laugh. In truth, old Mr. Watajak had become quite fond of the boy. He considered keeping him there. He was a strong kid. He might be able to bring some of the paddies back to life if the rains ever came. He might even make some money from the people putting in fish farms. There was a lot of potential, yet now the bamboo hut was empty but for Mr. Watajak. He was so mad about it all he had a drink. And, after the first couple of swigs, the brew reminded him how lonely he was. He was going to miss the little moron.

* * *

They'd told him. They'd all told him. The neighbors and the travelers and the kids out at the temple school. He'd kept asking because he wanted an answer that wasn't "twenty miles." Twenty miles didn't work for him. He wanted something like "a long time" or "several more nights of getting bitten by mosquitos" or "longer than it takes for a body to rot." By now, Mr. Geung could tell them the names of every town he'd passed through, probably could remember the names of everyone who'd been kind to him on the way and their kids. But he still couldn't get his head around twenty miles and what that meant as to when he'd be at the morgue to see what had happened there.

They'd told him it didn't matter. They could wave down a truck driver, get him on a bus. When he was ready to go to Vientiane, arranging a ride for him would be easier than getting wet in a river. But, for some reason, nobody was really surprised when they went to see young Geung at his house that morning, not to find him. It was the day of the big treaty signing with the Vietnamese, and the government had called a two-day holiday. The father couldn't tell them where his genius son had gone, and by the looks of him he was too drunk to care.

Geung had started off early. The sun was behind his left shoulder and he stuck to the edge of the road. Walking was the only sure thing. Every time he'd found himself in a vehicle it had taken him in the wrong direction. Things had always turned out badly. No more cars or trucks for Mr. Geung. No, sir. He was ready for this last test. His shoulder wasn't worrying him anymore. His blisters were dry and painless and his muscles were rested. His sunburn was healed and he could hear again.

He felt bad that he'd had to stay so long in Thangon. That old man, his father, made him feel sad, but he wasn't sure why. Some voice in his head had told him he ought to stay. It wasn't the voice that reminded him constantly of his promise and his obligations. The past few days had been confusing for Geung. He didn't know which voice to listen to, then Dtui came back. He was glad to see her. She sorted it all out for him.

She reminded him of this thing called love. It was something she liked to talk about a lot. She told him that even though there were times it didn't seem possible—times when you'd much sooner find fault and hate—these were the times you most needed to love. She told him his father deserved it. He didn't have to earn it. He was family, and there was a rule that members of a family got a share of love from each other just by being born of the same blood. Geung wondered when he'd be getting his. But perhaps it was something you only got back if you gave it out. His father had nothing. Even Geung could tell that. A little something would probably do him good. That's why, on the night before Geung restarted his long march, he'd kissed his drunken father on the forehead and told him he loved him.

The confused man had pushed his moron son away in disgust and wiped the gesture from his skin as if it were a slithering insect. He told his son things that could have hurt but didn't. Geung said how proud he was to have a smart father who came by every month to tell him news and see how he was. As he turned in for the night, he could see the old man doing a lot of thinking about things. He might have even cried a little, but rice whisky does that to a man, too.

Geung walked with confidence now, certain it wouldn't be too long before he saw familiar surroundings. He hoped the feeling of nausea that rose in his throat would pass, but it didn't. The headache stayed with him, too. It had been five days since the dengue mosquito had chosen him, and this would be the day when the fever arrived. Already the virus had been replicated in his blood and his gums were beginning to swell.

In Vientiane, a fountain pen, shaken once to unclog the ink, was scratching the names of all the delegates on the Treaty of Cooperation and Friendship. It officially tied the Lao to twenty-five more years of bullying. Even before that ink had dried on the parchment, those in attendance would be loaded into air force transporters and helicopters and flown off to Huaphan. They'd be wined and dined and treated royally (although that adverb would never be mentioned). At 7:00 PM they would decide which gray safari shirt to wear, have a final cocktail, and walk to the concert cave to watch a spectacular display of Vietnamese talent.

Of these events, Mr. Geung knew nothing. All he was sure of was that the morgue hadn't been swept for—goodness knows how many days. The cockroaches would have colonized the examination room. There was probably a mountain of dead bodies piled in front of the door, and all because Mr. Geung had broken his promise to his friends. Unacceptable. Totally unacceptable. He deserved whatever punishment he got. He fell to his knees and threw up into the slender panic grass beside the road.

When Everything You Think You Know Is Wrong

It was the day of the concert. Although they could have gone in for the kill on concert eve, Siri and Dtui decided that one more day of interviews and fieldwork would leave no doubt in their minds. There was also an important phone call from Vientiane expected. The guesthouse landlady was devastated that these medical people were still there, still occupying two valuable rooms. Thank goodness the "evidence" had been removed or she'd have had to explain that to Comrade Khong from Vientiane, too.

On the afternoon of the day before the concert, Dtui took Panoy back to her village. These were the days before the exodus to the big cities, when "neighbor" still meant more than just the person next door. Panoy's mother lived opposite a woman who had been widowed in the same conflict that had claimed Panoy's father. She took the little girl from Dtui as if there was no question as to where she would grow up and who would care for her. Just like that, the village had painlessly filled the gap in Panoy's life like white blood corpuscles healing a wound and leaving no scar. There had been no debate, no discussion.

Dtui was breathless with admiration for these people. Her own mother had been one of their kind. Dtui had been born in such a village but had no recollections of it. This was Laos. These were Lao people. Her people: kind, selfless, and honest. Ninety percent of Lao tilled the soil and cared for each other just like this. Dtui sat under an awning in the central square of this thirty-hut village, and saw what her country could so easily become if it was left to manage itself.

The village children were already playing gently with Panoy, recognizing her frailty. People nodded and laughed about simple things. They brought sweets and drinks for the nice nurse who'd rescued this child of the village from the edge of death. Everybody was busy, but at the same time relaxed. They all had time to talk with Dtui, and if they had no questions to ask, they would just sit with her and put their hands on hers.

And while she sat there, she noticed something else. As in every other village, the livestock, the babies, and the dogs all shared the same dust. The chickens pecked away all day at ants that barely carried a calorie among a thousand of them. Toddlers built up immunity from disease by growing up with dirt, but it was one little boy's playmate who caused Dtui to take a second look. It was an odd creature like nothing she'd seen before. From a distance, it looked like a small black pig. But there was something different about it. Where it should have had trotters, it had paws. Its tail was short and curly but it wagged from side to side. Whereas you'd expect it to snort and oink, this animal yapped at the little boy and was apparently enjoying their game.

It would have been quite simple to ask someone. She could have gone closer to confirm that this piglet had mud on its feet and a heavy cold, but instead she decided it was time to go. Even though she was in an animistic village in what was now officially an agnostic country, she had a few words with the Lord Buddha before she left. She promised never again to joke about the laws of nature. The lesson had been learned.

She kissed Panoy on the cheek, knowing the girl would never remember her if they met again. She thanked everyone, although none of them were sure for what they were being thanked, and walked out of the village. Her mothering instincts had swollen in her chest, and at that moment, she'd reached a point where nothing seemed more important than marriage and a family of her own.

In Comrade Lit's mind, there was only one reason why Dr. Siri and Nurse Dtui were in Vieng Xai. The Cuban-in-the concrete case was closed and yet they were still there. Security arrangements for the concert had kept him busy since filing his report. He'd stopped by at the guesthouse the previous day but nobody had seen hide nor hair of the two. He'd called again in the evening but they still hadn't returned. His mind should have been focused on the day's big event, but he couldn't get Nurse Dtui out of his head.

He'd come to the conclusion that Dr. Siri had agreed to act as her witness when she accepted Lit's offer of marriage. Siri had phoned and asked him to pick them up in his jeep. He dropped off his deputy to oversee the final arrangements at the concert cave and drove to the guesthouse, his heart thumping. When he saw his betrothed on the front steps, the early-morning sun bringing out the natural rouge of her cheeks, he could hardly breathe. What a fine choice he'd made.

But when Siri and Nurse Dtui got into his jeep, there was no talk of wedding arrangements. Siri asked him to drive them to Xam Neua. It was terribly inconvenient under the circumstances, but the doctor assured him this was a most serious matter that couldn't be avoided. Neither of his passengers would tell him the purpose of their journey. Left to his own imagination and the silence, he conjured up a trip to the central market to buy good northern silk for her wedding gown, even a visit to a fortune-teller to learn of an auspicious day for the ceremony. Perhaps this was how it was done. He'd never married before so he could hardly know. But he was too pleased with himself to spoil the day by complaining.

In fact, he didn't become anxious at all until the doctor directed him into the makeshift hospital compound and asked him to park in front of the director's office.

"What are we doing here, Doctor?" he asked.

"We've come to visit Dr. Santiago."

Lit was enraged by this announcement. "We've what? Why didn't you tell me this was your destination?"

"Would you have come if I had?"

"I . . . I have no business here."

"No? What about the business of revenge?"

"I have no idea what you're talking about."

"Yes, you do. You've been petrified of Dr. Santiago for too long, Comrade Lit. It's time to stand up to him."

"You're wrong."

"Am I? Then would you like to tell us what happened to that finger of yours?"

"I don't . . ." He looked at Dtui in the rear mirror. What effect would this have on her? Would she lose respect for him? Nothing showed on her face. Siri climbed down from the jeep and pointed to the key in the ignition. The confidence on the doctor's face buoyed Lit somewhat. It made him momentarily believe there it might be possible for him to escape from beneath the shadow of the damned Cuban. He turned off the engine and stepped down from the jeep.

Santiago didn't look up from his papers when the three uninvited visitors entered his room, but he smiled and said something to Dtui.

"He says he's been expecting you for some time," Dtui

told Siri. She stood to one side. Her role throughout this interview would merely be that of interpreter. She would translate Siri's questions as best she could and try to catch the Cuban's answers. She wouldn't become involved in any conflict that might arise. This was what they'd agreed.

His eyes sparkling with mischief, Santiago looked at Lit as he entered the office. Again he spoke.

"Dr. Santiago thinks it's very brave of you to get so close to him again. He asks whether your magician friend—that's you, Doc—has given you the confidence to come here after all this time. But he warns you that Dr. Siri won't be able to help you."

Siri noticed a pallor wash over Lit's face and began to understand the hold Santiago had over people.

"In that case, perhaps, before he dispatches us all to hell," Siri smiled, "he'll allow me to run my theory by him. Tell him he's free to correct any mistakes I make."

"He wants to know if this is really necessary," Dtui said.

"Perhaps the doctor would allow me just a few moments' indulgence," Siri began. "Comrade Lit, as you've learned from painful experience, Dr. Santiago is much more than just a brilliant surgeon. He is also a senior practitioner of Endoke. It would appear to many people that he is an extremely competent performer of this dark art. In fact, if you check the records, you'll find that his transfer to this godforsaken communist outpost had nothing to do with his medical skills, great though they might be. It was his last chance—the only work he could get. They kicked him out of his own country because he was a menace. Isn't that right, Doctor?"

Dtui tried her best to keep up. She told Siri the Cuban didn't want to interrupt his story.

"Oh, yes. I think he knows we're getting to the interesting part." Siri leaned back in his seat and looked into the mocking eyes of his old friend. "Because, you see, Comrade Lit, when Odon and Isandro arrived in this country, they had no knowledge whatsoever of the spirit world. They were hardworking, studious boys who wanted to come to a struggling Third World country and share their skills. They learned our language and took pains to understand our culture. The reason they were popular wasn't because they cast spells to make people like them. They were popular because they were truly nice boys.

"One of those boys, Isandro, met a patient at the hospital, the beautiful daughter of a Vietnamese colonel. Her name was Hong Lan, and in the two months she remained convalescing at Kilometer 8, the two of them fell deeply in love. There was nothing improper about their relationship. The girl was ill and he was her nurse. They talked and got to know one another, and whatever chemical it is that makes a relationship fizz and bubble, that's what happened to Hong Lan and Isandro.

"The girl had many suitors but had met nobody like this boy. He was handsome and intelligent and very kind. She was so confident that this was the man she wanted to spend her life with she even told her mother. That, as it turned out, was the biggest mistake she could have made. A foreigner—and a black foreigner at that—whatever could she have been thinking? Her mother was devastated; her father incensed. Word could never get out about their daughter's insanity. They transferred the girl to another hospital, but the humiliation wouldn't go away. The blacks had to go. Our friend Dr. Santiago was entrusted with that duty."

When he heard this translation, the Cuban twirled his hand arrogantly in the air like a musketeer. Siri smiled, shook his head, and continued.

"Fortunately for him, the doctor had experienced his own small disaster around the same time. Some children playing in the tunnels, ones they'd been specifically forbidden to enter, came across a peculiar altar. They told their parents, who reported the matter to the authorities.

"This, Comrade Lit, was the altar I told you about at the Sheraton de Laos. It had been the scene of small sacrifices and the casting of evil spells. It was Dr. Santiago's personal temple, the shrine at which he practiced his magic, where he put together his potions and curses. Dr. Santiago doesn't wear his amulets to protect himself from other exponents. He is a devotee. They are his chain of office. The altar had nothing to do with the interns, but, by accusing them of using black magic, showing people the so-called evidence, making up stories about their activities, he was able to turn everyone against them. The Vietnamese were only too happy to accept the possibility that Isandro had bewitched their daughter with his spells.

"To the boys, Santiago was a sympathetic countryman, a kindly old uncle. He told them he believed they were innocent of the accusations, but public opinion had left him no choice but to have them return to Cuba. It was all very neat. The colonel came one day with soldiers to arrest them and transport them by force to Hanoi. Up to that point, everything had gone very well for everyone except the boys. They could have left Vietnam then and that would have been the end of it. Only Isandro's love for Hong Lan and Odon's friendship with Isandro were stronger than their will to survive.

"They escaped before they could be put on a plane, and somehow worked their way back to Huaphan. It must have been a journey riddled with difficulties, fraught with danger. No help from anyone—soldiers everywhere who would probably have mistaken them for American servicemen. But they beat the odds. When they got back, they hid where they knew they'd least be expected to, in the old cave of the president. And they brought Lan to stay with them. It was no kidnap. Once she got word from Isandro that he'd returned, the girl had happily conspired with them to arrange her own rescue.

"Isandro and Hong Lan knew by then that her cancer was incurable, that she had no more than two months to live. She didn't want to spend the last of her days with a mother who taunted her daily, reminded her how she'd dirtied her family name. No, Hong Lan wanted to be with the man she'd fallen in love with. She wanted the last weeks of her life to be the happiest."

Dtui's translation flagged as she fought back tears.

"Apart from foraging for food," Siri continued, "hunting game, and keeping his lover free from pain, Isandro was also gathering his thoughts. There must have been many conversations, the three of them holed up in the cave with nothing much else to do. They knew the altar at the Sheraton had to belong to someone. There weren't that many Cubans to choose from. Perhaps they heard from Hong Lan that it was Santiago who had made the accusation to her father about the boys. Or perhaps they remembered the rumor about a pretty young nurse, with a fiancé back in her home village, who seemed to have fallen for Santiago. Nobody could understand why she was so eager to fall into the old doctor's bed."

Santiago laughed when he heard the translation and asked why Siri was so jealous. Was it inconceivable the old Cuban was attractive to young women?

Siri ignored the comment. "Perhaps they remembered the Cuban accountant who had suffered from an infection of the throat. How they'd questioned the need for a tracheotomy for such a small ailment, then recalled that he had been forced to return to Havana before completing a full audit of the doctor's books."

Unseen behind his desk, Santiago had worked open a drawer. At the front was a small wooden box with a colorful Hunan Tea emblem on its top. But the gray powder it contained had taken many months to blend and infuse with magic.

"Or perhaps they'd heard of your own unfortunate run-in with the doctor, Comrade Lit," Siri continued.

"I don't think . . . ," the security head mumbled nervously.

"Come, Comrade," Siri told him. "You have nothing to fear here today. Trust me."

Lit did draw confidence from Siri's words. He was angered by the constant grin the old Cuban wore on his face. He sighed and told a story he'd avoided relating to anybody.

"We'd had one of our many disagreements," Lit began. "They'd told me Dr. Santiago was to be the overall supervisor of the project, but the Vietnamese soldiers were annoyed because he knew nothing about engineering. Some of the decisions he made they considered to be downright dangerous. I remember . . ."

"Go on."

"I remember pointing my finger into his face and telling him he was wrong about an important issue. He stared at me and told me that was the last time I'd ever use this finger. He said I was wrong to underestimate his ability. I laughed at him and left, but when I woke the next morning, this finger was already bloodless. In a few days it had begun to wither. I know he did it. I don't know how, but from that day on I stayed clear of him. I, too, have heard stories of his wizardry."

"Well, now you know," Siri said. "And so did Isandro. I imagine he was quite upset when he realized the doctor had set them up and caused them all this hardship."

"So, if you're saying the two boys had no connection to

black magic, why did Odon have the scratches on his chest?" Lit asked.

"Yes, I admit it took me a while to work that one out. It especially threw me that Odon had the marks and Isandro didn't. Then I got to wondering what benefit the boys could gain from their knowledge of Santiago's little hobby. If, for example, they threatened to expose him, write to the project directors in Havana, and tell them what their resident representative was getting up to out here, what did Santiago have to offer them in return? And that's how we come to the deaths. They all knew Hong Lan would soon die. But Isandro couldn't bear the thought of losing her. They wanted their souls to be reunited for eternity. Odon told Isandro about an old Palo practice. An elderly couple in a town near his own had taken poison. A shaman had been recruited to unite their souls in death."

Santiago asked Dtui how her doctor could know such a thing.

"I spent a very pleasant time with Odon last evening," Siri smiled. "Tell him he'd be surprised at the information two men without a common language can share with the aid of a little mime and a pointed stick."

Dtui enjoyed translating these words.

The coroner continued. "The Cubans decided if Santiago here was such a great priest, he would know of the ceremony and agree to perform it in return for their silence. But Santiago refused to perform it himself. He did, however, agree to teach Odon. The scratches were a part of the ritual preparation, I imagine. My technical knowledge is lacking from here on. I wonder if the good doctor would be kind enough to talk us through the ceremony so we may better understand what happened that night."

Santiago was taken by surprise. He'd been busy maneuvering open the lid from the tea box without being noticed.

But he agreed to pass on the secrets of the ceremony. Siri was curious as to why he would give up such presumably classified information so readily. But he went into great detail and seemed inordinately proud to be passing on his knowledge. It appeared that for the rites to work, the hearts of the lovers had to be fresh. Santiago suggested that it would be best of all if they were still beating when they were removed, but conceded that this was often a little too gory for most people. The important thing was for the bodies to stay in perfect condition for as long as was possible after death.

"Hence the watery grave," Siri concluded. "But why?"

Santiago told Dtui that the couple would appear together in eternity the way they looked when the fusing of their spirits had been completed. As even the undead have a sense of the aesthetic, they prefer their loved ones to be relatively free of rotting flesh.

For three nights before the ceremony, the priest would mix a special concoction, a paste. Only the very best priests knew the ingredients and the incantations used while mixing them. The Cuban began to boast to Dtui of his skill; he told her he was one of the greatest exponents of the dark arts.

Siri interrupted her translation. "Dtui, thank the doctor for his commercial. But perhaps he wouldn't mind getting back to the night in question."

Santiago laughed.

"What's so funny?" Lit asked Dtui.

She squirmed in her seat before replying. "He said he can tell us everything we want to know, because . . ."

"Because what?"

"Because the three of us will remember nothing of this meeting. He says when the sun comes up tomorrow, we won't even know who we are." Dtui and Lit were intimidated by this announcement. Only Siri saw a funny side to it.

"I look forward to that," he said impatiently. "But Civilai and I have done that trick no end of times with a bottle of rice whisky. It isn't so hard. Now, the ceremony?"

Santiago told the doctor that he admired him for the bravado he managed to display when he was soon to meet a horrible end. He agreed to describe the rites in detail. The priest, he said, removes the hearts from the lovers. These he cuts into very small pieces on the altar and mixes them with the blessed paste in a pestle. Over and over he chants the incantation, over and over till he falls into a deep trance. He knows nothing beyond the actions he is to perform. On the altar, the same altar where he has minced the hearts, he models the paste into the shape of a bird. It is a bird in flight. There's no need for the priest to be a great artist. Just the crude shape of a bird is enough. This figure must then be concealed. Nobody must see it or touch so that the bird can develop its own life and symbolically fly to eternity. Then the lovers will be together forever.

"And how long does this process take?" Siri asked.

Santiago thought for a second before replying. It was hard to say. Weeks? Months? Sometimes years. Sometimes not at all. It depended on the will of the lovers. Then, all of a sudden, Santiago sighed and removed his glasses as if he'd said enough. His demeanor changed. He removed the tea box from the drawer and placed it on the table in front of him. His voice became gruff and his eyes bloodshot as he growled at his guests.

A tremor entered Dtui's voice. "He . . . he says he's enjoyed talking with us but now it's time for us to go." She abandoned her role as translator. "Doc, I don't like the look of this. I don't think we should let him—"

Before she could complete her warning, Santiago had seized the box in his left hand and scythed it through the air in an arc. The powder it contained blew in a cloud around the three guests. They could smell the scent of long-dead beasts and the stink of putrid spices. They could hear the loud angry chant emerging from between the Cuban's nicotine-stained teeth. Although their eyes stung from the dust, they could see Santiago back against the wall, extending his arms to an unseen God.

Dtui expected some manifestation—blisters, horns sprouting, a feeling of dread overwhelming her—but all she could manage was a sneeze. Lit also sneezed. Siri emerged from the cloud of powder with his hand over his mouth and nose and stared at the Cuban, now prone on the floor behind his desk.

"You can tell him to stop all this rot, Dtui. It didn't work," Siri said.

"But why didn't it?" Lit asked, taking his gun from his belt and pointing it at the confused Cuban.

"Because it never does," Siri told him. "Our Dr. Santiago here is a phony—a charlatan. He's only the great high priest of Endoke in his own mind. He couldn't conjure up a bubble in a bottle of Lao beer."

"But that isn't possible. You said he was thrown out of Cuba because . . ."

"Because he was a nuisance, not because he could actually perform any of the magic he professed to know. They thought he was a nutcase. His experiments got in the way of his medicine. Nobody was going to hire a surgeon, no matter how talented he might be, who believes the dark spirits are guiding his hand on the scalpel. Dtui, do you want to get him up off the floor before his joints freeze?"

Dtui helped the old doctor back into his seat, still mumbling an ancient curse, unable to believe that his intended victims were still conscious and coherent.

"I'm not saying he didn't study the dark arts," Siri continued. "I'm sure he did. I'm sure he's a veritable authority

on all the rites and rituals of Santeria and the Palo Mayombe. But the fact is, any old José can't just declare himself
to be a Grand Mage any more than I can announce to the
world that I'm Mr. Universe. You have to have something
special. You have to be touched by the spirits. Our Santiago
here, despite his enthusiasm, just doesn't have it."

Deprived of the benefit of translation, the Cuban sat at
his desk with a curious look on his face.

Lit stood, shaking his head. "But he did . . . he must have.
What about this?" He held up his finger, which drooped
sadly like a fractured stick insect. Siri walked to the towering
refrigerator in the corner of the office and opened the
door to reveal thousands of trays of neat petri dishes.

"Comrade Lit, if a man has no natural ability to perform
miracles—and most men don't—they resort to trickery, to
conjuration. Once we established that our friend here was
a fraud, it was just a question of going through the tricks
he'd performed to explain them. Some he just made up.
Others had more rational explanations. Take his supposed
love potion, for example. We met the young nurse who
had been charmed into his bed. But it wasn't a spell that got
her there. He'd caught her stealing medications to send
back to her village. Her body was payment for him to keep
his mouth shut. Simple blackmail.

"Many of his other spells can be explained scientifically.
Among other things, he is a brilliant chemist. I've been
trying to work out how he caused your finger to atrophy. As
you were all billeted together in the same caves, I have to
assume he infected you with some virus. He has a vast collection of cultures. It wouldn't have been difficult for him
to creep to your bunk at night and touch you with some
contaminated sample."

Comrade Lit was crestfallen. Could he really have been
duped like a simple villager?

"Every odd event that happened here," he said, "I marked down to Santiago and the supernatural. I was too afraid of my superiors' reaction to report what was going on. I was too afraid of him. Do you suppose he might have had something to do with Colonel Ha's death? His reaction to the ambush was inexplicable."

"Once a popular myth begins, son, it takes on a life of its own," Siri said. "The colonel had been so devastated by the news of his daughter's condition that he'd become dependent on opium to pull him through. I'm afraid the ambush came at a time when he was too drugged and grief stricken to appreciate the reality of the situation. His batman told us that the colonel wasn't fit for duty. He shouldn't have been on that patrol. But his reaction had nothing to do with witchcraft. The drug had unsettled his mind."

"So the last hope of Isandro and Odon was a mirage. They'd been fooled, too."

"Yes and no. Santiago refused to perform the ceremony because he knew he didn't have the ability to produce the result they all hoped for. By handing over the responsibility to Odon, he also removed the pressure from himself. You see? Dr. Santiago believes wholeheartedly in his magic. It must be terribly frustrating for him to be such a failure at practicing it. But I sense—and perhaps he did too—that Odon had some innate ability. By preparing Odon to perform the rite, I imagine the doctor could vicariously experience success."

"Are you saying that Odon was a shaman?"

"No, just that he was probably able to channel. He believed all the mumbo jumbo would work, that his friend and his friend's lover truly had a chance to be united in eternity. That made him a very appealing vessel for the spirits."

"You think he might have been successful?"

Siri's thoughts returned to his first visit to the president's cave, to the wardrobe, and the shadow of the mysterious bat. "It isn't impossible," he said. "He might actually have hit on the right formula for once."

"Should I tell him his magic worked then?" Dtui asked.

"Goodness me, no. We don't want to confirm him in the belief that he actually possesses the ability to send people off into eternity. The less enthusiasm he has, the better. I get the feeling Dr. Santiago will soon be recalled from his post here. Civilai tells me the embassy was very interested to hear about his background. I think he may be going home any day now."

Dtui looked down at the old Cuban, still vainly searching for an appropriate spell to dispatch his guests. "OK, perhaps one last question," she said. "If the ceremony was successful, and Isandro and Hong Lan are now sitting under a bo tree in heaven somewhere sharing a bottle of fizzy nirvanic nectar, why is Odon's spirit so restless?"

"Ah, yes. Good question," Siri agreed. "Originally I thought his spirit just wanted a hunky, physically perfect body in which to dance the nights away. That's why he chose me, of course. Then I started to wonder what might have happened to unsettle him. I found the answer when I met the Hmong scout, the one who led the raid that night. He's an interesting old character. An eccentric. In fact, he wears the nails on his little fingers long and varnished. It's a traditional thing."

"The nail in the mummy's tomb?"

"Right. But I didn't pursue that. He told me that night, when the laborer arrived to report his sighting of the two Cubans, the raiding party had already been selected and was ready to attack them."

"How come?" Lit asked.

Dtui was the one who answered his question. "They'd been tipped off."

"And I think we can guess by whom," Siri added. "Santiago wanted the ceremony to go ahead. He was curious. But he was also afraid that Odon might blackmail him when it was all over. Or maybe he was afraid word would get out that he, the great doctor and magician, was a fraud. I doubt Santiago expected the Vietnamese soldiers would kill Odon. Perhaps he didn't care, but once the young fellow was out of the way, he made sure that there was plenty of circumstantial evidence to suggest that Odon had been the Palo priest."

"So Odon's spirit knows that and he wants revenge," Dtui said.

"Which leaves only one thing to do," Siri decided. He went to the desk and smiled at Dr. Santiago. The Cuban seemed to have recovered from his shock and was again looking confident. "Could you tell the good doctor that we know everything. I can't pretend to like what he's been doing, but I still have great respect for him as a surgeon. I'm sorry he won't be able to practice his profession anymore after this, but I wish him good luck in the future."

While Dtui translated, Siri offered his hand to the Cuban and gave him a warm smile. Santiago slapped his palm into Siri's and returned the smile. He seemed surprised at the strength of Siri's grasp. And then he appeared to understand.

The Cuban screamed and tried in vain to remove his hand from Siri's. A force passed swiftly between them. Dtui watched Dr. Santiago squirm and shift on his seat. His posture improved and his demeanor seemed to change. By the time Siri pulled his hand away, a different person seemed to be seated at the desk.

Comrade Lit also noticed the change. "Dr. Siri, can I ask what just happened?"

In the light of everything the security chief had just heard, Siri decided there was nothing to be gained by keeping secrets. "Comrade Lit, for the past week, I have been hosting the spirit of Odon. He first came to me at Santiago's altar. At the time I thought he was trying to abuse Nurse Dtui, but, as it turns out, his aggression was directed toward Santiago. I should have realized that earlier."

"What? That no self-respecting spirit would want to abuse sweet little me?" Dtui asked. She had abandoned all attempts at translation. She felt no obligation to be polite to the old Cuban now.

"That there was no logical reason for it," Siri said. "Spirits are predictably logical. Odon wanted to clear his name and that of his friend, for a man's reputation survives his death. And to point us in the right direction. Now he's taken over the man who caused his death."

"So what should I do now?" Lit asked.

"Oh, I think the doctor will be quite cooperative. He may even confess to a thing or two. You should offer him temporary accommodation in your security complex for the night, perhaps have a little chat with him tomorrow together with the Cuban delegation. I think they'll be surprised to hear what he has to say. I imagine they'll want to contact the families of Isandro and Odon and see what they want done with the bodies. I'm sure our politburo would gladly ship them home."

"Shouldn't Hong Lan be buried with them?" Dtui asked.

"Oh, I don't see why," Siri replied. "They're just bodies. Their souls are already together."

The Plimsoll Pirouettes

The concert was scheduled to begin at six thirty. It was almost eight and Dr. Siri still sat beside an empty chair fifty yards from an empty stage. The first twenty-six rows had just started to fill, giving him a view of the backs of famous Lao heads and heads that were probably famous in other communist countries. The politburo members were there with their wives, including Civilai and his companion, the lovely Mrs. Nong. There was a cordon of uniformed troops seated between the VIPs and the common people in the rear where Siri sat near the back, saving a place for Dtui.

People were shown to their places by ushers who had once been senior military officers under the Royalist regime. They had undergone almost two years of reeducation and were considered to be trustees. They wore borrowed shirts and ties and expressions of defeat. Today's assignment was barely a humiliation compared to some of their experiences out in the jungle. Many of them didn't know that their king and queen had joined them in their exile, and most could not have cared less.

Fashionably late, the president and prime minister and the heads of the Vietnamese delegation arrived to thunderous applause from the audience. They turned and returned the applause before sinking into the sofas and armchairs that formed the front row. As was the case at any event, large or small, in the People's Democratic Republic of Laos, proceedings couldn't begin without an insufferably long speech mentioning everybody involved in the revolution and their grandfathers. Dtui turned up toward the end of it.

"I thought you weren't coming," Siri said, not bothering to keep his voice down. Most people in the commoners' section were chatting and having a good time. Socialist microphones had an extra notch to cope with Lao audiences.

"I was busy having two traumatic events," she told him.

"You saw Lit?"

"That was the first. It wasn't exactly like breaking his heart. More like disturbing his life schedule. You know what I mean. Actually, I had the feeling our little show this morning might have already put a few doubts in the comrade's mind about my suitability as a mate."

"He knows you weren't involved in any of the shenanigans."

"Yes, but he must have noticed I wasn't particularly surprised either. I didn't scream or fall about in panic. Perhaps that's what he expects from a woman. He still seemed a little shell-shocked by the whole affair. He didn't beg me to reconsider."

"Just as well. You'd already made your decision."

"Yeah. But it would have been nice to have had a suitor for a couple of months. I might have taken him to a dance or two and shown him off to the girls. I could have introduced him to Ma."

A blade of accidental static from the microphone cut through the audience. The people hushed guiltily.

"And you spoke to your mother?" Siri whispered.

"Yeah. That was the second trauma."

"Goodness me. Why?"

"She read me a letter."

"Bad news?"

"I'm not sure."

"But it traumatized you?"

"It shocked me out of my bloomers."

"Are you going to tell me what it said?"

A procession of pink-and-yellow-clad musicians filed down into the orchestra pit with their instruments. It seemed a terrible shame that such pretty costumes should vanish from sight so soon. The sound of music rose from the pit almost immediately, and the elaborate speaker system sent it rolling around the dome of the roof. The chamber vibrated. Natural acoustics, without electronic supplementation, would have filled the cave with a much friendlier sound. Siri felt Dtui's warm breath as she shouted into his ear.

"It was from the examination board."

"What did they say?"

"I have to be ready to leave for the USSR in December."

"You passed?" The overture came to a sudden halt just as Siri whooped with joy into the silence. Some of the senior cadres looked over their shoulders but the commoners laughed as they put their hands together for the unseen musicians. Siri felt no embarrassment whatsoever. He was so delighted he would happily have run up onto the stage to make the announcement public. He kissed Dtui on the cheek and then held on to her hand throughout the concert smiling the whole time.

The proceedings went on into the night. Beautiful Vietnamese ballerinas in army uniforms pirouetted in plimsolls. Acrobats did unthinkable things with chairs. A girl balanced upside down on a donkey, which ran in circles on the stage and pissed on the electric wiring, which smoked briefly. A small choir of angels in red scarves and berets sang Party songs, the ballerinas returned for a rousing dance with rifles, and a North Vietnamese pop star sang a romantic ballad that brought tears to the old men's eyes.

The final performance of the night was a Lao *ramwong* dance that snaked down from the stage and collected members of the audience. Civilai was one of the first out of his seat. He waved when he caught sight of Siri, who hoped his friend had left his feathers in Vientiane. Those behind the army cordon were not allowed to join the main snake so they stood where they were and danced in place. Dtui and Siri faced one another, bobbed to the music, and gestured like mismatched reflections in a mirror.

Behind her head, in the shadows of the side caves, in the nooks and crevices, Siri could see the departed assembling. They waited patiently for their turn. Once the old men had gone back to their houses, there was to be an official shindig for the young and the young at heart. As a special dispensation, the young Lao would be able to dance till the early hours. Although the partygoers would suspect nothing, Siri knew the spirits wouldn't want to miss anything as fantastic as a chance to strut their stuff with the living.

Civilai had no place in his heart for modern music, so he'd flown back to Vientiane directly after the show with the other party poopers. There was room on the helicopter, so he wangled spots for Siri and Dtui. The journey was made all the more pleasant for Civilai by having Siri yelling the events of the previous ten days in his ear above the chop of the rotors. His own life had become so predictable and pointless, it was a tonic to hear Siri's marvelous tale.

"How come the Vietnamese didn't find Isandro when they discovered the body of the girl?" Civilai asked; he never let Siri get away with any gaps in his reasoning.

"I have to assume Odon buried his friend first and disguised the grave so it wouldn't be discovered before the process was complete. He was just about to do the same to Hong Lan when he was disturbed by the arrival of the soldiers."

"You don't want to make this a police matter? You have enough evidence against the Vietnamese militia and the guide for murdering Odon?"

"I get the feeling the army will take care of this in its own way."

"As they seem to take care of everything else." Civilai almost had all the facts straight in his mind. Only one question remained and he knew the reply would be conjectural. "Any idea how the couple died?"

"The bodies were too far gone to tell. The girl may have died from her disease. If she was still alive, I imagine the lovers drank some poison together once they got to the cave. It was a love pact, after all."

"And do you honestly believe the hocus-pocus worked and the lovers' souls were reunited in the afterlife?"

Siri thought again of the locked cupboard and the unseen creature that had escaped from it. "I can't be sure. But I'd like to think so."

"After all these years, you're still a romantic."

"When you get to our age, older brother, you start to wish you'd devoted more time to romance when you still had the chance."

"You're right." Civilai leaned across to Mrs. Nong and whispered something in his wife's ear. Whatever it was, it caused her eyebrows to rise and a blush to suffuse her cheeks. She looked out of the far window and smiled uncontrollably.

"I hope you didn't just make a promise an old fellow like you won't be able to keep," Siri said.

Dtui and the doctor had arrived in their crowded suburban shelter for the homeless at 3:00 AM. The mongrel bitch was still asleep on her nest and a company of geckos were gathered around the porch lamp like three-dimensional wallpaper. The human guests were sleeping, too. Siri did a quick head count and found he'd inherited one new housemate since they'd been away. Apart from Monoluk, Dtui's mother, there had been Mr. Inthanet from Luang Prabang; Mrs. Fah, whose husband had passed away; and her two children. And now there was a monk, of all things, asleep on Siri's hammock in the back yard. None of these people stirred.

Siri and Dtui ate and slept a little, but by six they were both as wide awake as the early-rising cockerels on the roof. Then they had to face an inquisition from their housemates. "Who died? How? Who did it?"

Apparently, dull radio dramas weren't stimulating enough for them. The doctor did as good a job as he could of summarizing their adventures in the northeast, but was glad when the time came for them to leave for work. Halfway into the city, he realized he'd forgotten to ask about the monk, or perhaps he hadn't been ready to get the reply "What monk?"

He and Nurse Dtui arrived at the hospital at their usual time. It was Monday morning and their stay in the northeast already felt like a different time in an entirely different country. Siri parked his motorcycle in his regular spot and Dtui unlocked the morgue doors. There was a stale smell inside rather than the familiar stench of bleach and disinfectant. They assumed this was the smell of a morgue unused for ten days. At least it was clean and everything was in its place, just as they'd left it.

They opened the windows to allow the hot air inside to change places with the hotter air outside. They sat at their respective desks, ready to collate their fragmented recollections of the Huaphan case. It was likely to take them the

better part of a day to put it into a form that even Judge
Haeng would be able to make head or tail of.

At twenty minutes after eight o'clock Mr. Geung staggered through the doorway like a drunkard. He hadn't
even stopped to take off his boots. Siri and Dtui looked up
to see him silhouetted there, swaying. The only thing keeping him up appeared to be the uneven smile on his face.

"Hello, Geung honey," Dtui said. "What in blazes has happened to you?" She stood and began to walk toward him.

Before sinking to his knees and crashing onto the concrete
floor, Geung heard the doctor's voice. It was such a wonderful sound—a sound he'd been afraid he'd never hear
again. He'd imagined this meeting as he staggered painfully
through the outer suburbs and across the city, as he fell into
and out of trances beside the busy streets. He'd dreamed of
seeing the faces of his workmates, and here he was—the
morgue and his promise intact. He couldn't have been
happier. This, too, was his destiny.

"Mr. Geung," the doctor had said, looking at his watch.
"You're late."

Beware the Snowy-Haired Avenger

As head of the National Department of Justice, Judge Haeng could, technically, have found a lot of things to keep him busy every day of the week. Yet, by hanging on to senior staff who knew the workings of the department far better than he, and by not initiating any new projects, he managed to arrange many large gaps in his daily schedule. These he filled with visits to his family fish farm, afternoon trysts with colorful nightclub singers, and, his particular favorite, just kicking off his shoes and taking nice long naps. If napping had been an event at the Asian Games, Haeng would certainly have been the Lao national champion. He had everything under control and was proving to everybody that he could capably fill the shoes of those corrupt Royalist rogues he'd condemned so often at village seminars.

He became particularly upset, therefore, whenever the politburo gave him tasks that took away his three-hour lunches and "just-say-I'm-in-court" afternoons. The signing of the Vietnamese treaty had turned his life into a hellish succession of meetings and formal dinners and interminable speeches, many his own. The Hanoi judicial delegation had been particularly irksome. They'd insisted upon seeing the inner workings of the Lao legal system. Not only was that mechanism lacking oil, it was also missing a number of irreplaceable spare parts. But he could hardly confess this. So Judge Haeng had set about orchestrating an elaborate deception.

He moved men from outlying police posts to fluff up the two stations visited by the Vietnamese and stage-managed a fake trial at the central courthouse. He shifted four brand-new microfiche viewers from the old USAID compound and set them up at the criminal records department. As none of the Lao records were on fiche, and nobody knew how to operate the equipment anyway, on the day of the delegation's visit there was a sudden and mysterious power outage, which meant the visitors had to leave without seeing the system in action. The judge was exhausted and thanked the heavens that the Vietnamese only had one more half day before he would be rid of them.

One member of the group was a doctor—a coroner, of all things—who had convinced his compatriots that a review of the justice system could not be complete without a visit to the morgue. Judge Haeng had argued against this with all his might—the smell, the sight of blood, the heat—but they all seemed to be in agreement with the annoying little Vietnamese doctor. It occurred to Haeng that perhaps every country had the thorn of a difficult national coroner in its side. But he had no choice. On the evening of the last day of the visit, following a farewell banquet at the old presidential palace, Haeng had his driver take him out to Dr. Siri's house, deep in the new suburbs behind the That Luang shrine. It would be his first visit to the place. It would also be the first time he'd seen Siri since his trip to the northeast, and since the removal of his moronic henchman from the morgue.

On the car journey there he took a number of deep breaths and prepared retorts for the complaints sure to come his way. Siri was insolent but occasionally competent.

The old man had done a reasonable job in Xam Neua. Haeng would begin by telling him so, get him in a good mood, inform him of how satisfied the Party was with his work. He would not allow the doctor to bully him about the missing moron. He was, after all, the head of the Justice Department and Siri was just a worker. But still he felt his hands tremble as he walked through the tall front gate and into a well-tended yard. The front door of the house was wide open, and he could see Siri in the back kitchen. Haeng clenched his fists and called Siri's name, but was totally unprepared for what happened next. Siri raised his arm in greeting, smiled, and trotted out to welcome him. He was so polite, so friendly, that Haeng wondered whether Siri had confused him with someone else. But taking the judge's arm, Siri led him inside.

It was an awful place, a menagerie: old people, invalids, brats running amok. Siri had turned perfectly good government housing into a slum. There would be a report made to the housing division about this, no question, but there was a more pressing issue. He hurriedly acknowledged the introductions and immediately dismissed the names of Siri's gang from his mind. As soon as he could, he herded Siri and Dtui onto the front step. He asked for assurance that they would be neatly turned out for tomorrow's visit, white coat for the doctor, crisp white uniform for the nurse. It was also vital that there be no—what he referred to as "patients." Siri asked whether he meant dead bodies, and Haeng acknowledged that was his meaning. If there were any bodies in the freezer, Siri would have to get there early and clear them out.

Siri had been so bold as to ask where they should dump a body, were it to arrive before the delegation turned up, but Haeng didn't give a hoot what they did with it as long as the morgue was spotlessly clean and presentable. Siri and

Dtui assured him there would be nothing dead to spoil the reputation of the national mortuary. They assured him it would be a day like no other. Haeng drove home that night with a lighter heart. The only possible flaw that might spoil an otherwise exemplary picture of Justice Department efficiency had been removed. And, miracle of miracles, there had been no mention of *that* matter. This Siri character was proving to be trainable after all. Haeng lay back in his seat and smiled for the first time all day.

The entourage of shiny black Zil limousines pulled up in front of the morgue at nine fifteen the following morning. The hospital director was there to meet the delegates. He had a speech written and planned to give each of them a wrist garland of orchids. But it was a stinking hot day, and the cars had kicked up a mist of dust. The Vietnamese wanted nothing to do with the director's foolishness. They wanted merely to get the final pointless visit over with and head off to the airport. They'd all been in Laos far too long already. They pushed past the director and a chorus of applauding nurses, and headed for the shade of the morgue entrance. The director recognized at least two senior Party members, a judge, and two police generals as they shoved him out of the way. But his camera still hung by his side, and he had no photographic evidence that his hospital had been so honored.

The delegates were met in the vestibule by Dr. Siri in a spotless white lab coat and, of all things, a shirt and tie. A gleaming stethoscope hung around his neck. He stood beside a beaming Judge Haeng and welcomed the Vietnamese in their own language. He had no need of an interpreter although this left Haeng at a slight disadvantage. Despite completing much of his undergraduate education in Hanoi, Haeng's Vietnamese was infected with a horrible

Lao accent, and his comprehension was lacking. The doctor said he regretted there were no bodies to show the guests but he invited everyone into the autopsy room regardless. The throng shuffled forward to find Dtui standing in front of the large freezer door. She was immaculately groomed and dressed in her whitest uniform. She'd even gone so far as to stick a bright pink *champa* flower above her ear. She smiled sweetly and pulled open the freezer door like the hostess on a Thai television game show.

The visitors stared into an empty freezer in a body-less morgue and wondered what they were doing there. Judge Haeng was glowing. It was as if he wanted to shout his delight, but somebody beat him to it. The deathly cry came from one side of the room, from behind the door that led to the samples store. That door suddenly flew open, inflicting a blow to the shoulder of a senior police person, and the most incredible sight presented itself. There was an audible intake of breath from every visitor. A dark-skinned man, perhaps of Indian origin, shirtless and unshaven, waded through the crowd of frightened onlookers to stand beside the judge. He wore only a very brief sarong and in his open palm he carried what appeared to be a human brain. It dribbled fluid onto the spotlessly clean concrete floor. He appeared to be laughing but no sound came from him.

Comrade Nguyen, the Vietnamese coroner, was the first to speak. "Judge Haeng," he said indignantly. "What's the meaning of this?"

It was clear from Haeng's expression that he'd suddenly recognized the half-naked man. Wasn't this the nutcase who strolled aimlessly around the city begging for food scraps? Wasn't this the serial flasher who had been arrested repeatedly and spent several nights in jail? This was the man they called Crazy Rajhid. What was he doing here in the morgue?

"Siri, what's the meaning of this?" Haeng demanded.

"Gentlemen, I suppose I should explain," Siri said. "You'll have to forgive the appearance of our new morgue technician."

"New morgue . . . ?" Haeng began. He felt obliged to laugh, to convey the impression that this was a joke and he'd been party to it all along. Siri heaved himself up onto the cutting slab and began to address the audience.

"You see," he began, "Mr. Rajhid here is the only person we could find who'd agree to work for the half salary we are allocated for this position." Rajhid had sunk to the floor and was molding the brain like silly putty into the shape of a mushroom.

"I don't think . . . ," Haeng began, still smiling but unable to form a sentence in Vietnamese with sufficient aplomb to rescue himself.

Siri continued. "We used to have a well-qualified—in fact, brilliant—technician who was perfectly happy to work for a pittance. He had more experience than either I or Nurse Dtui here."

"What happened to him?" Nguyen asked. The other delegates had shuffled forward, entranced by the first authentic show of their visit.

"Well, I'm sure he had a good reason, but Judge Hae—I mean, the Justice Department—fired him."

"I didn't actually fire h . . . ." Haeng tried again. His smile was wilting.

"Why?" Nguyen asked. "Why fire a perfectly good technician?"

"Because . . ." Siri paused for effect. "Because he had Down syndrome."

A mumble rose from the group.

"You fired a man because he was a mongoloid?" the leader of the delegation asked with an expression of disbelief on his face. It was conceivable he would have done the same—probable that none of the assembled dignitaries would have hired the handicapped in the first place, but group dynamics work wonders for one's indignation.

"I . . . I didn't fire him," Haeng said. "I reallocated him."

"Why?" Nguyen asked. "Wasn't he serving in a valuable capacity for the socialist state? Wasn't he contributing to the community?"

"He certainly was," Siri replied.

Rajhid had put the brain on his head and was now modeling it as if it were a hat. One of the generals looked at him in disgust, then turned to Siri. "Can we talk to this retard—see for ourselves?"

"I'm afraid you can't," Siri told him. Both the doctor and Dtui lowered their heads. "You see, he was shipped north under armed guard. He was sent all the way to Luang Prabang but such was his loyalty, such was his love of his job and his responsibilities here, that he turned back. He walked—yes, Comrades, he walked—all the way back to this morgue. For ten days, beneath the biting summer sun, he marched"—a sob was heard from the direction of the freezer—"three hundred punishing miles he walked. But, as you can imagine, the journey weakened him, and on the way he contracted dengue fever. When he arrived here he was barely alive. He collapsed right there behind you."

The crowd turned back as if expecting to see the body still there on the concrete. Siri took the opportunity to look up at Haeng, whose teeth were so tightly clenched they could easily have been welded together. The delegation turned back to see the young nurse with tears rolling down her round cheeks.

"He's dead?" someone asked.

"He might as well be," Siri replied. "It's touch and go." He could see the Vietnamese glares slicing through the judge, who stood exposed and unarmed beside him. Siri expected one last defensive volley from him and he wasn't disappointed.

"We . . . we're doing everything we can to keep him alive," Haeng said, not terribly convincingly. He'd had no idea the moron had come back. "If he makes it, naturally we'll honor him for his courage and dedication."

"Let's hope you do," said the senior cadre. "This is exactly the type of spirit we want to see in a socialist state. It would be a marvelous incentive for normal people. If a mongoloid can show so much dedication to the Party . . ."

"Exactly," someone agreed.

"A medal at least," said Dr. Nguyen.

"Walked all that way—marvelous," said the policeman.

Soon the morgue was awash with enthusiasm and hope for this slightly defective but nonetheless courageous soldier of the revolution. Someone suggested they visit the brave warrior to show their support. They trooped out of the morgue and across the hospital grounds to the intensive care unit. Crazy Rajhid joined the pilgrimage, so the only ones left in the cutting room were Dtui, Siri, and his old friend Dr. Nguyen.

"I think that went quite well, don't you?" said the Vietnamese.

"Thanks to you," said Siri. "I'm in your debt."

"I'll think of something, don't worry. Maybe ask you to send me some of these pretty nurses." He smiled at Dtui. "I think I should join my team, don't you?"

They laughed and shook hands, and Nguyen walked jauntily out of the autopsy room.

"Well," said Dtui. "I had no idea what you were all talking about, but I can still see bits of Haeng's face littering the floor so I know it worked."

From the shadows of the vestibule came another figure. Haeng's chief clerk, Mrs. Manivone, walked out into the fluorescent lighting, slowly shaking her head. She'd watched the whole thing from the wings and knew her boss only too well.

"He'll never forgive you, you know."

"I know," Siri said and smiled his most devilish smile.

"I'm serious. He can make life very difficult for you, Dr. Siri."

"You don't suppose he'd fire me and banish me to the countryside?"

"You'd like that, wouldn't you?" Manivone started to laugh. She walked over to the coroner and sniffed at the air by his cheek. A Lao no-contact kiss. "I suppose you know you're my hero," she said.

Siri squeezed her hand, blushed a little, and walked out of the cutting room. Manivone put her arm around Dtui.

"How's Geung, really?"

"He'll live," Dtui said. "In fact, this morning he was looking a little too flushed. Dr. Siri had me talcum-powder him down."

"You want to swap bosses?" Manivone asked.

"Not on your life, sister. Not on your life."